DUPLICITY

WHEN TRUST IS TOO HIGH A PRICE

JO WILDE

CONTENTS

PRELUDE

When I left my abusive boyfriend, I thought all my troubles were behind me. But to my horror, it was only the beginning. Without breathing, I stared across the cabin into his pleasant face. I wondered … how could I have not known he was a *monster*?

FLEE

*L*ife sucks! When it storms, it blows in one kick-ass blizzard. It seems my life once again is at a tailspin. Why do I keep falling back into the same old pattern? It's like I don't have a cell in my brain. I keep picking the wrong people over and over. Stumbling in the rabbit hole has become a bad habit of mine.

Fright racks my mind as I finish shoving the last piece of clothing in my overstuffed bag and snatching it up and sprinting for the front door with keys in hand. I'm not running from my troubles. It's my life I'm fleeing from.

I knuckle the blood from my busted lip, darting downstairs, two steps at a time, dragging my heavy bag with me.

The crisp night smells like ice. It bites my bruised cheek and swollen eye. I lift my eyes to the ominous canopy of clouds. The meteorologist finally got this prediction right. The frozen grass crunches under my feet while icicled trees slump low and ice flakes cover my long, black hair and shoulders like a white, wintery shawl.

A shiver runs through me as I try to ignore the throbbing pain. I can't catch my breath. It feels like someone's hand is clamped around my lungs and squeezing as I beg for air. But I can't slow down. I have to get out of town quickly before my boyfriend, Tad, returns.

Why do I push his buttons? I know the outcome. We had gotten into a terrible argument. And for the first time in our relationship, I stood up to him. I will pay dearly for that mistake. I should've kept my mouth shut. I lost my temper and made him hit me. It's my fault. If I'd just left ... turned and walked out the front door, he would've never known that I had returned home.

Screw him! I refuse to be his punching bag any longer. I should've ended this two-year relationship long before now. I've invested my time with a man that has no idea how to be in a committed relationship.

Why do I do this to myself? A dark cloud seems to always hover over me, and the promise of trouble is a mere whisper away. Will I ever stop being a loser? Can't I do anything right?

Of all things, I caught Tad in bed with my closest friend, Susan. I knew this incident meant the beginning of a colossal mudslide. The whole scene is as fresh as the cut on my busted lip and as deep as the bruise on my cheek.

Strangled with cheap, heavy perfume, I stand in the doorframe of our bedroom, gaping at Tad and Susan entangled between the sheets in the throes of sex. I drop my bag.

"What the hell?" Shock, hurt, and betrayal slams into my chest as I stand there gawking, frozen like an ice sculpture.

Susan yaps and scrambles for her clothes, scurrying past me, darting for the front door. I glower at my friend but let her go. Why bother? She has bigger problems than me. Dealing with her six-foot-four husband should serve her right.

My eyes target Tad as he takes his time slipping on his jeans. The fat grin beaming across his face suggests his lack of remorse. "What are you starin' at?" His voice is cold and aloof.

Tears well in my eyes as I ask, "How long has this been going on?" I cross my arms, holding his baleful gaze.

"Stop your snifflin'. I-dee-clare, Ms. Baker. I do be-

lieve I'm a grown man. Don't have to answer to you," he mocks.

"A man!" I scoff. "Half the time you're unemployed and the other half you're at some bar getting shitfaced."

"So, what Anna! I'd rather be with anyone else than the likes of you!" His words feel like stones being thrown at me.

"No one is forcing you to stay. Leave!" Tears streak my cheeks.

Tad steps up in my face, his lips quivering with bitterness. "I'm not goin' anywhere, bitch! I like it here."

"Of course, you do! Why would you not? You have free rent, food, and a comfortable bed to screw your best friend's wife!" I shove his chest, causing him to stumble. A big mistake.

"Never put your hands on me!" Anger flickers through his hard, black eyes as he cold-cocks my cheek, clipping the corner of my eye.

I fall to the floor, cradling my throbbing face. Before I have time to see past the spinning stars, he wrings a fist full of my hair and drags me to my feet. Taking his rage further, he backhands me. Immediately, I taste blood on my lip. I stagger backward but remain on my feet. Tad comes at me again, rearing his fist back to take another.

But I spy my bag on the floor in the bedroom doorway. I duck and make a swan dive for it. Thrusting my hand inside its content, I pull my hand free, revealing a small pistol, my Smith & Wesson six-forty-two. I aim *right between Tad's eyes, gritting my teeth and tasting the sweet nectar of revenge.*

"Make one more move, and I swear, I'll shoot you where you stand." My finger caresses the cold steel trigger. One easy pull and it'd be over. I'd get off too. Self-defense with all the bruises on my face.

Tad's eyes fill with a mix of emotions: anger, fright, shock. "You gotta be kidding?"

"Nope! I'm done with you hurting me." I cradle my gun in both hands, pointing straight at him, daring him to move.

He throws his palms up. "Good riddance! In a few short weeks, I'll have enough money to live wherever I want, and it sure as hell won't be with you!" He sneers, spinning on his heels and storming out the door. I lower the gun as I hear Tad starting his truck to a roar, and headlights quickly flash through the window.

After a moment, the truck's engine, and light fade. I take a deep breath, collapsing my trembling body to the floor and raking in air.

Putting Dallas, Texas and Tad Taylor in my rearview mirror is the best idea I've had in a long time. I'm getting the hell out of Dodge and never coming back.

Destination … *New Orleans.*

My older brother, Jeff, invited me to stay at his pad for an undisclosed time. He's a second-year resident at Tulane Medical Center, only a block from the French Quarter. A great location to live. And since Jeff works ungodly hours, I'll have the place to myself the majority of the time. A perfect solution to a terrible ending and a much brighter future. At least, that's the plan.

NEW BEGINNINGS

*A*fter eight hours of driving, I arrive at my brother's apartment complex at 925 Common, in the central business district. I check the address again just in case I'd read it wrong. "Nope. I'm at the right place," I mumble to myself as I drop my chin in shock, tilting my head back and gaping at the tall building. Such an improvement from his last cramped, one-room apartment. It didn't even have running water. He had to shower at the hospital.

My eyes rake over the high-rise. I see that big brother's hard work has paid off. Jeff explained to me that the property is older and was once an office building. I like it; it goes with the vibe of the city.

The area is mostly high-rise buildings in the heart of the busy city. I'm used to traffic noise and busy streets, so, I shouldn't have any trouble adjusting. But even more so, I'm happy my brother is opening his home to me. I don't know what I would've done if it hadn't been for his generosity.

I spot Jeff waiting by the curb. I'd called my brother letting him know that I was only fifteen minutes away. Or at least that's what my GPS said.

Excitement warms my heart, seeing Jeff's big smile light up. It's been a few months since I last saw him. He approaches the car just as I pull up and park. Boy, luck must be on my side today. Catching a convenient parking spot in the city seldom happens. Maybe Jeff will have an extra parking spot for me. Valet parking sounds dope!

I climb out of my packed-to-the-hilt car as a crisp breeze tousles my hair. I forget the winters are milder in Louisiana. I'm glad too. Driving on ice sure ain't for this Texan. Louisiana has milder winters but hotter summers. Which reminds me of Jeff's infinity pool he's bragged so much about. Living here is going to be a nice vacation.

I plan to get a job and take a couple of courses at the local community college. I'm the black sheep of the family. My parents were big on education. Jeff pursued his dream of becoming a doctor. Unlike Jeff, I have failed miserably sticking with a job or getting an education. But it's time I grow up. I have to get my life on track and expecting Jeff to support me forever is unfair to him. I don't want to be a bum.

But I have high hopes. From this point on, my life can only get better. Why wouldn't it? My big brother is helping me.

"Hey, Jeff!" I smile back and reach up on my tippy toes to hug my six-foot-three brother. To look at us, one would never think we're siblings. We look nothing alike. Jeff's tall, blond, and blue-eyes. I'm five-two, Arabian hair, and hazel eyes. "You're lookin' good, bro."

He pulls away, holding me at arm's length. "You're looking a little fluffy," he teases as I slug him in his arm.

"Shut up, Jeffie! I'm not fat, you nerd," I laugh and slug him again. Truth is … I'm not a big girl, but I do have some junk in my trunk.

Jeff grabs my bag. "C'mon, let me show you the place. I'll get my neighbor to help with your stuff in a bit."

"Okay, but you don't think anyone will break-"

"Nah," he shakes his head. "Most of us tenants here are nerds. We wouldn't know how to smash your window or pop the lock," he chuckles, glancing at my car. "No one's going to want your junk anyway."

"You're pushing it!" I glare at him, but internally I'm laughing.

We enter the lobby and pass the clerk sitting behind a long counter like a fancy hotel. I look at Jeff. "Wow! Impressive." I nudge him with my shoulder.

"It's alright," he shrugs. "I'm just a resident. But it ain't too bad."

"Why Jeffery Dan Baker, I do believe your southern accent is comin' out when you're embarrassed."

"Hush up before I kick you out," he teases, or at least I think he is.

My brother and I are all we have. Our parents' lives were taken by a drunk driver in a head-on crash. The drunk lived, my parents were not as lucky. I was eighteen and my brother was twenty-six and in the middle of medical school. Somehow, he pushed forward, determined to stay with it, and now he's a resident at one of the best hospitals in the country. I think he just dug his heels into the ground and kept his mind on his studies. Now look at him … a surgeon.

Me?

I wear the jewel crown of a troublemaker. The one that stayed out past curfew, smoked pot, and had a fair amount of underage drinking. Most of my teenage years, I think my parents' favorite catchphrase was … *you're grounded*! Despite their efforts, I still managed to defy them. I can't count all the times I'd climbed out my window and shimmied down the old oak tree to meet up with my friends.

But that cold winter night, three days before Christmas, our parents were coming home from a party that my dad's company had thrown in his benefit. Dad owned a couple of retail stores that sold uniforms and western wear. Mom was a part-time nurse and worked for a private doctor. I guess that's where Jeff gets his talents.

I'm still trying to figure it out. But one thing I can say … after that unfathomable night of losing our parents, I stopped getting high, and I cut out drinking.

My biggest regret is that my parents had to die first, before I cleaned up my act. I was young and stupid.

And I struggle to forgive myself.

Years have passed, and I'm still digging my way out of the rabbit hole. I should've seen the trouble coming with Tad. But I wasn't any better at picking girlfriends either. Now I've ditched all that excess baggage in Texas and, hopefully, I've left my poor choices there too. I'm done with love; I have terrible taste in picking men.

The bell dings and the doors slide open with a mechanical thump. Jeff and I step inside the elevator and he pushes button ten. I gape at him, surprised. I remember when we were teenagers. No matter how much I bribed him, he refused to ride Judge Roy Scream, the baby rollercoaster at Six

Flags. No one could talk him into it either. "I thought you were afraid of heights?"

He looks at his feet. "People change."

"Yeah, uh, hmm. Why is it I don't believe you?" My mouth curved into an unconscious smile, knowing damn well his curtains are closed tighter than a camel's butt during a sandstorm.

We step out onto a long corridor with one door after another. Finally, we reach the last door on the left and stop at number 1025. Jeff pulls out his key from his jean pocket and slips the key in the lock. We enter and I stop to gape. Jeff stops behind me and sets my luggage down.

The apartment is better than decent: white marble counter-tops, stainless steel appliances, wood floors, and huge windows at every angle, bathing the space in bright sunshine. It's perfect! I can imagine at night the panorama view of the city lights as far as the eye can see. I gasp with excitement.

I peel away my eyes and spot black leather furniture. I turn to my brother as I make my way to the center of the apartment. "Wow! Did you decorate?"

Jeff hides a smile behind his hand. "Some. But I had help."

"Great help!" My eyes stop at the center window. "The cars look like toys. So tiny." I turn to Jeff. "Why so high? You're terrified of heights."

A faint smile tips the corners of his lips. "People do change."

"Do you ever enjoy the view? I can't wait to see the city lights at night."

"I usually keep the blinds drawn."

"Whatta waste." My eyes brush over the space. "Where will I be sleeping?"

"Follow me." Jeff nods as he heads to the other side of the living room.

Down a short hallway, we come to a halt at the second bedroom. I step inside as Jeff leans on the doorframe. Standing in the middle of the room, I wash my eyes over the room. A little tight in size but still nice. The window isn't as large as the living room but it still brings in a generous amount of light. I can't wait to gaze at the nightlights as I drift off to sleep.

I notice sheets, a blanket, and two pillows stacked on the full-size bed. The fresh scent of "new" fills the room. A small dresser stands in the corner and a bathroom is off to the left. Unlike most women, I didn't have a lot of clothes, so the fair size closet will accommodate my belongings. I didn't have anything of value anyway.

I face Jeff and say, "Wow! New bed and covers too."

"Yes, I'm not letting you ruin my new couch." He looks at the floor, shifting his feet, smiling.

After our parents died, Jeff became the parent

and pushed me to clean up my act. I'm not an addict, thank goodness, but it could've happened if I had not stopped.

I reach up and hug my brother. "Thank you for all your trouble. It's wonderful!" I smile up at him with awe.

"Well, you know how I feel about Tad. I'm glad you left him. I'm just going to be frank with you, sis. You are better than him. And … and the kind of friends you pick …" Jeff's lips thinned.

At that moment, I couldn't look my brother in the face. Just as if he were my parent, guilt strikes at my chest. "I know. I'm trying. I really am."

"Are you? Because from where I stand, I don't see it." There's a critical tone to his voice.

"Okay, I pick crappy friends and a boyfriend that half the time didn't bother coming home. I know … *I screwed up!*" I huff.

"You've got to start learning to love someone who's good for you."

I get what Jeff's saying. I know how much I have worried him and our parents when they were alive. I correct one problem, and five more pop up in its place. "I know I deserve a good chewing out, but can I at least settle in a night before you lecture me?" I'm not ready for the heavy yet.

"Okay, fine!" He rakes his fingers through his hair. "I have a shift tonight. Let me go get the neighbor and we can unload your car." He pushes out a smile but I know, inside, he's disappointed in me.

"I can help!" I try to be cheerful.

"What? And ruin our male ego?" he teases.

"Alrighty, then." I clasp my hands together. "I guess I'll get my suitcase and take a shower."

I feel awkward not helping, He's always there for me. Such a dependable brother. I don't know what I'd do without him.

Jeff had supplied me with all the makings for a great shower: body soap, shampoo, even toothpaste and a toothbrush. He thought of everything.

I quickly dress, hoping to catch my brother before he finishes the last load. The least I can do is carry in the small boxes. I snatch up my overnight bag and tug out a T-shirt and my favorite pair of cut-offs. My brows dip into a scowl as I hold up my shorts to the light. Most of my belongings are still in Texas. Especially the good stuff. No biggie, though. Out with the old and in with the new. And that means new clothing… that is, after I land a job.

I make my way into the living room and stop in my tracks. My eyes go bug-eyed. A stranger is halfway buried in one of my boxes. My eyes freeze on his long, lean physique. I bite my bottom lip, pausing a moment, enjoying the firmness of his tush. After an enjoyable moment of ogling, I begin to feel like a perv. Awkward.

Glancing over my clothing, I come to a sharp

realization that I'm not prepared to meet any guest. I'm a terrible mess, even for a blind man. My hair is dripping wet and saturating my T-shirt. And here I stand in my short, short cut-offs that have more holes than thread. I clear my throat. "Hello."

I startle the mystery man and he shoots to attention. Our eyes latch. "Oh, hey!" he drawls. "You must be the little sister?" He wipes his right hand on his jeans and steps forward. "I'm Ethan LeBlanc. The neighbor."

I meet the smile and hand which is offered. "I'm "

"You're Anna Lee Baker. I've heard a lot about you."

"Oh. Well, I hope it's all good." I jump on that a little too fast. "Hmm." My gaze combs the living room. "Is Jeff downstairs?"

"Jeff left for the hospital, bitching about no hot water." His glint churns with amusement. He's teasing me.

"Oh, yeah … hot water." Jesus! I'm rattling on.

"Hey, I hate to run, but I have to get ready too. My shift at the hospital starts in half an hour."

"Oh! You're a doctor like Jeff?" That explains the smooth hand but unlike most, his is warm. I smile inwardly.

"You are correct," he flashes a lopsided grin. "After the shift, you should come join us. We usually stop at a local bar and shoot the breeze. You know, wind down from a taxing night."

"You guys go drinking in the morning?"

"*Laissez les bons temps rouler*," he rattles off perfectly. "Bars stay open a little later here, and especially if the owner is a good buddy." His lips draw back, revealing straight white teeth.

"Oh, I see." I bite my bottom lip. "You speak Cajun French?" He does have that French vibe, light sandy hair, tawny skin, and dreamy green eyes that screams sex.

"I do," his eyes sparkle. "Do you speak French?"

"Oh no!" I giggle. "I did a little research about the city."

"There's a lot of history in this old town. More than a hundred years ago my people moved here from Canada. A long line, born and raised right here in this city." He unconsciously scratches behind his ear. "Anyway, it's nothing special. The food's pretty good too. Especially when you're single. Boiling water is not in my skill set," he laughs, a nice rich rolling laugh like molten chocolate.

"Boiling water is a necessity to survival," I tease.

"I've heard that. It's a wonder that I've survived for the past thirty years." His eyes glisten with mirth.

"I have a book with instructions. You're welcome to it."

"I just might have to take you up on that offer."

Our eyes lock as a silent moment settles between us.

I break contact first. Stuffing my hands in my back pockets. "As generous as your offer sounds, I have to sit this one out. Maybe next time," I smile, kicking myself.

"Sure, no problem. Nice meeting you." He edges his way to the door, toting a smile. "Have a nice evening."

"Hmm ... thanks for the help."

"You bet!" Ethan smiles, leaving as I lock up behind him.

I pause, leaning against the door. Suddenly, the apartment is quiet, and a quick bout of loneliness stabs me. After living with Tad, I should be used to it. This move is a good thing. I think.

One thing for certain, I can't get into another relationship until I figure out what to do with my life. I inhale a deep breath. Ethan leaves a great first impression. Not only is he easy on the eyes, but he's nice too. Two attributes you rarely find in one man.

Even if I wanted to meet up, I couldn't intrude. Apart from my brother, I've always felt guys like Ethan were out of my league. You know the type: mild-mannered, smart, quiet, and sweet. With my record of screwing up, I don't understand what a nice guy would see in me.

I'm my worst enemy. I have a knack for finding men that are incapable of feelings. You know the type. They show up for the date, absent-minded of their wallet, sticking you with the bill and daring to expect sex afterward. I think I need to take a break from men. I should get my life in order first. A man would only prolong my problems.

Shifting the focus from the hot neighbor to my boxes, I huff. Might as well get started. My things aren't gonna unpack themselves.

JOB HUNTING

I get up early and get dress. I have my thick mane-like hair blow-dried, flowing to my waist and straight, just precisely the way I like it. I decided to make myself presentable for any worthwhile entry-level job that pays minimum wage. Dress for success, or in my case, dress for any job that pays even pennies. The holes in my pockets are getting larger. I need a job and pronto. I dig out my only dress and borrow Jeff's iron. Can't have wrinkles on a job interview. I don't want to give anyone the impression that I'm a slob. I am, but that's not the point.

After I pour my body into the garment, I stand staring at myself in Jeff's long-length mirror that I'd swiped from his bedroom. Eh, the black dress is a little short, and form-fitting. My knee-high boots will disguise the short length. But just in case, I ought to wear a coat to cover my ass.

Apart from the relentless monsoon seasons and the monstrous hurricanes, New Orleans might not be such a bad place to live. Lots of life in this city. It's rich, with so much diversity and culture. All the more intriguing.

I'm not sure where to apply. I'm sort of lost in the world of job marketing. For the last two years, I've been living with Tad, he'd demanded that I stay home. Now that I'm out from under his perpetual control, I'm like that little bird released from her cage and confused where to fly. Regardless of my newfound freedom, it's a little intimidating. I don't have any training in any particular field. I am a disaster with computers, my experience waiting tables is hazardous from breaking dishes, getting orders wrong and pissing off customers. Maybe a department store can hire me. I'm pretty good with a register.

Unlike my brother, I barely finished high school. My senior year was the year we lost Mom and Dad. I wanted to drop out and get my GED. Jeff wouldn't stand for it. He insisted I finish or else he'd kick my ass. I graduated, but not with the best GPA.

I'm stuffing my face with cereal when Jeff comes through the door. I take one look and see the exhausted lines cleaved in his face. "Hey, rough night?" I smile, taking a bite of corn flakes.

"You could say that," he mumbles as he pads his way to the fridge and grabs a bottle of Fiji water and joins me at the island. "Did you sleep well?" He opens the cap and turns his head back, taking a deep gulp.

"I did. Thanks!" I smile before stuffing a large bite in my mouth.

"I see you found your way to my Frosted Flakes."

"You know I did, Jeffie," I grin, stuffing another big bite. It's my favorite too. "Why aren't you at the bar with all your doctor friends?"

A fine line appears between his brows, "How do you know where I hang out?"

"Your neighbor, Ethan, invited me to meet up with y'all," I shrug. "I didn't want to invade your turf."

"Oh, stop it! You're welcome anytime." He suddenly frowns. "I lost a patient."

"I'm sorry." I pause. "Such a terrible night."

"It never gets easy losing a patient. And of all things, it had to be a car accident."

"Do you think about Mom and Dad?" Such a painful reminder. We were robbed of our parents at such an early age. It's not fair. Life is not fair, and I hate accepting that fact.

"It's not just Mom and Dad's death, Ann," his

voice appears edgy. I never liked that tone. "Another human life is gone needlessly."

"I'm sorry."

He stares at the window and cuts his eyes back to me. "It's fine. I'm just drained." He goes quiet as he takes another drink of his water. "So where are you going all dolled up?" He eye-balls me.

"I'm going job hunting. I can't be mooching off my brother forever." I take another bite of corn flakes.

"Yeah, that'd be nice for a change."

"I figure New Orleans is a big place. I might get a bartending job. They make good tips."

"Anna, I understand that you want some spending money, but I have another idea, and I'm willing to help."

Oh crap, here we go.

"What?" I drop my spoon in the bowl.

"You're not going to make a living as a bartender or depending on a boyfriend to support you. Look at Tad. That is when he actually worked. Hell, half the time I paid your rent, groceries and anything else you needed."

"Jeff, I'm going to pay you back every cent!" I feel on the defense. Listening to him tick off all the things he has done pierces my heart to the point that I want to run back to Texas. Though running away is becoming an unabating habit. It's time I grow up and take some responsibility.

"You can pay me back by pulling yourself out of the gutter and going to college. Get a degree, or even training in something that will keep you afloat. How many times are you going to suffer the backhand of creeps like Tad, so you can have a place to live?"

"That's not entirely true. I really cared about him."

"Like hell you did! Ann, I love you, but I know you better than anyone. You're a loafer. Always moving from one person to the next, not giving it much thought. And no plans for the future. You're not getting any younger. Before you know it, you're looking at fifty. Too late in life to start a career."

"That's enough!" I snap.

"Is it? What are you going to do? Find another guy that gets liquored up and decides to kill you?"

"That's not fair!" Guilt is eating at me from the inside.

"Fair or truth?" his lips tighten. "That jerk put you in the hospital, and you went back to him after I begged you to come home with me. It took that son of a bitch to get caught with his pants down with your trashy girlfriend before you decided to leave." Jeff slices through my raw wound like I'm a piece of cake. "He hit you again, didn't he? Your make-up can't hide the bruises."

Jeff's right. I know how to pick 'em. "Okay, okay!" A suffocating sensation tightens my throat.

"You're right. I'm the loser sister you wish you never had!"

"Those are your words, not mine! I care about you, but I'm fed up with picking up the pieces and trying to make you well. I just don't understand why you keep picking these losers and ruining your life. You're better than that."

It feels as if my throat is closing up. I can't listen to Jeff's scolding any further. I quickly push from the island, sliding off the stool and snatching my bag. I don't disagree with Jeff. I need a moment to breathe before he rehashes all my stupid mistakes.

"Look, I'm sorry! I can't do this right now. See you later." I dart out, slamming the door behind me and rushing down the corridor. I stop at the elevator and jab the button several times, taking my anger out on it. Sometimes it's hard letting Jeff hammer at me.

Boy, what I'd give for a drink … *several*. But that would add one more to Jeff's endless list. Still, sometimes, I just don't give a rat's ass.

Jeff's right. Tad is trouble. He put me in the hospital with a broken jaw and two cracked ribs. I can't remember what we were arguing about. How stupid is that? I wipe a fallen tear with the back of my hand. Crap! Hope my mascara doesn't run. I blow out a sharp sigh. What great memories I have. Tad spending the night in county jail while the police tried persuading me to press charges. How could I do that to him when I'd provoked him? Don't men think with their fists?

The elevator door dings and opens. I start to board but my eyes collide with that cute neighbor, Ethan Something. Dang, I can't remember his last name, but he looks good in his light blue scrubs. I suddenly realize I'd been crying and it's apparent as I see the startled look in his sea-green eyes. I swallow the lump in my throat as I say, "Oh, hi." Jesus! Perfect timing!

"Hey, you okay?" He holds the door open, his eyes piercing, full of pity.

"Yeah, it's nothing. Really." I can't step into that elevator and have my brother's friend see me collapse into pieces. "You can go on down. I'll wait for the next one."

"C'mon," he smiles amiably. "I'll ride with you. You look like you could use a friend." Oh geez, he feels sorry for me. Not cool or sexy.

"Alright," I force myself to smile as I step inside. The door rattles as it closes, and I take a long breath. I suddenly smell cologne, an outdoor scent like fresh pine. Whatever he's wearing, it's enticing.

All at once, I feel nervous as I shuffle my feet. Ethan stands next to me, quiet, though I sense his eyes on me. Just break the ice, will you? "Where are you heading to?" Geez, now I sound nosey. Talking about the weather would've been better.

"Oh, I just got off my shift. Thought I'd walk

you out. You know, make sure you're okay." A gentle smile dances in his soulful eyes.

"You really don't have to bother. I'm alright. Jeff and I sorta had a disagreement is all. No biggie." Nervously, I moisten my lips.

"You look nice. I like your hair, but I prefer the wet look," he smiles as humor flashes in his eyes.

"Thank you." My cheeks flush.

The first floor dings and he holds the doors for me to exit. As we make our way to my car, he asks, "Do you have somewhere you have to go?"

"Uh … I'm job hunting. Thought I'd go drop off applications to the local bars around here. How hard can it be serving beer?" I shrug.

"It's early. Why don't you let me take you for coffee? Have you eaten?"

Oh, geez! Another person trying to give me advice is more than I can handle this morning. "It's sweet, but I can't. Maybe next time?" I dig out my keys and unlock my car door.

He scratches his day-old stubble. "No problem. Another time, then," he flashes a brief smile.

"Thanks for walking me out."

"Any time," he winks.

As I climb in my car, I watch Ethan saunter back to the building. His movements are swift, full of grace, and virility. I sigh, feeling the devil of disappointment. Why couldn't I have met this guy first?

I may not have truly loved Tad, but the impact

of his infidelity still left a mark on my heart. My raw memories of our argument still lingers. For the life of me, I can't understand why I stayed as long as I did. This girl is hanging her Texas hat elsewhere. When I say I'm done, I am done!

I pounded the pavement, hitting every bar on Bourbon Street. Most places directed me to apply online. I just figured I could go marching in and get hired. Boy, was I wrong!

I return home heavy-hearted. No job, no gas, and no money to even buy a piece of gum. Then, a brilliant idea knocks me in the head like a fallen brick from the sky.

I'm standing at my neighbor's door, ringing the doorbell. I rock on my heels until I hear feet dragging across the floor. Seconds later, the door squeaks open and Ethan appears, eyes heavy with sleep, dressed merely in heart-covered boxers. "What's up?" he speaks in a groggy voice.

Oh, snap! "You were sleeping." My eyes pause at his boxers and my cheeks flame.

"It's fine," Ethan yawns, running his fingers through the tousled, sandy curls that sweep into his face. "What can I do for you?"

"It can wait." Shaking my head, I back from the door and turn, tossing over my shoulder, "I'm sorry to have disturbed you."

"No, it's okay," he calls out, opening the door. "I

have to get up anyway. Come in." He steps back, seemingly unbothered that he's shirtless.

Nice abs, by the way. The boxers are pretty darn cute too. I bite my bottom lip to hold back a giggle.

"Oh … *ooo-kay.*" I keep my eyes up, forcing myself not to peek … *much.* He's adorable but hands-off. After all, he's my brother's friend.

"What's up?" He makes his way over to the coffee pot and flips it on.

I glance around. Apart from the décor, his apartment looks like my brother's, but only on the opposite side. Hands down. This is a bachelor's pad, alright. A little on the messy side. A few shirts lay around, tennis shoes by the recliner, and a big-screen television. And I can safely assume that he likes video games, I think when I spot a pile of gaming devices by the shoes.

"Umm … as you know, I'm looking for a job." I walk over to the island and lean over it, on my elbows.

"I recall." He rubs the bristle across his face.

"I'm thinking, how about I clean your house and cook?"

"You can clean and cook?" There is a trace of amusement in his voice.

I'm almost offended, but I swallow my pride. "That's right. I'm pretty good at it too."

"Does that include you washing my dirty drawers?" he asks while pouring a cup of coffee. He turns to me with his mug in his hand, "Care for a cup too?"

"I'm good. Thanks."

He leans against the counter directly across from me and sips his coffee, not saying a word.

I'm beginning to think I made a mistake. "Well, I see you could use the help." Despite his lack of interest, I push forward. "And if you pay me well enough, I'll be happy to wash anything you like." Holy crap! That came out wrong. I clear my throat. "Uh ... you know what I mean." I squirm as I divert my gaze to the coffeepot. My cheeks all at once blister enough to light the sky.

"Really? Even my shorts?" I catch a glance of a smile behind the brim of his cup as he takes a sip.

"Never mind! I shouldn't have-"

I turn on my heels heading to the door. I'm worn out from pounding the pavement, and the sting of my brother's lingering words. Now I have to take this jerk's jabs too?

"Wait!" Ethan rushes in front of me, slapping his palm flat against the door, blocking my escape. "Hang on!"

I suddenly feel his coffee breath against my neck. I freeze.

"You're right, I could use a housekeeper. How about you come clean my apartment, five days a week, when I'm at work. I'm a light sleeper. Noise keeps me up."

JO WILDE

I face him, my eyes wide and liquid. "What time and how much?"

He laughs. "Pushy, aren't you," he sighs. "How about you start tomorrow evening at six. I go in for my shift at that time. I'll drop my key off tomorrow."

"Okay, and how much?"

He grins, revealing a dimple on his right side. "Fifteen an hour. Deal?" he extends his hand.

What does this guy have about handshaking? I clasp my hand to his. "Deal! I'll see you tomorrow."

"Alrighty. Six sharp." He steps back and opens the door.

I start to head out but stop. Our eyes meet as I smile. "Thank you." I linger, holding his gaze. I think how little effort it would take getting lost in those pools of green. Specks of gold churn within the green, full of mischief like a little boy, and yet a man with desire.

Without another word, I break the hold and leave, hearing the door shut gently behind me. I giggle, full of excitement. Now I have to face my brother, but at least I have a job. I am so excited that I do a little twerk down the hall on my way to Jeff's apartment, two doors down.

FOE OR FRIEND

 enter the apartment, prepared for another one of Jeff's *Come to Jesus'* speeches. I soon realize that he's gone and I'm alone. I kick off my boots and head for the couch. My feet are killing me.

Getting lost in watching some mindless movie sounds like heaven to me. I wonder if I can get *Ghostbusters*? An oldie but a goodie. Maybe I'll snack on some junk food too. I find the remote in a pouch on the side of the armrest. Just when I pick it up, my cell lights up with a silly tune. The stupid one with the dogs barking. Just as I expected, Susan, the backstabber calling. The one I'd caught in bed with Tad.

I grab my phone out of my purse and glower at

it as her number hits my phone. I inhale a deep breath and slide the button.

~

"Hello!" I don't bother hiding my aggravation.

"Hey, Annie! Umm … glad you picked up. Can we talk, please?" The plea in her voice sends waves of betrayal through my body.

"Make it quick," I say coldly.

"Listen, you may not believe me, but I'm sorry for hurting you. I don't know how it happened, but I've learned my lesson," she sniffles.

"Go on," I insist.

"Look! It started over Tad and me having a few drinks. He'd been complaining about you not understanding him and you refusing sex."

I interrupted. "And you thought you'd give him a helping hand." I spit out the words as if I hate the taste. Susan's betrayal angers me more than Tad's. It's an unspoken girl code that you don't mess with your girl's man. *Unfuckingforgivable!*

"Yeah, kinda," she admits.

"Wow! So, you're saying that it's my fault you climbed in his bed?"

"It kinda is. If you'd been tending to your man, he would've never looked at me."

Why do cheaters always blame everyone else

instead of owning their shit? "How long? How long have you been sleeping with Tad?"

"To be honest, it started about six months ago."

"Six months ago! I was in the hospital with two broken ribs and a busted jaw. Is that what you mean by me not being there for Tad?"

"I don't know! But you started that fight with him. You know to leave him alone when he gets in one of his dark moods."

"You mean his *drinking* moods?" I want to reach through the phone and strangle this girl.

"He likes to drink. If you would've joined him with a drink or two, he might not have gotten so mad at you. And then your brother hatin' on him didn't help the situation any."

"Don't talk about my brother. He's done nothing but help, Tad and me!"

"Your brother told Tad if he ever hit you again that he'd turn him in to the police."

"So that makes Jeff a bad person?"

"No, not bad. He should've kept his gay ass out of yours and Tad's business."

"Susan, what do you expect? Jeff was defending me!"

"I get that, but frankly, you should've had Joe handle it. Not your doctor brother."

"Why your husband?"

"Joe whooped Tad's ass and," there's a sudden silence between us. I hear her breathing. "Joe kicked me out, and Tad says I can't stay with him. It's over. I think he was sleepin' with me to make you jealous." She's flipping this around making herself the victim. Why did I see her as a friend?

"Whoa! That's rich! Tad and Joe both have dumped you?" I mock.

"Look! I'm the worst friend ever. I done you wrong," Susan whimpers. "I don't blame you for hatin' me. But can't we get over this one little hump? Remember the good times you and me shared?"

"You ruined those memories by sleeping with my boyfriend in my bed!" My patience veers quickly. "Good-bye, Susan!"

"Wait! Don't hang up," Susan begs. "I need your help. I got nowhere to go. Joe kicked me out, and you know my family won't take me back. I need a place to stay. Can I sleep on your couch for a few days?"

There's a moment of icy silence between us. "You blew our friendship. Your homeless ass is not my problem. Don't call me again."

I hit the red button on my phone and block her number. If there is one thing I can say that's nice about Susan ... that she's resourceful. The girl will find someone to fall for her pity story. I wash my hands of the whole mess. She's proven where her loyalties lie.

Besides, Jeff would hit the roof if I brought that skank home. Piqued, I toss my phone on the other side of the couch and sink into its cushions. The deluge of problems seems to increase. Why can't I be more like Jeff? He's the king of discipline.

Me, I'm the one that flies by the seat of my pants and seeming to land on my nose. Will I ever learn to make better choices in my life? Like, pick better friends? Looking back, Susan and her husband, Joe, were closer friends with Tad than me. The three of them were fishing buddies.

I wipe the tears from my face with my sleeve and drag out a long sigh. I think of myself as a glasshouse, and everyone in my upside-down world is throwing rocks at me. Any minute, I expect to shatter into a million pieces.

THE JOB

The next day, straight up 5 p.m., I hear the doorbell ring and my heart leaps. "Oh, God! It's Ethan!"

I rush to the door and stand on my tippy toes, looking through the peephole. Quickly, I run my fingers through my hair and straighten my top. Can't let him see me looking a fright.

I swing the door open and he's standing there, devilishly handsome, holding a key between his fingers and carting a smile. "Here you go," he says. "I won't be home until six in the morning." Curiosity flashes in his eyes as he glances over my head. "Where's your brother?"

"Jeff's pulling a double shift. He slept at the hospital last night."

A faint line appears between Ethan's brows, "Oh, yeah. Those are the worst." He slips his hands in his pockets casually. "Well, gotta run! Don't touch my Xbox," he teases, breaking into an irresistible smile.

"I think your Xbox is safe," I giggle.

"See you tomorrow," he winks, turning on his heels.

I watch as he rushes down the hallway, drinking in his attractive male physique. Scrubs never looked better. I sigh, half wishing he could've hung around. I shut the door as I lean against it for support. Ethan is a rare find. His well-groomed appearance is congruent with his suntanned skin. Then, I come down off my high. No matter how much I'm crushing on Ethan LeBlanc, he's off-limits. First of all, I'm not his type, and secondly, he's my brother's friend. For all I know, he's gay and my brother's boyfriend.

Jeff came out of the closet after our parents died. He'd kept that secret to himself for a long time, even from me. Despite these modern times we live in, coming out as a gay man or woman is very difficult. Not everyone is accepting. Jeff has had a hard time swallowing his truth. I think he's torn between society's beliefs and where his heart lies. He hides who he is, fearing it will affect his career. I've seen him go on dates with women, and the females go crazy over him. With his thick blond curls and blue eyes and his towering height, who wouldn't be attractive to him? Jeff's a great catch. His heart is bigger than the Grand Canyon. Although, if he marries a woman, I know he's not being fair to himself or the girl. Though, the chances of Jeff marrying are improbable. I don't think he's dating anyone unless he's seeing the neighbor, Ethan. They do seem to know each other pretty well, looking out for each other. Although, I don't get the gay vibe from Ethan.

～

Off I go to Ethan's apartment with a mop under my arm and a box of cleaners and supplies that I borrowed from Jeff. I enter the apartment and lock the door behind me. A gal can never be too careful.

I start with the dishes. He's collected quite a bit of pots and pans and several plates. For a man who never cooks, he sure has a large number of dirty dishes. I spot two long stem glasses still half full of a dark cherry substance. I pick up one of the glasses and notice a smudge of crimson lipstick. I sniff the drink and pull back.

"Yup, it's wine," I mumble.

A little green sting all at once strikes. He's dating! If he's in a relationship with Jeff, then he's cheating on my brother. If he is with a woman, that means my assumption is wrong, but on a positive note for me, he's not gay. On a negative note, he has a girlfriend.

Bummer, either way. I rake in a sigh and get busy washing. I don't know why it bothers me. He's not shown me any genuine interest. I'm merely his friend's little sister. "Just plain Anna Lee!" I mumble sourly.

He'll never look twice at a girl like me. I'm damaged goods with nothing to offer. I don't fit in a doctor's world.

But it's time that I stop thinking of guys and focus on myself. Jeff mentioned college. I know what that means, buckling down and keeping my nose to the books. What would I major in? There's not a lot of subjects that interest me. Back when I was younger, I used to write. If I get an English degree, I could teach. A teacher's salary wouldn't compare to what Jeff makes, but the satisfaction of helping others is rewarding. Still, I have a hard time finishing projects. Shoot, getting a degree would be major. Unlike this job, house cleaning; I'm already bored.

After I finish the kitchen, I find the vacuum off to the side in the living room. Note duly taken. Ethan intends for me to earn my money. I plug in the vacuum and then tidy up the living room before

I head back to his bedroom. I stop at the doorframe and glance inside.

I feel like I'm invading Ethan's personal space. I notice the California king-size bed. Why would a single man have such a large bed? Unless he has plenty of overnight guests? Then again, Jeff has the same size bed. I need to get my mind out of the gutter and stop worrying about what Ethan does in his spare time. The man's personal life is his own business. I'm the maid.

I brush my fingers over his sheets. Wow! They're amazing. I search for the tag and find it. The name brand is Frette. Not a cheap brand by any means. I sigh, stroking the satin-like fabric. I wonder what it'd be like sleeping on these sheets naked? I *gotta* stop thinking about sex.

I start with his sheets, tugging them off the bed and gathering them in the basket. I dare not attempt washing his comforter. It's heavy, and I assume it's expensive and requires dry cleaning. It's best I steer clear of that.

I turn to head to the washer, but stop. Something glittery catches my eye, hiding in the thread of the carpet. I bend down to find a diamond earring. Large honking one too. Jesus! He must be dating a rich chick with expensive taste. Ire bristles my neck.

I look for a place to put the earring and spy a

glass dish on his dresser. My guess it's where he lays his keys and shades. I drop the diamond earring into the bowl as if it's searing my palm. The thought of another woman is getting under my skin. I'm acting ridiculous; I don't have any right to get jealous. Yet, it eats at me all the same.

I quickly move to the washing machine. I toss the sheets, a little too hard in the washer, taking my frustrations out on Ethan's bedding. Then I get grossed out, realizing I just handled sex sheets. Yuck! I adjust the water and pour bleach in the drum. Then, a little voice whispers in my head. These sheets are special care, no bleach. Frantically, I open the lid and stare down at the saturated sheets. Jesus! I just lost more than a month's wage. That is, if I still have a job. The sheets are ruined!

I slam the top down as a loud thud ricochets off the wall. I slide down the washer to the floor, resting my back against the cool metal. I stare at the ceiling. My heart has sunk to an all-time low.

"Damn!" I blow out.

I suck at everything! Tears start to collect, and I just want to go home and crawl in my bed and cry. Is there anything I can do right?

When the wash is done, I rush to check the sheets. Just what I feared. The sheets look like a blast from the past … *tie-dyed*. Ugly gray with white swirls.

"Geez!" I gape at the mottled sheets. I'm in big trouble, and I can probably kiss my job good-bye. Jeff is going to have a field day at my expense. That is after Ethan gets done with me. I'm a dead girl walking.

I inhale a deep breath and check my watch. It's 10 p.m. Ethan won't be home until the morning. There's a Wal-Mart around the corner. Jeff was nice enough to loan me some money. I think I have enough money to find sheets similar to these. Maybe then, I can break it to Ethan slowly. Very slowly. I bite down hard on my bottom lip, thinking. I rush for my bag and lock the door behind me.

When I return from Wal-Mart, I rush with my sack in hand, heading to his bedroom. I first stop at the laundry room, dragging out one of the ruined sheets, comparing the color. It's close enough that I think he won't notice. I'll have enough time to beg, borrow, and steal the money to purchase the real deal.

I tear into the plastic covering and pull out the new sheets. I didn't think Wal-Mart carried California king-size, but "whew!". Glad I was wrong.

In no time, I have the gray sheets fitted on his bed and nicely tucked in the corners. The fabric is much more course than the pricey set. Eh! He's a dude, he won't notice. Then it hit me. "Oh geez! The new smell?"

I sniff the fabric. I draw back, my nose wrinkled. "Phew! Wal-Mart scent! I'm screwed! I am so Wal-Mart screwed."

I run to his bathroom, digging in his bottom cabinet until I come across a can of starch. The can looked like Ethan found it at a junkyard, corroded and dented. But I have an idea. The starch will mask the smell. He'll think I starched it. My spirit of hope soars.

I go to work spraying the sheets. When I finish, I damn near use up the whole can. The sheets are dripping wet. Then something occurs to me, "Jesus!" I didn't think about the sheets fading. This just keeps getting worse by the minute. My heart races as I quickly pull back the sheets, and I'll be damned forever!

I nearly screech to the heavens. The sheets bled through, dotting the stark white mattress with gray smudges. I twirl on my heels, tugging at my hair, having a conniption fit. What do I do *now*? Go buy him a new mattress? How much will that cost me? I rake my fingers through my hair, freaking out.

Then I go to thinking … Jeff has a California king, and I think it's the same brand. I pull the damp sheets from all four corners, looking for the tag. Bingo! I spot the tag. Same mattress. The little light goes off in my head, and I almost jump with joy. I can switch mattresses! I break out into a euphoric dance.

Jeff will never notice, and neither will Ethan. And if I manage to *not* get fired, by the end of next year, I'll have the money to replace Ethan's mattress and sheets. When Jeff figures out what I've done, it won't matter. By then, I'll have an apartment, so all he can do is yell at me over the phone. I start to chew on a fingernail. A bad habit, but I'll ignore it this once, given the circumstances.

I rush out the door and into Jeff's apartment, headed straight to his bedroom. Quickly, I strip his bed down. I stand there huffing, eye-balling Jeff's huge bed. This isn't going to be easy. I go back to the living room and push things out of the path to make room for this monstrous mattress.

I return to the bedroom and begin tugging at its corners, pushing the mattress to a vertical position. Attempting to hold it straight up and shoving it through a narrow pathway down the hall and through the front door is harder than I anticipated. I could've at least worn loose clothing. My jean cut-offs and tight T-shirt are too tight for this manual task. Dragging this monster of a mattress with my butt cheeks hanging out, along with my boobs spilling over the top of my shirt, is not how I saw this going down. Glad it's late at night, and everyone is sleeping. I'd die if I ran into anyone.

I manage to shove the heavy mattress out Jeff's

front door and slide it to Ethan's. I heave and groan, scooting it down the hall. Ethan's only two doors down, but it feels like a hundred. When I'm halfway to Ethan's, I lose my grip, and the mattress tumbles flat to the floor, a thud echoes down the dim corridor. Relief washes over me, knowing that folks are asleep at this time of the night. I bend over and lift the heavy thing, cursing under my breath and breaking out into a sweat.

After I'm done switching out mattresses, I'm back at Ethan's, collapsed on the bed, dragging in oxygen from my deprived lungs. My heart finally settles, and my breath returns to normal as I'm back up finishing the last touches to Ethan's bed. Once I complete the task, I go to the kitchen and pull out a large pot pie from the Wal-Mart sack, Marie Callender. The best money can buy … or at least on Jeff's budget.

I turn the temperature to 350 Fahrenheit and set the pie in the oven. I put the timer on 45 minutes.

When the pie is ready, I take it out and place it on a plate and leave it on top of the stove to cool. I go check all my bases around the apartment and pass with flying colors. Now all I have to do is tie up a few loose ends, and I'm done. I wrap foil over the pie and place it back in the oven. I write Ethan a quick note letting him know there's food for him and thank him for giving me this opportunity. I lock the door behind me and head to Jeff's. I check my watch. It's a quarter to two in the morning. I'm so beat that I could fall asleep standing up.

I drag myself to my bedroom, not bothering to change into my pajamas, and flop on my bed, face down, and in seconds, I am out.

All is well in the world.

THE TALK

I'm half asleep when I feel my bed shake. My eyes pop open, and I'm staring up at Jeff as I break into a wide yawn. "Hey, did you just get home?" My voice is groggy.

"I made some coffee. Why don't you have a cup with me?"

"Don't you need to sleep? Coffee will keep you up." I cover my mouth, yawning again.

"I caught some sleep last night at the hospital. It was slow." He taps my shoulder. "I got cream and Splenda. Just like you like it."

"Okay!" I stretch and yawn.

Moments later, I'm dragging my feet to the island. I spot two huge mugs, and Jeff is pouring black coffee in one. I slide onto the stool next to Jeff.

He glances up at me and sets a full cup with all

the works. "There you go, Sis." He pours his cup and sets the pot back on its plate. "You hungry?" he nods over his shoulder at the fridge. "I have eggs and bread."

I band my fingers around the handle of my mug, staring into the steam curling above the rim. "No, I'm good, but thanks." I know my brother well enough that his catering to me is a ploy to get me prepped for the talk. Oh, boy! Here we go. "What's on your mind?" These discussions set my teeth on edge every time. He means well, and he's always right. Still, it doesn't make it any easier.

Jeff takes the stool next to me. "I think we need to talk."

I blow on my coffee and take a tiny sip, "I thought we did that already." Jesus! Last night just came rushing back. Hope he doesn't catch on about my little stunt. When he finds out I switched his mattress, Jeff's going to blow up. I hold my breath.

"There are other issues I want to discuss."

Staring in his big blue eyes feels as if a machine gun is firing straight at me. "Okay, can you just say it?"

"Sis, I'm tired of worrying that one day I'm going to get a phone call that you're dead. Seriously, the company you keep is disturbing."

"Duh! That's why I left Texas. You do not need to worry."

"Ann, you don't seem to understand. It is a

matter of time before you pick another Tad and maybe worse!"

"Stop predicting the future for me! If it's a problem me staying here, I can leave." It stings that my brother doesn't see that I'm trying.

"No! I don't want you to leave." His lips pucker with annoyance.

"Then, what do you want from me? Plain English, please." I push my coffee away.

"Apart from a job, I want you to go see a psychiatrist. I'll cover the expense. All you have to do is show up and work on yourself."

I stare at him as my mouth drops open but then I halt my protest. This might be a good idea. I'm fractured and finding the reason why would help me to understand myself better. "Okay, I'll go." My shoulders slump. It's not easy admitting defeat.

"You have no idea how happy I am to hear this. One more thing." Jeff pauses.

I'm not sure I can take much more of his demands. "What else?"

"I'd like to see you get a part-time job and enroll in classes at the local college."

I fiddle with my hair, not sure how Jeff will take this. "I have a job."

My brother leans back, brows fly up. "When and where?"

"I worked last night at your friend-friend's apartment. I'm his housekeeper now."

"Ethan?"

"Yep, your friend-friend," I toss him a grin.

"Will you stop that? Ethan is not my friend-friend. He's merely a friend. Ethan is straight. Not my type."

"Oh, I thought since you guys know each other so well that-"

"That what? We're lovers?" His blue eyes are sharp and pointy.

"Well, yeah. Ethan's hot."

Jeff rolls his eyes. "I disagree, but Ethan and I are just friends. And you don't need to get tied up with him either." He shakes his head, "How the hell did you end up cleaning his house?"

"I just asked," I shrug.

"Is he there when you're cleaning?"

"Why the concern?" I stare at Jeff suspiciously.

"I'm wary you're going to get hurt."

"Hurt? Like mass murderer hurt?" Despite Jeff's disapproval, I'm stoked to hear that Ethan's straight.

"No, of course not." He slides his coffee over to the side of him. "Ethan is a ladies' man. He doesn't date, if you get my drift."

"Oh, that kind of guy. Love 'em and leave 'em kind."

"I just don't want you getting your hopes up. Besides, since you were recently in a relationship, don't you think you should hold the brakes?"

My brother, the mother. "You don't have anything to concern yourself with. I'm not Ethan's type anyhow."

"Why do you say that? Ann, any great guy would be lucky to have you. Apart from your outer beauty, I don't know anyone who has a bigger heart than you."

"That's really sweet." I wish I saw myself as Jeff does. Maybe a therapist would be good for me.

THE THERAPIST

The therapist happens to have an office at Tulane Medical Center, where my brother and Ethan are residents. I look at my phone to recheck the suite number: 102. On the first floor, I follow the arrows and turn left down a bright bleach-white hall when I spot my therapist's office.

I enter through the heavy glass door and go up to the receptionist's desk. A gray-haired woman with thick glasses opens the small window and asks, "How can I help you, ma'am?"

"I have an appointment with Dr. Kim Rice."

"Your name, please?" The woman's voice is flat and rushed. The normal clinical voice that you hear at every doctor's office.

"Anna Lee Baker. My appointment is at ten this morning."

The woman checks her computer. After a moment, she looks up and says, "Yes, I see your appointment. Is this your first time to see Dr. Rice?" She hardly glances at me.

"Yes," I say. My heart is pounding my ribs. I guess I'm nervous. First time to see a shrink.

The receptionist hands me a clipboard with a stack of papers to fill out and a pen with a silly flower on the tip. "Please fill these out and return them when you're done."

"Okay, thank you," I take the clipboard and go to find a seat. I always hated filling out forms. It's awkward enough with the clipboard since I'm left-handed

I spot a seat and just my luck, the only one available is next to a woman that looks like she's been road raging for the last month. Wild red hair, eyes like she's been electrocuted. I hesitate, thinking about rescheduling. But no, I promised Jeff I'd do this. So, despite how much I'd like to flee, I force myself to take the chair. I remind myself that this is for me too.

After the clock's hand climbs the circle, pointing to the top, I've covered every freaking magazine possible. I start playing Candy Crush Saga when I finally hear my name called. I quickly gather my bag and follow the nurse as she leads me down a narrow hallway. Framed pictures of doctors hang on the stark white wall as we pass. I notice one picture of a woman. I don't catch the name, but I wonder if that's my doctor. If so, she's very attractive.

We come to a halt at a door on the right that is about halfway down the hall. The nurse opens the door and invites me to step inside a small room. I hesitate. I know once I enter the land of Oz, my life will change forever. I'm not sure I'm ready for this, but what choice do I have? I cautiously enter the room. I spot a couch and two chairs on the opposite side.

The nurse draws my attention, "Dr. Rice will be in shortly. Make yourself comfortable," she smiles, exiting the room.

With a wary sigh, I brush my eyes over the small space as I take a seat on the bright yellow couch. The cushion gives under my weight, making me feel uncomfortable. I stuff a pillow behind me and lean back, folding my hands in my lap.

I check my phone as I've been waiting for a half-hour. The door is calling to me. Just a few feet and I'd be free. I could reschedule. Lying to Jeff wouldn't be so hard. Then I remember, Dr. Rice and my brother are friends. And he works right down the hall. Jesus! I feel trapped. Which only makes me more agitated.

Sitting there, biting my nails, I hear footfalls clacking down the hall and a soft woman's voice. The door opens and in steps a woman in a white jacket. I read her tag: Dr. Kim Rice. That *was* her in the picture. I catch myself from gaping. Attractive, tall, slender with long brunette hair and wearing a hip-hugging dark navy dress with killer heels. She's beautiful. Not what I'd expected for a psych.

The doctor steps up to me and reaches out to shake my hand. I gather to my feet and accept her offer. My eyes fall on her perfect cherry-red nails. She should be on the cover of *Vogue*.

"Hello, I'm Dr. Kim Rice. Make yourself comfortable." She tosses a crimson-lipstick smile, lovely, but I detect no emotions. Weird.

"Thank you," I say, feeling underdressed. I'm wearing a blue blouse and faded, ragged-out jeans with wedged heels. It's a warm day even, though it's almost December.

The doctor gathers back her perfectly groomed hair, and I choke. My eyes draw to her ears like a man discovering water in a desert. Holy crap! Her earrings match the one I found in Ethan's bedroom. The small room suddenly starts to spin. *She's Ethan's girlfriend!* I heard her mumbling words, but it's like I'm in a tunnel.

"Oh, I'm sorry." I snap out of it. "I was admiring your earrings," I say, cheeks flushed.

"Yes, a very close gentleman friend had given these to me." She flashes straight white teeth. "Now, tell me why you are here today?"

I inhale and exhale, regretting my promise to

Jeff. "Umm … I seem to be following a destructive path. I just got out of a bad relationship with someone."

"I see." She locks her fingers together and lays her hands on her lap. Our eyes catch. "I understand that your parents were killed in a car accident when you were eighteen. Do you think the loss of your parents has anything to do with your lifestyle now?"

I gather my thoughts for a minute and say, "No, I was a rebellious teenager until my parents' accident. Afterward, I straightened up and started walking a straight line. I have a lot of guilt for their death."

"Guilt, like you feel it's your fault they died?"

"Umm … no, of course not, it wasn't my fault. I feel guilty that they had to die first for me to stop my reckless behavior."

"So, you no longer drink or do illicit drugs?"

The doctor picks up a notepad and pen and starts jotting notes, or that's what I assume. The relentless scraping of the pen across the paper is like chalk across a blackboard. I desperately want her to stop. I'm more than just notes on paper.

"Uh … I only smoked pot. And correct, I've stopped."

"Yes, of course." She pushes out a synthetic smile. "You're saying basically, you have traded one bad habit for another, by choosing abusive men. Is this correct?"

"I don't know." I shift in my seat.

"And the relationship has dissolved."

"Yep." So many questions, I'm nearly going cross-eyed.

"How long did you stay with him after he started hurting you?"

"Umm … maybe a year. I, umm … I caught him in bed with my best friend. That's when I left."

"At this point, you felt the relationship couldn't go on any further?" Her voice is soft but very clinical.

"That's true." Jesus! My nerves are spastic.

"I'm assuming you fled Texas for your safety?"

"Yes, true. I want a new start too," I shrug.

"How was your childhood?" she asks as she jots something.

"It was great. My parents were loving and took good care of my brother and me."

"What were you like growing up?"

"Uh … it was childhood," I shrug. "You know, birthdays, family vacations, playing with the neighborhood kids."

"Can you remember your favorite birthday?"

I shrug. "Umm, I was twelve, and …" I suddenly draw a blank.

"Why did you stop. Go on," she coaxes.

"I'm a little foggy with the memories."

"Do you find this as odd?"

"I guess," I give pause. "Don't most people forget parts of their childhood?"

"Some, yes. What about before ten? Do you remember any birthdays?"

I shrug. "Maybe. I don't think about my childhood much."

"Why is that, Anna?" she asks.

"I don't know. I guess I'm living in the moment."

"It's normal to reminisce. Especially over our childhood."

"I guess. I just never think about it," I say.

Dr. Rice jots something on the pad and then looks up at me. "Are you and your brother close?" It feels like she's going down a checklist.

"Yes, especially after the accident."

"I'm sorry for your loss and I'm glad you have your brother's support," she half-smiles.

To me, her sincerity seems disingenuous. "Thank you," I say.

"I'd like to talk about the past." She pauses. "Let's touch more on your childhood memories. I want you to try to remember one birthday, before the age of ten?"

I look down at my hands on my lap, thinking. I look up and reply, "I don't recall any."

"Did you have friends when you were young?"

"Umm … maybe. I recall having an overweight

issue. Kids picked on me. My brother, Jeff, when he was around, defended me."

"Was this before twelve or after?"

I pause, trying to recall. "I think it was after."

"Why do you think your parents allowed you to gain weight?"

I shrug, "Mom worked part-time and, on her free days, she liked spending time catching up on her soaps. She'd make dinner when Dad came home. During the day, I wasn't restricted from eating junk food."

"At the age of ten, did you have friends in school?"

"Uh … I don't recall any friends until high school. I went on Weight Watchers and lost weight. It changed my life. I became more outgoing and started making friends. Though most had a wild streak. I found it to be invigorating."

"What do you mean 'wild streak'?"

"My friends teetered on the defiant side, and they accepted me. For the first time, I felt like I belonged."

The doctor checks her wristwatch. "It looks like our hour is over. Anna, I'd like to see you twice a week."

"That would be fine." I gather to my feet. "Umm, thank you for seeing me." I make myself smile as I grab my purse.

"It was a pleasure."

The doctor remains poised. I wonder if she ever lets her hair down, is less plastic and more human? Although, I see why Ethan likes her. She's stunning, and I'm a little jealous. I shouldn't be, but I can't help it. Knowing that my therapist is the woman that Ethan is seeing grates me.

After I pay the receptionist, I dart out the doctor's office. I rake in a long breath of fresh air as I open the heavy glass doors leading outside. Back in that tiny office, I felt stifled. I'm not sure if I like Dr. Rice. Time will tell.

As I cross over to the parking lot, a crisp breeze coasts under my thin blouse. I wrap my arms around my waist. Geez! In the last hour, the temperature has dropped at least ten degrees, and a cold chill fills the air. I peer up at the ominous clouds, looking bruised and angry. A faint taste of rain in the atmosphere promises a downpour. When does it not rain here? I sigh, eyeballing the gloomy clouds.

I spot my old silver sedan down three rows and make my way toward it when I catch sight of a familiar head, light brown hair to the shoulders and a quick side glance of an unkempt beard. Oh, my God! It couldn't be *Tad*. Jesus!

Alarm ices my blood. All at once, my feet feel heavy and cemented to the concrete. I stretch my eyes in every direction, but I see no one. The parking lot is eerily quiet. And the person I thought

I saw has vanished. My neck suddenly bristles. Could I have been mistaken? Perhaps, I'm just being paranoid, and my eyes were playing tricks?

I pick my feet up heading to my car, clenching my keys in hand. I need to get out of here before I lose it. I begin to tremble all over. Geez! This doctor is already messing with my head.

I reach my car and just when I start to unlock the door, a deep male voice drops on my neck, sending a flurry of chills over my body. My head whips around as I gasp. "Oh, Ethan!" I grab my chest as my heart jumps into my throat.

"Hey, I didn't frighten you, did I?" His hand gently touches my shoulder as a faint line appears between his brows.

"No, I'm fine," I say, slightly breathless. "What's up?"

He stuffs his hands in his pockets. "I just wanted to say thanks for cleaning my domain." His eyes dance with humor.

"Your domain?" I giggle. Cute but, of course, he would think of me as a maid. Unlike Dr. Rice. "Thanks."

"You up here to see Jeff?" A swath of sandy hair falls casually on his forehead.

Dang! He looks like a model for *Vogue*. "No, I had a doctor's appointment."

"Are you ill?" he asks, looking as if he's about to check my temperature.

"No, it's just a checkup," I lie. No way am I telling him that I'm not only seeing his girlfriend, but I'm also sick in the head as well.

"Oh, well, since you're done, why don't I take you to eat? I'm starving, and I hate eating alone."

There goes that white, dimpled smile taunting me again. I'm holding my breath that he hasn't figured out about the bed swapping.

"Umm ... thanks, but I'm not hungry."

"Then coffee?"

Having coffee with Ethan is very tempting. Though, I may be asking for trouble, considering Jeff's warnings, and the fact that he's dating my shrink. Yet, I like this guy. There's an inherent strength to him that I find hard to resist. I bite my bottom lip, thinking. "Do I meet you there?"

"You can ride with me. I'll bring you back to your car afterward."

Afterward? Sounds like sex. I got a little tingly over that delicious thought. I clear my throat. "Alright, you talked me into it. Lead the way." I shamefully cave.

It would be a delightful thought if he looked at me as girlfriend material. The problem I keep bumping into is that the men I like generally are not the one-woman type. Here I go again, liking someone that isn't available, and it just so happens that he's dating my therapist. The earring is a dead giveaway. If that's true, then why is he asking me to lunch? Does that mean he's two-timing my doctor? That makes me the other woman. Not cool.

I walk beside Ethan as we head to where he's parked. When we walk upon it, I stall, gaping. "A *Harley*?" Our eyes lock. "You want me to ride on the back of this?" Dread shoots through me. "I can't ride this."

I could see laughter behind his eyes, "Don't worry. I know how to handle my bike." He grabs up his helmet and hands it to me.

"You just have one helmet?" My eyes go wide.

"I got this," Ethan smiles wide as he straddles the bike and cranks its motor. He extends his hand, giving me a gentle tug.

I step up on the peddle and swing my leg over. I shout over the hum of the motor as panic churns my stomach. "What do I hang on to?"

Ethan tosses over his shoulder, "Lock your hands around my waist and hang on tight. I can't have you falling off."

"Umm …okay," Geez! My body trembles as I scoot closer to him to where even a thin shaft of light couldn't squeeze between us. I clench my hands around his waist. I feel the ripple of his firm abs. Hot damn! This is kind of sexy. A tinge of excitement surges through me, though I don't want to get used to this. He's just being nice since I'm his friend's little sister.

Then Dr. Rice comes to mind. I would be stupid

to think I have a chance. Anyway, it doesn't matter. He's taken.

"That's good," he pats my hands and lingers for a moment.

My body reacts as chill-bumps betray the obvious. I've never responded this way to Tad. I can't recall a time feeling excited over a man until now.

We roll up to a small diner on St. Peter Street called Spitfire Coffee. Once we park, Ethan kills the engine. I hop off and proceed to take off the helmet.

"Hold up," Ethan says. "Let me help you with that snap." His long leg swings over the bike with grace and ease, wearing his powder blue scrubs and his hospital tag.

I bite my bottom lip to keep from groaning.

He steps up to me and works his fingers, loosening the buckle, lifting the helmet off my head. I hide behind my lashes, feeling his warm breath on my cheeks. "There you go."

Suddenly, our eyes hitch and it feels like time has stalled. Ethan inclines his head, slowly. I swallow my breath, unsure if he's moving in for a kiss. My eyes go wide, holding my breath.

Suddenly, he tucks a wild strand of hair behind my ear and says, "You have the most striking eyes I've ever seen. They're hazel, but you have green specks that glisten." His eyes study me with an approving grin.

My cheeks blush five shades of pink. "Thank you, but I think you need your vision checked."

He flashes a smooth lopsided grin. "Did the bike ride make you nervous or is it me causing your heart to pound?" He lays his palm gently above my right breast, his green eyes dancing with amusement.

"Don't flatter yourself." I sock him in his stomach.

He flinches, laughing. "You're a spicy girl." His hands move to my hips.

"No, I'm not!" I step from him, making my way inside the café. Faint laughter wafts behind me as my face deepens to a bright red. I roll my eyes, thinking he's just messing with me now that he knows I'm a little timid.

We enter the coffee shop and make our way to a quaint table for two by the window. Quickly, I conclude that there's not a lot of space, only four tables to be exact. While I take a seat, Ethan goes and retrieves our order.

I stare out the window, watching the clouds grow dim and menacing. I wonder if we might get caught in the rain as the clouds grow darker. Yet, for some unknown reason, I'm not bothered.

Soon, Ethan returns with two large espressos and two muffins. One pumpkin and one oat-bran. Ethan takes his seat across from me and slides a coffee and muffin to me. He takes a large bite of his oat-bran muffin. "Hmm, this is out of this world." He closes his eyes and savors its taste. Then he plucks off a bite and reaches over the table. "It will melt in your mouth."

Feeling a rush of awkwardness, I open wide as he slips the bite into my mouth. I pause a minute, chewing as Ethan's eyes are fastened on me. "Oh, wow! That *is* good!" I chew with my mouth closed.

"I love this little place." He rests his elbows on the table and asks, "Have you had a chance to sightsee the city?"

"No, not yet." I glance outside. "I've been trying to get settled, so I haven't had time to think about anything else." I fold my hands around my cup. Its warmth soothes me.

We both lean in toward each other. It's like the whole world doesn't exist and it's just like two star-crossed lovers gazing into each other's eyes. I wonder if love feels this way.

"One day when I'm off and have had some sleep, we should take a tour." His smile reaches his tender green orbs.

"That sounds like fun." I take a sip of my coffee to mask my surprise.

"Just curious," he states. "What brings you to New Orleans?" His eyes hold me captive.

"I was tired of Texas and wanted to start something new," I shrug, fearing if I tell him about my abusive ex, it would turn him away. My life hasn't exactly been pristine.

"I guess what I'm asking is … if you are in trouble?" His eyes feel as if they're boring a hole through me. "Before I get too invested, I want to know if you're a straight shooter. Like, do you use illicit drugs or have a drinking problem? Why are you living with your brother instead of in your own apartment? Something had to happen for you to move in with your brother."

I glare at him. "Invested? How do you know I want to become *invested* in *you*?"

"*Touché*," he says softly. "I'm sorry. I'm a forward person. I have to be. I can't jeopardize my career." He leans back in his seat, staring at me with his piercing green eyes.

"First of all, you're the one pursuing me. The only thing I've approached you for was a job," I respond harshly, setting aside any pretense.

He stiffens as if I'd slapped him. "I've upset you."

"You think?" I'm not upset. I'm pissed. "You know what? Take your old stuffy self and take that woman with the fancy earrings to this diner. By the size of those diamonds, I doubt she'd come to a place like this."

"The woman with the earrings?" He looks puzzled, then a light of understanding flickers in his glint. "Oh, the earring you found." He clears his throat. "I wouldn't call her my girlfriend. More a friend, if you will."

"I don't understand how you can sit here, talking about investing in me when you are seeing someone else."

He arches an eyebrow questioningly. "Why do you think I'm seeing someone?"

"How did a woman's earring end up in your bedroom if you're not involved? Did it leap in your room?"

"Oh." The line of his mouth tightens a fraction more. "I know what it must look like. It's not what you think," he sighs. "Some folks just hook up, leaving any sort of attachment at the door."

I scoff. "So, you're telling me that you gave diamond earrings to someone you're not committed to?" I hold tight to my dirty little secret, knowing his lover is my doctor.

He laughs. "Huh ... that's a pretty pricey indulgent to give to a woman I'm not emotionally involved with."

Was it possible Dr. Rice had been speaking of another man? Even still, whether he bought the earrings or someone else did, the fact remains that he is sleeping with her. "So, the earrings are not a gift from you?"

"Hell, no! I'm just a third-year resident. I don't make that kind of money," he laughs.

"Judging by those earrings, she must be something else. Beautiful, expensive, high maintenance."

"True. The lady is a handful." He twists his lips into a faint frown. "I don't care for her type." There's a mystery behind his glint. "Beauty is nice, but I prefer a woman that's more natural, more heart. A gal that likes the outdoors and has a soft spot for big fluffy dogs."

"Oh, I see. I think you're a hypocrite. You were not planning to tell me about your rendezvous with this woman, but you expected me to divulge all the gory details of my life."

"I didn't see it necessary to elaborate," he shrugs. "She's in the past. I'm a single man now." Gosh, he sounds convincing.

"I'm confused. Is this how you ask women out?" I exhale loudly. "Do you always do interviews and background checks with every woman you potentially date, or is it just me?"

"My apologies for coming on strong. You moving in with your brother seems sudden and then, that day I ran into you in the elevator, you were crying. I can't help but question if you're in trouble."

"I'm not in trouble. And, just for the record, I don't drink, and I don't do drugs. I don't have any arrest records either. Does that make you happy?"

"Yes, very. I wouldn't want you hurting yourself. I'm sorry if I've offended you. I can't take any risk that might jeopardize my career."

"I get it. You don't have to worry about me. I don't foresee us dating. And for the record, I will keep turning *you* down."

He grabs his chest as if he's having a heart attack, "Ah, you sure know how to shoot a guy down," he teases. "Let's start over." He leans in and takes my right hand. "Would you care to go on a date with me? I'd like to show you the town."

I bite down on my bottom lip to smother a giggle. "Why are you interested in me? We are polar opposites."

He pauses as one corner of his lips tips upward, suggesting a smile. "I like you. You're cute and you make me laugh. Yet there is a mystery behind those beautiful hazel eyes." His eyes latch on mine, and I smile unconsciously.

He thinks I'm funny and my eyes are pretty. I inhale, fighting back the bubbles inside. "That's not a reason to like someone."

"Sure, it is!" He pauses, grinning. "Your brother and I know about the mattress switch. A neighbor shot a video of you lugging each mattress. Jeff and I couldn't stop laughing."

I'm gawking as my whole body breaks out into a sweat. Jesus Christ! They both know. I thought the neighbors were asleep. Geez! "You *know*?" Shock soars through me.

"Yep, and I found my tie-dyed sheets tucked behind my tools in the pantry," he chuckles.

"I can explain!" Talk about egg on one's face.

"No need." Ethan's shoulders bounce. "I've never laughed so hard in my life. You're only 5' 2" and weigh about a hundred pounds. You've got muscle, girl." He shakes his head in wonder. "Jeff and I switched the beds back, and it took both of us to move the mattresses."

Slugging him would give me great pleasure, but I deserve his taunting. "I ... I plan to replace your mattress and the sheets. It was a stupid, stupid accident."

"Actually, I haven't laughed that much in a long time. Even the neighbor came over and joined in on the fun, watching you tugging those mattresses. I didn't know a body could go in all those positions," he snickered.

"Wait! You saw my ass?"

"Well, what can I say, I'm a guy." He grins as my face heats up more than I thought possible.

"Am I fired?"

"Oh, absolutely. But you can come over and watch TV and play a video game with me."

"Gee, I feel lucky," I smile. "You're not mad at me?"

"Heck, no! I will treasure your video forever," he snickers.

I shake my head. "Oh, brother." I roll my eyes.

"Does that mean you'll go on that date with me," he gently nudges.

I want to say yes, but I think I should bow out gracefully. It would be easy to fall fast for this guy. And right now, that makes Ethan off-limits. I huff a discouraging sigh. "It sounds like fun, but I can't. I need to clear up some things in my personal life first before I take the plunge in dating."

"Oh, I assumed you were single?" His eyes study me.

"I am. I mean, I was in a relationship, but we broke up."

"I'm relieved to hear that you're a free woman. You're too young to be married."

"I'm not that young. I'm twenty-five." Wait! Did he just say he was *relieved*?

"Twenty-five. Damn, I thought you were eighteen," he teases. "You're too old for me."

"Really? And just how old are you?"

"I'm the big three O, plus two, thirty-two. I feel it too."

"Thirty-two isn't old. Your body aches because you work ungodly hours at the hospital," I laugh. "Besides, if thirty-two is old, I have only seven years before I need a walker."

"Since I answered all your personal questions, it's my turn." An impish grin toys with the corners of my lips. "Have you ever been in a serious relationship?"

Ethan's mood swiftly changes as he shifts in his

chair. "I was married once, for ten years, a few years ago. It didn't end well."

"Divorce?"

"I'm free of any obligations if that's what you mean." A muscle jerks at his jaw

I sense that he's holding back. "Any children?"

"Nope. No kids."

Switching the subject, I notice his tone is deep and rich. "I like your accent. French kinda."

"It's Cajun French. Our French has more slang."

"Say something!" I request.

"I don't know," he laughs, shaking his head.

"Oh, come on! Teach me something?"

He sighs. "If you insist," he pauses. *"Tu as mis un cunja sur moi.* You have put a spell on me."

I laugh. "That is very impressive. I assume you speak it fluently?"

"Yes. As a child when my dad was still living, we spoke nothing but French. Dad insisted. He didn't want us to lose our culture. Something important to my parents."

"Sorry to hear about your dad passing. What was it like growing up in your family?"

"Dad, Louis Leblanc, was a farmer … sugarcane. During planting season, he'd have me out there on the tractor. I loved helping him too. There's nothing like sowing a fertile field and watching your hard work grow. Nothing but sugarcane sprouting as far as the eyes can see. Holidays were nice too. Dad'd go shoot a wild turkey, and we'd have the neighbors over for a holiday feast. Mom makes the best sweet potato pie too."

"Any siblings?"

"No, Mom couldn't have any more kids. Just me."

"I'm sorry. I can't imagine being the only child. I don't know what I'd do without Jeff."

"You guys do seem close."

"We are, very much so." I smile faintly and quickly switch the subject back to Ethan. "What about childhood friends?" I lean in closer. I love listening to him talk about his life. His eyes glisten with joy.

"I had a neighbor friend, Frank. We used to go down the basin and fish. He hated hooking worms. I'd do it for him and tease him. Frank would get so blooming mad. Sometimes, he'd walk off, leaving me. That boy used to crack me up. He was some cool cat too.

"I don't see him as much now. I think he does hair. Life on the farm didn't last either," Ethan sighs. "When Dad died, Mom sold the land and all our farming equipment to the highest bidder and kept her shop, called *Old World Witchery*. Occasionally, Mom pulls me in to help, but with my residency taking up all my time, I'm pretty worthless helping her." All of a sudden, Ethan's brows shot up. "Hey, I have an idea. Mom could use some help. You got a problem with spooky things and voodoo magic?"

"Is it like fortune-telling and Ouija boards?" Chills run down my arm.

"Yes, and some other eerie items to ponder over."

"It sounds intriguing," I shrug.

"I'll talk to my mom. I think she needs a clerk, but you can't do any mattress switching. No matter how bad you stain the mattress with cheap sheets," he snickers.

I narrow my eyes but am laughing inside. "Oh, shut up!" I throw an empty creamer cup at him as he continues to chortle.

"What was it like growing up for you and Jeff in your family?"

All at once, I swallow my laughter, and I'm lost for words. Should I tell him about my problem? "Uh … just like any other family. I was the little sister that annoyed big brother. I was a rebellious teen and Jeff was the nerd."

"He still is," Ethan laughs.

"Yep, a typical Class A personality. But I am seeing a therapist. We're trying to figure me out."

"I've been there before and needed someone to vent to. Who are you seeing?"

I hesitate. Revealing the doctor's name may throw a wrench in this budding romance, but I never was one for keeping secrets. "Dr. Kim Rice."

JOB INTERVIEW

*A*fter I'd revealed the little tidbit about my therapy session with Dr. Rice, the woman that Ethan's been having noncommittal sex with, I'll never forget his pale face and spewing coffee over himself and half the shop. Once he contained himself, he was obliging enough to enter the address of his mother's shop in my phone.

So, here I am just a few cars down from *Old World Witchery*, located a street over from the French Market on Decatur Street. As I step out of my car, the scent of gas exhaust and a faint hint of salt wafts in the morning air.

I notice the hustle and bustle of downtown life —cars lining both sides of the narrow street and people walking up and down the sidewalk with aimless chatter. It's electrifying, I think, as an easy smile caresses the corners of my mouth.

I find myself gaping at the majestic architecture; the colors and marksmanship are one of a kind. I'm falling in love with this city and all its vintage charm.

I come to a stop at 1219 Decatur, blowing out a nervous sigh. Job interviews always churned my stomach. Taking a moment, I pause at the window and peek inside. The shop is small but packed with all sorts of oddities to explore. I spy these strange dolls that appear like they'd been made out of straw. Next, I spot candles and tarot cards.

I don't know much about magic and all it entails, but I do know how to work a register efficiently and count money. I hope that'll be enough to get the job. If not, it'll be a major disappointment. I've already fallen in love with this place.

I walk in as the bell on the door jingles and make my way to the sales counter. I spot an older woman busy ringing up a customer while several others fall in line. I stand off to the side and wait. More customers start piling in line. I notice another register that no one is working on. It looks like the one-million-and-one registers I've used before. It's been a while, but I'm sure it will all come back. I used to bartend, and the cash register was my thing. I usually kept my money balanced. Never had a problem counting money.

The line keeps growing, and the cashier is quickly getting behind. Some folks are starting to stir impatiently, checking their phones, and shooting frowns at the cashier.

Taking the initiative, I make my way behind the counter to the other register. I smile at the cashier and call out, "I can help someone over here."

Time passes without a hitch, and the crowd finally clears. The cashier turns to me, "You must be Anna Baker, my son's been talkin' about. Hi, I'm Maybelline, Ethan's mom. Most everyone calls me May." She extends her hand, and we shake. "Let me close for lunch, and then we can sit down and talk."

"Yes, ma'am," I smile, nervous with jitters. I see Ethan favors his mother. They both have the same striking green eyes.

After May flips over the "Gone to Lunch" sign, I follow her to the back. I notice a heavy scent of sandalwood drifting through the store. I inhale deeply. I love the scent of incense. It reminds me of my pot-smoking days. I don't miss pot, but I do miss that wonderful aroma.

We step into a small office as May offers me a chair. I take a load off as she makes her way behind a cluttered desk. She groans softly as she eases into her chair. "Whew! That was a load of customers. I appreciate the hand," she smiles, tapping a pencil against the desk. "I understand you're new in town and needing a job. My son says a lot of good things about you."

"Yes, ma'am. I just moved here." I sit with my hands clasped, feeling a little uneasy. It's been a while since I last worked and the fear of screwing this interview up weighs heavily. After all, this is Ethan's mother.

"What kind of experience do you have with witchcraft and the tools that are used in rituals?"

My brow flies up, surprised. "Huh … none," I rush to finish, "but I'm a fast learner."

"Well, I notice you know how to handle a register and you ain't shy. That's more than most. You're pretty and you're not too bad with customers either." She pauses, studying me. "When can you start?"

I almost drop my jaw, but rush, saying, *"Now!"* My eyes widen with excitement.

"You sound eager. I like that," May smiles. "I open at 10 in the morning and close at six. Get here at 9 a.m. sharp. You'll get Tuesdays and Sundays off, and I pay a little more than minimum wage. This shop ain't normal like most, and folks ask peculiar questions. We have customers that practice Voodoo and will teach you a thing or two. Get prepared. This is Nawlins, and there are all sorts of strange and eerie things and people in this town." She grabs some forms and hands them to me.

"Make sure you fill out these papers and bring them to me in the morning."

"Thank you." I smile, taking the papers.

"My son seems to like you, and if he says you're the girl, then I have to listen to him. Ethan's great at judging character." She checks her watch. "Oh, Lordy! Time to get back to work."

I left the store feeling like I'd won the lottery. I have a real job and one, I think, will be very interesting. This new adventure has a good feeling. I carry a smile all the way to my car.

The first thing I want to do is tell Jeff the good news. I wonder if he takes lunch. I decide to take a chance by dropping by the hospital. With any luck, I can catch Jeff when he's between patients. I'm excited to share my good news. Of course, my silly little cashier job is nothing to Jeff's second year of residency. I just want him to see that I'm trying. It's important to me that I make him proud of me. After all the times I've let him down, it's time I start carrying my own weight. I'm changing. I see it. No returning to the old Anna. I see things more clearly. For starters, my pernicious relationship with Tad and that toxic environment I once thought was normal, was acid to me. And as time passes, I will see that more and more.

Moments later, I'm walking through the double-glass doors to the hospital's main lobby. If I'm lucky, Jeff might be in the cafeteria. I walk up to the main desk and ask, "Hi, I'm Dr. Jeff Baker's sister. Can you check to see if he's on lunch or available?"

A red-haired lady asks, "Do you have ID?"

"Yes." I pull out my driver's license and hand it to her. "Here, you go."

"Let me see if I can locate Dr. Baker." She points to a section of blue cushion chairs. "Just have a seat. It shouldn't take me but a minute."

"Thank you." I turn around, and my breath catches in my throat. I spot Ethan lost in the eyes of the gorgeous, Dr. Kim Rice. I can't see his face, but I see hers. The lovely doctor could light up the French Quarter. Now she's laughing, as she grazes pink manicured hand across his chest and adjusts his tag as if she's his wife or ... *girlfriend.*

Then anger hits me like a hot branding iron. That douche has some nerve to ask me on a date when he's in a relationship. I should've known. It's sort of hard to deny, especially after I found that ridiculous earring. A wave of sickness clenches my stomach. I can't watch Dr. Rice's outrageous flirting and Ethan standing there lapping it up.

I snatch up my bag and dart for the door. I hear the lady behind the counter call out to me, "Ms. Baker, your brother!"

I hear the confusion in her voice, and I toss over my shoulder, "I'm sorry, something has come up."

I swing the glass door open and trek across the parking lot, breathing in the cool breeze back into my lungs. Realizing that Ethan's been lying to me is a humiliating, deflated feeling. Call me gullible. I fell for the oldest trick in the book. Cliché, yeah! But so is his stupid game.

I should've listened to Jeff. Now, what do I do about my new job? Jesus! I want to scream to the heavens. Once I reach my sedan, I rest against the door, raking tense fingers through my hair.

Despite Ethan and his lying ass, I'm taking the job. I don't care! I need it. Just because he put in a good word for me doesn't mean I owe him any special treatment other than a thank you. He can forget about that date. *Damn him!* Why did he have to make me like him?

"Grrrr!" I kick the tire as my eyes fill with tears.

THE APOLOGY

*T*make it back to Jeff's apartment, and throw myself on my bed like a blithering baby. My bedroom's the only place I feel safe enough to cry.

My mind flashes over the hurtful memories of Mom and Dad's car accident. All the things I did as a troubled teen and my poor choices with friends in general. I'm not any better than I was in Texas. Still making the same mistakes.

Why do I set myself up for failure? I close my eyes, feeling utterly miserable. I should take Jeff's advice. Focus on my road to recovery. Getting tangled in a love triangle is crazy. And clearly, Ethan is a lying douche bag. Deny all he wants, but he and Dr. Rice are lovers. It was written all over her face. A woman in love. And I refuse to be the other woman. I guess Ethan thought he could fool this ill-educated girl. Boy, does he have another think coming!

I jerk a tissue from its box and wipe away my tears. I'm glad I found out before I got involved. But then, why does my heart feel like it's been snapped in two? I kick my feet against the mattress. Angry at myself for letting my guard down.

I wish I were like Jeff. He never gets in situations like this. I'm trying to be as perfect as him, following in his footsteps … who am I kidding? I'll never be as disciplined as my brother. Picture perfect. Yeah, right! I envy him a little, but I don't fault him for his success. He's earned it.

When our parents died, he took on all the responsibilities. Even though I sobered up, I wasn't there emotionally for him. Have I ever? How can I help anyone when I can't stand on two feet myself? I yank the covers over my head, bringing my knees to my chest.

After I have no more strength to cry, I start to fall into a slumber when my phone lights up. That stupid frog jingle penetrates my dream and in a fit of anger, I throw the covers off reaching in my bag on the floor beside me.

I answer without looking. "Hello."

A male's voice speaks. "Are you having a good time at your brother's?"

Geez! I thought I'd blocked him. Then I remember. Tad has several burner phones. "What do you want?"

"Why are you avoiding me?"

I remember how much I hate his snarky tone. "Tad, I'm not avoiding you. We broke up, remember?" My voice is flat and hard.

"Look, I screwed up. Your bitch of a friend kept coming on to me. I didn't want that skank. She wouldn't let up!"

"Are you telling me that you screwed my friend to get rid of her?" I laugh. "That's rich!"

"Look! I'm trying to say I'm sorry. I dumped that whore, and I want you back. I miss us."

"Well, I don't miss your fist giving me black eyes. And I don't miss the broken jaw and ribs either."

"Look! I'm gonna change. Listen, I got a construction job with a local lumber company. The work is steady. You come back, and you won't have to go to work. I know you like soap operas. We can get married. Make it official."

I scoff. He doesn't know me at all. I hate soaps. "Do you think it's that easy? Tad, I can't do this anymore."

"I'll admit, I've been a real dick to you. I'm going straight. I'm not selling drugs anymore. That part of my life is over. I swear to you. I'm gonna work an honest job. Stop drinking too and no more snorting blow, I swear!"

"Wait! You're a drug dealer *and* a user?" That explains his bizarre outburst.

"I didn't tell you because I know how you feel about drugs since your parents were killed by a drunk driver, but—"

"Tad, stop!" I rub my forehead, trying to ease a brewing headache. "I left Texas, and I've left you. I'm not coming back. We're done. Count your blessings and do whatever! I don't care."

"You bitch! You sittin' at your brother's place, acting like you're all high and mighty. No decent man is gonna want you! You should count your blessings that I put up with your dumb ass. You can't cook, and you're the worst lay I've ever had-"

"Five minutes ago, you were begging me to come back to you. Don't call me anymore!"

I hit the red button on my phone, and a surge of anger flies through me. Without giving any thought, I throw my phone against the wall, shattering it. I stare at its tiny pieces scattered all over the floor. Whatever I saw in that loser will puzzle me for the rest of my life. I see Tad for his true self unstable and dangerous. I'm lucky I'm alive.

I hear keys rattling in the door. Then the door swings open and I flinch, but then I relax. I can tell by the familiar breathing that it's Jeff. Besides, who else would have a key?

I quickly make myself presentable and make my way to the main room. I turn the corner and Jeff's drinking milk from the carton. I smile shaking my head. Some things never change. "Hey, you're home early!"

"Oh … yeah!" He puts the cap back on the milk and sticks it back into the fridge. "I'm off. I tried calling you. Katy at the desk said you came by, but you took off without saying a word. I worried that something was wrong. I've been trying to reach you."

Oh, crap! "I'm fine," I frown. "I sorta took my anger out on my phone. Tad called." I shrug as I mount one of the stools at the island.

"Tell me you're not going back to that piece of shit."

I shake my head. "You haven't got anything to worry about."

"I hope you mean it this time," he says in a biting tone. "I swear if you go back to that loser, I'm washing my hands of you. I can't keep sending you money when Tad is sitting on his ass, not working, and putting his hands on you."

"I know! I know!" I throw my palm up, surrendering. "I have done some idiotic things and hooking up with Tad was the worst. But I'm trying to change." I pause, deflecting the subject. "I do have some good news. I got a job. A real one!" I almost jump with joy.

"Oh really? I like the sound of that." Jeff reaches in the fridge and pulls out the sandwich meat and bread.

"It's a magic shop, all that Voodoo and stuff, called *Old World Witchery*," I giggle.

Jeff drops his sandwich, gaping at me. "Please tell me that's not Ethan's mother's store?"

My smile drops. "Yeah. Why?"

"Why are you getting involved with Ethan? Do you ever learn?" Jeff throws his hands on his hips, lips tight with frustration.

"At least I'm not cleaning his house. And you don't need to worry about me getting involved with your friend, Ethan," I snap. "It's a job and I can still go to school and see that doctor you've arranged for me."

"Okay, just don't let Ethan charm his way into your ... you know."

Silence lingers for a moment as Jeff finishes making his sandwich while I pick at my nails. After he puts the food away, he turns to me and asks, "How did your appointment go with Dr. Rice?"

I scoff. "You mean the Sex in a Dress?"

Jeff rolls his eyes. "Her appearance has nothing

to do with her profession. She's one of the best. Stop being so judgy!"

"It's sorta hard not to notice. Overall, it went well. The doctor wants me to see her twice a week. I must be totally screwed up, or she's hard up for cash," I joke.

"Don't say that. You need to understand yourself, is all. Why your life is one long plight."

"I know. That's why I am going to this overly priced doctor. By the way, thank you for paying for it." I cross my eyes.

"I'm guessing your phone is damaged to the point of no repair, right?"

I drag in a deep breath, "Uh, yep."

"I doubt your plan covers broken phones. Go down to MetroPCS on Rousseau Street. Their phones are reasonably priced, and when you get your first check, you're paying me back." I know Jeff's tone far too well. He means business.

"Alright already!" I slide off the island and walk up to my brother and hug him. "Thanks for everything."

"Hey, some of my friends are meeting up at a favorite bar tonight. We thought we would grab a bite to eat and just unwind. Why don't you come?"

I squinch my nose and shrug. "I don't think I'm ready to meet anyone." I prefer to stay in the confines of my comfort zone. Jeff's friends are overachievers, and then there's me.

"I'm not taking no for an answer. Come with me. You'll have fun."

"Jeff, I don't have any money, and I'll feel weird if you pay for everything."

"Since when has that ever stopped you?" he mocks.

I roll my eyes at him. "Shut up!"

"I will, if you come tonight."

Staring into his impassive face, I know he isn't going to let this go. I have no choice but to go. I guess I'm obligated after everything he's done for me. But I don't have to like it. "Alright! I'll go!" I throw my hands up heading for the TV.

"Don't turn that box on loud. I can't sleep with that thing blaring. By the way," he tosses over his shoulder. "I'm glad I got my bed back," he chuckles as he heads to his bedroom.

I gawk at his back and laugh to myself. What was I thinking? I shake my head as I hit the button to switch on the big screen and slide down into the soft cushions. Soon, I get lost in Bravo's house-wives. That's a show that makes me feel a little normal.

MEET THE FRIENDS

I get the pleasure of riding with Jeff as we head to Bourbon Street. I think he just wants to show off his classic Mustang, ox-blood red. Keeping my thoughts to myself, I prefer to take my sedan and follow him, in case I decide to leave early. It's nice to have the option to duck out if I'm not feeling the company. I guess tonight, grin-and-bear-it is on the menu.

I'm anxious about tonight, though I should be a good sport and take it with a smile. I should be more infused in his life, opening myself up to his circle of friends.

It's bad enough meeting his well-educated friends, but of all places, we have to meet at a bar. Because of my past problems with alcohol, that's the one place I prefer to steer clear from.

Jeff swears this bar, Lafitte's, is the hot spot of New Orleans. I think most of his friends hang out there after work because it's convenient. Only a few blocks from the hospital. I'm happy he has melded well with fellow doctors from the hospital and this unique city. He's usually a straight-laced sorta guy, dull and boring. Unlike most gay men, Jeff is one of a kind. Nothing wrong with that.

We enter the smoky, candlelit bar, and the clanking of glass and aimless chatter fills my brain as the smell of liquor and various perfumes linger. Instantly, I sneeze. Cigarette smoke and heavy cologne do it to me every time.

As we make our way through the crowd, I spy a man on a small stage playing a piano and singing. His voice is rich with that deep southern twang. Nobody does Cajun French better than a New Orleanian.

Jeff spots his friends and breaks into a wide grin. That's odd. Jeff never smiles like that.

We make our way to the back two tables, which are pushed together. Some are still wearing powdered blue scrubs, and others have changed into civilian wear. Everyone appears excited when their eyes fall on Jeff. I stand behind my brother, hiding in his shadow. A couple of women jump up and hug Jeff. The two men reach up and give him a bro hug—you know the one, where they grab each other's hand and lean in, pounding each other's back.

"Good evening, everyone," Jeff says. "I want you to meet my little sister." Jeff places his hand on my shoulder, guiding me to the forefront of the group. "This is Anna," he announces.

The tall black man reaches over the table. "I'm Dr. Ivan James. Just call me, Ivan." Nice spoken man, easy on the eyes with a bright, pleasant smile.

"Nice to meet you, Ivan." I smile and shake his hand.

Jeff proceeds with the introductions. "This is Dr. Jim Brown, another resident. Betty Price and Joyce Jones. Our dedicated nurses that work so diligently."

Both women laugh. Betty, the freckled face with red-hair, speaks up. "Yeah, we do all the work, while your brother dictates."

Laughter circles the table.

"It's nice to meet y'all," I say, sticking my hands in my jean pockets, feeling uncomfortable. I hope tonight goes fast. Maybe they'll talk about work. That'll keep them occupied from drilling me with personal questions.

"Don't listen to what your brother says about us. He lies," Ivan teases.

I laugh but not internally. I've always had trouble blending in social circles. Jeff can get along with a Tasmanian devil. He and I are as different as night and day.

We join everyone at the table. I'm sitting next to

Betty, and Jeff is on my right side, sitting next to Ivan. I feel like a sandwich, and my breath feels stifled. I keep quiet, feeling pathetic. What can I contribute to the conversation? *Has anyone ever taken a left hook?* That would sure get heads snapping. I coax myself to breathe. Just breathe.

When the waitress comes to take our orders, she goes around the table jotting down each person's drink. When she comes to me, Jeff abruptly takes the liberty to order for me. "Uh, she'll have a Coke," he points at me, "and I'll have Schneider Weisse. Put it on my tab too."

The waitress nods and the table suddenly becomes quiet. My face blisters, though I keep a smile glued to my face. I could die. Without realizing it, he strikes me down twice. Apart from ordering himself a beer, he embarrasses me by ordering a soda and announcing that he'd pay. I just want to crawl under the table, or better, go home and never show my face again. Geez!

Quietly, I sip my Coke and study the bar. I find myself wishing to be anywhere but here. My mind begins to drift, listening to everyone's blather. It only makes me feel more isolated and alone than usual, but I keep a smile on my face, for Jeff's sake.

All at once, the night brightens when I glance over my shoulder as my eyes latch onto Ethan's dazzling white smile. He's dressed casually in a blue hoodie and faded jeans. An excellent match for those green eyes of his. A tingle warms my toes.

He approaches our table, laying both hand on the sides of my shoulders as his warm lips graze my earlobe. "Hey, beautiful, would you care to dance?"

I'm almost embarrassed about how happy I am to see Ethan. Even if everyone is staring, including Jeff.

Ethan appears amused. "Sorry to intrude. I'd like to take this lady off your hands for a minute." He smiles as he takes my hand and pulls me from my seat.

I nervously clear my throat. "Excuse me. I'll be back," I say to Jeff and company, and I smile politely.

"Pardon me." Irritation swirls deep in Jeff's sharp eyes. "I'd like for Anna to get acquainted with my friends."

"I'll have her back before you know it." The amused look suddenly leaves Ethan's eyes.

I watch both men shoot each other a look of warning. Jeff doesn't like the idea of me hanging out with Ethan. I'll have to reassure him later that he's worrying about nothing. After I caught him flirting with my therapist today, the chance of this guy getting a peck on the cheek is zero to none. And dancing with him is the last thing I want ... although, he gives me the perfect excuse to leave.

"What's wrong with your brother?" Ethan glances at Jeff's scowl.

"I could use some fresh air."

He steps back and flashes his charming smile. "Whatever the lady wants," he drawls, placing his hand at the small of my back and giving me a grin that sends my pulse racing.

That smile of his is lethal. I bite my bottom lip, breaking into a giggle. It's no mystery why women are drawn to him. He's got that southern charm, a twist of Cajun French and sexy as hell.

We pass through the doors and a cool breeze tousles my hair and soothes the beads of sweat across the bridge of my nose. I move from the door, out of the incoming traffic's way, and lean against the building.

My pulse is beating fast. I try not to be so evident with the consumption of oxygen. Unknowingly, Ethan saved me from a horrible embarrassment.

His sharp eyes roam over my body and draw back pinched brows. "Are you ill? Your face is pale." He steps closer, putting his hand flat across my forehead. "You're burning up."

He caresses my cheek and slides his smooth hand down my neck and stops on my throat. Our eyes lock and linger, drinking in each other. A tear slips down my cheek and Ethan tenderly takes his thumb, wiping it away. "Who has hurt you, *bab-ee*?"

His lips gently brush across mine as he speaks, "Tell me what's wrong." His words are demanding, yet tender.

I stiffen as his warm breath fans my cheeks. "I-I-I just needed some air," I say as a brief shiver flows through me. Why can't he leave me alone? He's involved with another woman. Of all people, my therapist.

"I would like to kiss you." His green eyes brim with desire.

"Ethan, why do you do this to me?" My voice quivers slightly as I step away.

He's silent for a moment as he scratches his chiseled chin. "Are you bothered by Dr. Rice?"

"Duh!" I cross my arms, overcome by jealous anger.

"Rice is not my girlfriend. I don't use that term toward any woman ... *ever*."

"Really? What term do you use to describe her, then? Lover, a friend with benefits ... a fiancé, wife?" I can't believe I'm letting him bother me. I might as well loop him in that type—the type of guy that never gets involved emotionally and is only a heartbreak away. The kind that takes privileges with whomever he so dares to and doesn't care about the consequences of the aftermath.

He stiffens as though I've slapped him across the face. "I don't understand why you're upset."

"I saw you today at the hospital with Dr. Rice.

The two of you, close and intimate, talking. It's obvious you're lovers." I divert my gaze across the street, fighting the knot in my throat. It's hard to keep myself together when I gaze into those pools of green.

Ethan's face glistens in the faint streetlight. He's stunning and, yet, I'm terrified of letting go of my heart. "You were spying on me?" His words sound accusatory.

"I wasn't eavesdropping!" I scoff. "I dropped by to see my brother, and I saw the two of you standing in the hallway up in each other's grill."

"Okay. So, you're upset that I was talking to Kim?"

Ethan seems confused. Do men ever get it?

I roll my eyes. "No! I'm upset that you'd asked me on a date when you're not single. It's obvious that you and Dr. Rice are a couple."

He whispers harshly, "Look! I was breaking it off with her. Kim and I didn't have the kind of relationship where we go to dinner or a movie. It was all physical."

"All I know is that I witnessed the face of a woman who's in love."

Ethan's response holds a note of impatience. "Kim likes to flirt. It means nothing."

I look away, my eyes fixed on a couple passing by. "Dr. Rice is beautiful," I say barely above a whisper.

"Looks aren't everything." Suddenly, his face goes grim. "I know her type."

"What type is that? Tall, dark, and rich?" I hold tight to my stance. I want to believe Ethan, but after Jeff's warning and everything else with Tad, I'm not sure I can trust him. My heart is flooded with doubt.

"I get why your brother is leery of me. He's just looking out for his little sister." He leans his forehead against mine. "I like you, Annie. You make me laugh. I haven't laughed like that with someone in a long while. I want to take you out. It's nothing more than a bijou date. That's all. I won't require you to sign your name in blood." He flashes that lopsided grin that gives me goosebumps.

He calls me Annie.

I bite down on my bottom lip. "I don't know. Jeff's gonna have a cow."

"Annie, your brother can't run every aspect of your life. Some choices should be left up to you."

"My choices get me in trouble," I shrug.

"If we didn't make bad choices, we wouldn't be human. We learn from our mistakes."

"Have you ever screwed up?"

Ethan gives a curt laugh. "Yes, ma'am, a bunch."

I sigh. "Where would you take me?"

"For starters, I'd take you sightseeing." There's a hint of hope to his voice. "We can do it during the day."

"So, I'm safe from your advances in daylight?"

He openly laughs. "I won't lay a finger on you unless you ask me to. Scout's honor!" He places his two fingers across his chest. Not sure it's the Cub Scout's honor, but it works for me.

I giggle. "Now you're a Scout?"

"Well, it was about twenty years ago, but I still wear the badge quite proudly."

I laugh and shake my head. I enjoy his sense of humor. "You are quite a bit older than me," I tease. "I'm not sure you can keep up." Our eyes lock.

"My beautiful Annie, I give you my word, I can do more than keep up." A hint of a challenge toys in his gaze.

"Let me think about it," I say, not trusting my heart to make a firm decision.

"No problem," he pauses, changing the subject. "Did you get the job?"

"Yes," I smile behind my lashes, feeling a little bashful.

"So, you don't get squeamish?" He looks at me with rounded eyes.

"Excuse me?" My eyes fly open.

"You don't know? You're hired to drain blood from the goats behind the shop. Mom uses them for rituals. She didn't tell you?"

"What!" I gasp.

OLD WORLD WITCHERY

I left early this morning to stop by MetroPCS to get a new cell phone. Jeff, as always, gave me the money. Bummer that I broke my old phone. I really liked it too. On the upside, Tad can't call me anymore, no matter how many burner phones he goes through.

I walk into *Old World Witchery* at 8:45. A brush of warm air flutters through my hair. It's unusually chilly today, and I'm wishing I'd been more prepared than wearing a light sweater.

I see Ms. May at the register counting money and setting up for the day. Ethan's teasing about draining blood from goats is a big fat tale. I roll my eyes at the vision of his amused face laughing at my shock. I still want to slug him.

As I make my way to the counter, Ms. May pops

her head up from the register and smiles. "Oh, hi hon!" She nods toward the back. "I have an apron for you. It's hanging on the coat hanger with your name on it too."

"Okay, thanks!" I find my way in the back and spot a dark purple apron right where she said. I quickly pull it off the hook and slip it on and head back to the front. "Alrighty, Ms. May! I'm ready to start the day," I smile.

"Well, ain't you pretty in purple," she smiles back. "And just call me, May. No point in being formal. Folks here are laid back and casual."

"Where would you like me to start?"

"Well, I got your register ready, but you need to count the money. We don't want any booboos. It'd be good for you to learn the merchandise too. People come in here, and they like to ask a lot of questions." She bends down under the counter and pulls out a small book. "This is a list of our items and their purposes and uses. Study it, 'cause it's gonna come in handy." She hands the book to me.

"No problem. I'll get right on that," I promise, feeling a little wary. When it comes to magic and Voodoo dolls, I'm lost. I look forward to learning, though. I'm not sure I believe in the practice, but it's intriguing nonetheless.

"We have some real characters that come in here. Down here in the bayou, folks take magic on a serious level. They don't play. I'll let you handle the tourists. They're in here to play and quench their curiosity. But the regulars, you should refer them to me. When they come in, you'll know it. There's an air about them."

"Got it!" I smile. "Umm … where do I put my bag?"

"Oh, I forgot. There is a locker in the back with a lock. No one ever goes back there but one of us. We don't have a public restroom if anyone asks."

"I will remember that." I made a mental note.

"Oh, did you fill out those forms I gave you?"

"Yes, just as you asked." I pull out the papers from my bag and hand them to her.

"Great! I'll put these up. And in the meantime, you can look over the merchandise and check each item off in the catalog. That's a good way to learn." May tosses a light smile and heads toward the back.

I begin sorting out each item. I notice different colored candles. Each one has a purpose but that's all I know. I flip open the to the section on candles and read.

Candle magic is a kind of alchemy, where all elements are represented, such as fire of the flame, air to feed it, melted wax for water, and solid wax for earth.

Okay, I didn't know that, but now I do. I spot funny looking dolls made of straw. I turn in the book and continue to read.

Louisiana Voodoo, also known as New Orleans Voodoo, describes a set of spiritual folkways developed from the traditions of the African diaspora. It is a cultural form of the Afro-American religions developed by the West and Central Africans' populations of the U.S. State of Louisiana. Voodoo is one of many incarnations of African-based spiritual folkways rooted in West African Dahomeyan Vodun. Its liturgical language is Louisiana Creole French, the language of the Louisiana Creole people. The language consists of elements of French, Spanish, African, and Native American roots.

That's interesting. I go about checking off other items when I notice a tall woman, wearing a hat, passing me. The woman's perfume is familiar. My gaze lifts, and I freeze.

It's my psych doctor, Rice. What is she doing here? May is in the back, and I'm the only one to greet her. Jesus! Does she have to come in here on my first day on the job? I'm behaving silly, I know.

The doctor has a right to go wherever she chooses. But did she have to invade my turf?

I inhale sharply, swallow a wry smile, and approach her, "Hello, Dr. Rice. Hope you're well today." I forge a friendly smile as her gaze meets mine.

At first, I don't think she recognizes me. Then, as if a light bulb flickers in her brain, her smile fades. "Yes. You're my new patient, Ann Baker."

I sense the good doctor isn't happy to see me. I have the same sentiments.

"It's Anna," I point out. "How may I help you?" I try to keep my voice light.

She pauses as if she's trying to be inconspicuous. It's obvious that she wishes to speak with May. What other reason would someone like her want to visit a shop full of Voodoo dolls and magic? Unless she's a witch. I wonder if she knows about Ethan and me.

"I came to speak to Mrs. LeBlanc. Is she here?"

I couldn't help but notice how Dr. Rice is dressed to impress. A very tight form-fitting dress … black, a V-neck that plunges low enough that it could reach China, and red-soled heels that can only be Louboutin Stilettos. It's like she's walking sex. I bet she causes car accidents wearing that getup. A dash of insecurity bristles my neck.

"Let me get her for you," I say as I head to the back. I peek just inside the office and clear my throat as May looks up from her paperwork. "I'm sorry to interrupt, but you have a visitor, Dr. Rice."

May's eyebrows shoot up, displaying surprise. I wonder how well they know each other. Are they friends? What if Dr. Rice tells May that I'm the reason they broke up? Would May prefer Dr. Rice for her son as opposed to a salesclerk? Or what if Ethan lied about their break-up? What if I'm the other woman? Gosh! I take a deep breath. Hope I don't get fired over this; I really like this job too.

May rises from her desk and makes her way out, mumbling, "What does that woman want now?" She sounds agitated.

The doctor is standing by the register when May approaches her. Her brows are tight, as if she's dreading the visit.

I keep my distance, remaining close to the front of the shop, hoping to stay out of earshot. No such luck. I can hear a pin drop in here. Taking a deep breath, I busy myself, taking inventory of the items and crossmatching them with the catalog, but my ears cling to May and Dr. Rice's conversation.

The doctor speaks first.

"Hello, Mrs. LeBlanc! I hope I'm not troubling you." Her voice is soft as it wafts through the air.

"Well, not so much if this is a quick visit. What can I do for you, Kim?" May's voice is flat, conveying no emotion.

"Yes, I want to pick up one of your pleasant

smelling candles for my office. It's quite soothing for my patients." She pauses briefly, like she's stalling. "I don't mean to alarm you, but Ethan hasn't been himself lately. We sort of had parting of the ways." She pulls out a monogrammed, crisp white napkin from her purse and sniffles. "I thought Ethan was going to propose marriage to me, but I think … well, I'm just going to say it … I think he's seeing another woman." She pats the makeup around her eyes with her fancy white napkin.

"… I make a point to stay out of Ethan's affairs. He's a grown man."

"I understand." Dr. Rice's lips tighten and then she breaks into a plastic smile. "You know how much I love your son, and we were practically living together. But the other day at my office, he gave back an earring he'd been keeping for senti-mental purposes and, out of nowhere, he breaks up with me. I'm shocked and hurt."

"I'm terribly sorry for your pain, but that is something you have to discuss with my son. I really don't ask questions concerning Ethan's private life. He'll tell me if he feels the need. Otherwise, I butt out," May says.

"Oh, I certainly think that's best. I worry over Ethan. I fear he's slipping. Of course, since the acci-dent … I am glad I was there to help him in his de-spair," the doctor smiles.

"Well, I'm no expert, but I know my son, and I haven't detected any trouble with Ethan's mental health. Matter of fact, he's been pretty happy lately," May smiles, suggesting she's taunting the doctor.

I almost laugh.

Almost.

"Do you think he could be masking his true feelings." The doctor places her hand on May's arm.

"Honey, I don't think Ethan is masking anything. He's fine. I'm sorry for your pain, but this break up might be for the best. You never know, there could be a suitable man right around the corner. You're plenty young and easy on the eyes." May pulls her arm free and pats the doctor on her arm. "I hate to cut you off, but I have to get back to work. I ain't a doctor like yourself. I can't afford to slack off. But thanks for coming by."

"Thank you for speaking with me. I do hope to get one of those candles. I swear." She delicately waves her napkin and speaks, her voice heavy with that southern accent. "Mrs. LeBlanc, you have the best smelling candles in all of New Orleans!" She gives a high pitch giggle.

"Which one would you like?" May asks.

"Oh, I hope you have gardenia. My favorite." Dr. Rice stretches her lips, revealing a set of pearly straight teeth.

"Hey, Anna!" May sticks her head up over Dr.

Rice's shoulder. "Please take care of this good lady for me!"

"Yes, ma'am. My pleasure," It takes a second for me to find the candle. Once I spot it, I grab it and take it to the front.

May turns to the doctor. "Thanks for coming by and you have a great day, doc." May smiles, edging her way to the back.

"Such a delight, seeing you again." The doctor flashes a cherry-red smile and then drops it as soon as May is out of sight.

An awkward silence stirs between the doctor and me as I ring up her purchase.

"Will there be anything else for you today?" I smile politely.

"That's all," she answers, eyeing me with open coldness. "I believe we have an appointment tomorrow."

"Yes, it's at eight in the morning."

"Funny," she shifts her hip, leaning on the counter. "I wasn't aware you worked here." Her suspicious eyes study me.

"I was recently hired. This is my first day." I smile sweetly, adding an extra dose of sugar as I sack-up her candle.

She hands me her card, and I run it through, giving it back to her, along with the bag.

"Such a small world, isn't it?" She gives a curt smile, but it doesn't feel genuine. "I'll see you tomorrow morning." Without further ado, she leaves.

I lean against the register. That woman sucks the air from the room.

Well, I suppose it's true that Ethan ended the affair with the lovely doctor, but if she's telling the truth, he wasn't honest with me. You don't cohabit with your booty call. That troubles me. A lot. And to be honest, I can't see her being anyone's booty call.

Then there's the earring. Did Dr. Rice lie about that earring as a gift from Ethan? I have an awful feeling about this. My mind fills with suspicion.

Jesus! I have to see her in the morning too. I can't back out either. I promised Jeff that I'd go. I can't ask him if I can change doctors either. He'd want to know the reason why and I'm not ready to go there yet. A frown pulls at the corners of my mouth. Damn! The last thing I need is a love triangle. I have to call it off with Ethan. We can be friends … from afar.

I'm too attracted to him to be in close range. And falling for him is out of the question. My heart can't take the risk. Staying busy will help distract me. I should look into doing some classes at the community college. Between this job, my therapy sessions, and school, I should stay busy enough to keep out of trouble and that means staying away from Ethan LeBlanc.

THERAPY: SESSION 2

$\mathcal{I}$'m sitting in Dr. Rice's office on the same lovely expensive couch, but someone must've replaced the cushions with needles. I get the feeling she suspects something about Ethan and me. I'm the other woman.

What if she's a wacko and comes at me with a knife or, even worse, a gun? I begin chewing my fingernails. I keep shaking my leg, waiting. I check the clock on the wall. It's nine minutes after eight. I only have a window of time before I leave. Work starts at nine this morning.

Finally, I hear footfalls. The door opens and in steps the doctor. I'm half relieved, and the other half prefers to be anywhere but here.

She smiles smugly. "Hello, Ann." There's that smile that never quite makes it.

"It's Anna. I go by Anna," I correct her, forcing down the sarcasm. I don't know why I bother. She doesn't look up from reading her notes, assuming it's from our last session.

She finally speaks up, eyes still on her notes, "I want to talk more about your childhood." Her soft voice drifts slowly across the room, with intention behind its cadence. "You say you can only re-member as far back as twelve. Most people recall their earliest childhood as young as three and a half. Have you asked yourself why your memories are blocked?"

"Hmm." I mull it around in my head a minute, yet my mind isn't giving me visuals. My gaze lifts to Dr. Rice, and I say, "No, nothing." Even more strangely, it's never crossed my mind. My happy childhood was more of a feeling than a memory. "I mean, yeah, I was a chubby kid. We had family meals, went to visit family out of state. My con-sumption of food was mostly eating junk food."

"These memories are after twelve, correct?"

I shrug. "Yeah, I believe so."

"I think we need to explore why. Don't you agree?"

I couldn't help thinking how this woman before me now is such a contrast to the person who visited the shop yesterday.

I whiff and answer, "I guess."

"How does it make you feel, not remembering a large portion of your childhood?"

"Umm ..." I exhale. "I haven't given it much thought, to be honest."

"Let's focus on your brother, Jeff, for a minute. Do you mind?"

"I guess not, but Jeff isn't the issue. He's been a great brother."

"I respect your closeness with your brother, and I certainly understand why after the loss of your parents."

I suddenly feel defensive. "This isn't about Jeff. It's about me and my destructive behavior."

I suppose she senses my frustration as she raises her palm to ease the tension. "I totally agree, Ann. But your brother is part of the equation, and I am merely exploring all angles. Perhaps, your brother can help jar your mind. That's all," she smiles and pauses.

I guess she's waiting for me to respond. "It's Anna. My name is Anna," I say softly. I'm not sure how I feel about this, but I'll only go so far with her scrutinizing my brother. "Okay, shoot," I say, warning myself to prepare for whatever she throws at me.

"Well, can you describe your earliest memories with your brother?"

"Umm ..." I'm squirming in my seat as I'm

trying to recall a time. "Uh … Jeff never liked me to tag along with him and his group of friends. I was the annoying little sister." I twist my hair, feeling her pointed gaze on me. "Oh, I remember going to a baseball game with him." I straighten my shoulders and cross my legs, folding my hands on my lap.

"Do you remember your age?"

I sit quietly a minute, thinking. "I'm sorry. I don't." Geez! Do I have holes punched in my brain?

"Can you think of another memory with your brother?"

"Huh, Jeff stayed busy with sports and school. I recall how everyone liked him. Or at least, I think they did. He's seven years older than me. When he finished high school, he left for college. Yale, in fact. I didn't see him much until Mom and Dad's accident."

"What kind of student were you?" She jumped on that question fast.

"Not great." I diverted my gaze to my feet. "I had a hard time focusing. I mostly daydreamed my classes away."

"Why is that? What was it that you didn't like about school?"

The doctor's eyes feel like a drill, grinding through my brain.

I scoff, "What's there to like?"

The doctor smiles. "There are lots of things. Reading fascinating literature, science, school recess, forming bonds with friends."

"I wasn't good at bonding with peers. I tried, but no one wanted to be a buddy to a fat kid."

"Were you rejected often by others?"

I exhale, not liking what I do remember of my childhood. Some memories should be laid to rest. "I hated recess because I worried who would play with me. It sucks being the kid that's most likely to fail. I remember whenever we played games in P.E. The coach would pick two kids to choose their team; I was the kid no one wanted. Even the teachers didn't like me. Let's face it, fat kids are not popular."

"I hear anger in your voice." The doctor drops her pen in her lap. Her eyes study me.

"No, it's just not a good memory for me. I think I was about thirteen."

"Where was Jeff during these times?"

"I don't recall. Maybe college." I toss my hair over my shoulder. Why is memory lane so tough for me? I can't wrap my head around it, even for one simple answer.

"Were you aware of your absent brother?"

My eyebrows pull into an affronted frown. "Why are you asking me questions about Jeff?"

"I'm just trying to understand your relationship

with your brother. There may be some correlation between the two of you that might jar memories."

"There's really not a lot. Because of our age difference, we attended different schools, and by the time I reached twelve, Jeff was gone to college."

"I see. Do you recall his relationship with your family? Did he have issues as well?"

"If he did, he never voiced them to me. Jeff was perfect in Mom's and Dad's eyes. He was an all-star linebacker and an honor student. I hardly made anything above a C."

"I'd like to speak to both of you in a session together. Do you think that can be arranged?"

I huff with annoyance, "I can ask, but I can't promise anything."

"I'll mention it to your brother and see if he can come to your next session. Of course, I'll need you to give me permission for Jeff to attend."

I shrug. "Okay, I guess."

"Great." She flashes those straight white teeth. "On your way out, please stop at the receptionist's desk. I need you to sign a permission form."

"Alright," I agree.

"Well, this ends our session." She kicks out a crimson smile. "I'll see you at our next appointment."

Dragging Jeff into therapy is a bad idea. He's not going to be happy about this either. I dread telling him and dealing with his explosive reaction. Is it not enough that I'm even willing to seek help? Why drag me through the mud too? Why can't I be a normal person with normal screw-ups? Everyone makes mistakes. On second thought, not everyone. Jeff doesn't.

The Memoryland of my childhood has me shaking in my boots. If I went into work today, it'd be a disaster. I can't function or think straight. My stomach is giving me fits and my hands are trembling. I snatch my phone from my bag and call May.

"Good Morning! This is *Old World_Witchery.* How may I help you?" she answers in a rush.

"This is Anna. I'm sorry to do this to you, but I just left my doctor's appointment, and I'm feeling ill. I'm not able to make it to work today. I hope you're not upset."

"It's no problem, hon. Are you okay? Nothing serious?"

"I will be. I think I have the stomach flu." I hate lying to May.

"You comin' in tomorrow?" she asks.

"Yes, I should be feeling better by then."

"Get well and don't worry about today. I was thinking about sending you home early anyway."

"Thank you, May."

"I'll see you in the morning. Get some rest."

"Thanks, I will. I'm headed home now."

~

I'm standing in the hallway in front of my door when I suddenly hear a deep, velvet-edged voice come from behind me. "Good morning, beautiful."

I whip my head around and my gaze falls on Ethan's chiseled face. He must've been jogging. His T-shirt's damp around the neck and lower chest. I suddenly remember how tight his abs are and I flush. Whatta delicious hot mess he is, with his disheveled dark golden curls. I catch myself from running my fingers through the strands that spill over his forehead.

Then my mood pummels. The vision of Dr. Rice talking to his mother yesterday still rides heavily on my skirt-tail. "Hey!" I snap, glaring at him.

Ethan's brow shoots up. "Somebody's not in a good mood."

"Nope, I'm not." I gather my keys out of my bag.

"What's wrong?"

Chafe rushes through me and hits my mouth before I realize what I'm saying. "Your ex-girlfriend came to see your mother yesterday. My first day on the job."

Ethan leans against the doorframe, crossing his

arms over his chest. "Really?" He shrugs dismissively. "And?"

"And she has a completely different story than you."

"What are you talking about?" The line between his brows deepens.

"According to the good doctor, the two of you were living together. Cohabitating." My hands fly to my hips. "Why would you lie to me?"

"I have never spent a night with Kim."

"According to the good doctor, it was more than a night." Why won't he just own it?

"In my defense, it shouldn't matter. I'm not seeing Kim any longer. Kim's too high maintenance for my taste."

I scoff, "Yeah, she looks like sex on a stick." Sarcasm rolls hard off my tongue.

Ethan takes a step, closing in the space between us. He reaches up to touch my cheek but then drops his hand and steps back. "You gotta stop battering me about Kim. I like you, Anna. But I can't see how we have a chance if you don't stop."

"If you want us to work, then you have to be truthful!"

He puts his hands on my shoulders and holds my gaze. "Kim Rice and I are over. Regardless of what she says, it's the past. She doesn't mean anything to me. We were basically each other's itch. That's all."

"Is that what I am to you ... an itch?" Whatta quick and disturbing thought. Yet I can't help myself; mistrust plagues my heart.

"We haven't even gone on a date, and you're expecting a ring on your finger!" His words burn like a red-hot iron.

"I didn't say anything about a damn ring. You know what? This is a bad idea! We both have recently gotten out of bad relationships. I can't handle this rollercoaster ride with you. I'm sorry!"

Smothering a sob, I flee inside the apartment, shutting the door in Ethan's face as he calls out my name, *"Annie!"*

Dropping my bag by the door, I rush to my bedroom, making a nosedive under the covers. Maybe if I stay hidden long enough, the world will fade away.

Since therapy, my brain is more scattered than usual. I sigh. I have to find the strength to push through my childhood issues. Although at this minute, I feel like I'm teetering on the edge of a cliff. Any minute, I'm crashing to my death.

Then, Ethan ... I think I should forget this guy and focus on my truckload of problems. I'm not in the right frame of mind to cope with all these uncertainties. He said, she said bull-crap.

The problem is, when I look into Ethan's green eyes, I lose my self-will. I am helpless when I'm in his presence. I sigh. I can't remember ever losing myself to a man like this: the tingling, my heart pounding whenever he's near me. All the more reason why I need to stay away from him. I laugh to myself. It's kind of hard when he lives next door. Why does life have to be so complicated?

THE WIND

I begin to stir when the doorbell sounds like it's coming off the hinges. I sit up, rubbing grit from my tired eyes, feeling like I'd just closed them only minutes ago. I check my phone. Huh, it's nine o'clock! I'd pretty much slept the whole day and most of the evening. I peer out my window. The sun had disappeared behind the horizon, and stars have speckled the dark sky.

The doorbell goes off again, and I throw the covers off and plant my feet on the floor. I drag myself to the living room, yawning, and thinking Jeff had lost his key. Strange, he's at work this time of night. Too late for the Jehovah's Witnesses.

I make my way to the door grumpy and don't bother to hide it. "I'm coming!" I shout. "Hold your freaking horses!"

I reach the door, twisting the knob angrily, and swing the door wide open. I couldn't have been hit any harder if I'd been slammed in the head with a live alligator.

What is he doing here?

My gaze collides with Ethan. I open my mouth to protest, but he stops me by raising his forefinger in my face. "Before you say anything or shut the door in my face, I'd like to explain myself."

I blow a strand of hair from my eyes. "Speak!" I grunt.

Ethan's gaze flows slowly across my body, as an impish grin lights his face. It registers that I'm wearing a white shirt barely touching my buttocks, and lacy red panties riding up my crack with a pair of mismatched, black-and-white socks.

My embarrassment quickly turns to ire. "Well, I'm waiting."

"I do like this look on you. However, the hallway is a bit drafty. Plus, there's the neighbor with the video camera."

I roll my eyes and step back, letting Ethan inside as I close the door behind him. I can't help but notice how his eyes dance with amusement as I tug on my shirt. I wish he'd stop staring at me like I was dessert. I clear my throat and ask, "You have something to say?"

"Oh, yeah, that," he smiles to himself. "If you would do me the honor, I'd love to take you to Café du Monde. It's a hot spot around here. The coffee isn't so bad either," he winks.

I pause, thinking what a weakling I am when it comes to this man that's not much more than a stranger. Then again, setting aside my disdain, I *could* eat. "I hear the beignets are calorie-free." I lean into the doorframe, smiling in his face, debating whether I should throw him out on that face or cave.

"That's what I hear, too." His sweet, silent eyes steal my breath.

"Alright!" I cave. "Let me get some clothes on."

"Great!" He saunters past me, grinning like an Olympian, winning the gold medal.

I turn to head to my bedroom, dragging my feet. "There's beer in the fridge if you want one," I offer, not glancing back, but I could feel Ethan's carnal eyes glued to my backside. Like I say, I have junk in my trunk.

"No rush," Ethan says lightly. Then, I hear him mumble, "No rush at all." He muffles a groan.

The involuntary arousal strikes, making me mad as hell. Stop thinking about sex! I scold myself. I am sexually flustered enough, and it deepens whenever I'm around Ethan. I've never been so aroused by a man like I have with this guy, and all he has to do is look at me with those big, dreamy green eyes.

I tug on my jeans, brush my teeth, take five minutes with my tangled hair and decide to leave it as is. When I finish, I stare at myself in the mirror. I never was one for makeup. Only on special occasions. I was blessed with smooth skin and a tawny complexion. Quite the opposite of Jeff.

I apply a light natural lip gloss, and spray a little Versace on my neck, dabbing some on my earlobe. I remember watching Mom use perfume. Dabbing a little behind the ears, down to her neck and behind the knees. It was like watching a graceful dancer. Even in her fifties, Mom was beautiful. I blow at my wild hair, staring at myself in the mirror. I favor Mom a lot. Dark hair, dark skin, and hazel eyes that pop. Tad used to complain about my eyes being too big. Oh well, he's part of the past and I plan to keep him there too.

Okay, ready or not, here I come.

We head downstairs and, as we pass through the glass door from the lobby, dread hits me. I stop and grab Ethan's gaze. "Are we taking your motorcycle?" I'm not feeling a bike ride tonight.

"Would you rather we catch an Uber?"

"We can go in my car. I know it's not as impressive as your Harley."

Ethan shrugs. "No problem. Where's your car?"

I smile. Tad always had to be in control. I like that Ethan is the sort of guy that goes with the flow. "This way." I nod over my shoulder with a little burst of glee.

I toss the keys at Ethan and he expertly catches

them. "Will you drive? I hate driving at night when I don't know where I'm going."

"No problem!" He smiles.

We enter the café as my gaze washes over the place. The twenty-foot ceiling is covered with deep, rich beadboard and low-hanging fans to keep a nice breeze flowing through the diner. Large, picturesque windows are embellished with deep green shades to protect from the glare of the sun during the day. The aroma in the air is a mixture of sugar and coffee. The thought of sinking my teeth into a sweet beignet is ever so present in my mind.

Not long after we take our seats at a cozy table for two, a waiter approaches our table. "Good evening!" The waiter has his iPad braced over his arm. "What would you like this evening?"

Ethan takes charge. "Two coffees and two beignets."

"Could we add lots of cream and Splenda with that order, please?" I ask.

"The lady likes a little coffee in her cream," he jokes to the young waiter. After he taps his iPad, the young man laughs and whizzes to the back with our order.

Elbows on the table, I prop my chin on my hands, drinking in Ethan's features. His handsome face is kindled with a sort of passionate beauty, and yet there lies a mystery behind those vivid, green eyes. Why is this man still single?

"This place brings back childhood memories. When my dad was alive, we'd come here a lot." Ethan's face takes on a faraway look as he scans the busy diner.

My mind drifts to our conversation earlier today and my smile fades. Ethan's fingers lightly strum the table, and I suddenly feel uneasy. "I need to explain myself for my behavior today."

"You do?" I reply.

"I have a hard time talking about my past. I'm a private person."

"You do?"

"I understand your reservations after getting out of a terrible relationship."

My brows furrow. "Did Jeff tell you about my ex?"

"No. He didn't have to. I figured it out when I saw the bruise on your cheek and busted lip. That's more than enough to know the guy's a shirt." Ethan's voice comes off harsh.

"Oh, you noticed!" I hide my gaze under my lashes. No matter how wrong it is for a guy to lay his hands on a gal, it doesn't dissolve the shame. A deep-seated shame that sticks to you like a bad rash on Good Friday. "There's a lot I haven't told you either."

"I feel we should be totally open with each other."

"I can appreciate your honesty." I manage a smile.

"First, I want to apologize for what I said earlier." His eyes brim with remorse. "I was wrong for lashing out."

I open my mouth to speak but halt when our order arrives. As the waiter places the dish on the table, I eye a plate of powdered sugar on top of square-shaped donuts. The sweet aroma stirs my senses, but my stomach is churning. All I can think about is why he brought me here. Unable to look at the sweets, I take my hot cup of brew and sip as Ethan thanks the waiter. My heart's thumping and I can't stop it.

When we are left alone again, an undeniable silence falls between us. After a moment, sitting in silence and sipping coffee, I speak up. "I suppose I need to apologize, too. I was pretty bitchy this morning."

"Don't mention it." He pauses. "I don't know how to tell you this other than just saying it. But Kim was a distraction."

"Meaning casual sex?" I ask half snarkily. I don't know why I'm angry about his involvement with this woman. But it grates on me like a bed full of fleas. Maybe I'm crazy.

"Kim came along when I was in a dark place. When my ten-year marriage ended, I was a shattered man. My wife and I were teenage sweethearts and married when we were barely out of school. We had our issues, being kids. We were so different.

"I come from farmers. And my wife came from a very influential family, and she was a perfectionist. Everything Heather touched turned to gold. She was an overachiever. I didn't have a problem with her drive," he laughs to himself. "But the Jenkins' had a problem with my unpretentiousness. Taking things in stride. Her family considered me a low-level minuscule doctor."

"You're a surgeon!" I gape. "What parent wouldn't want their daughter married to a doctor?"

"Apparently, they didn't." Ethan smiles, but it doesn't reach his eyes. "Heather went to Yale. She took law and finished in the top ten in her class. Anyway, she started her practice while I continued my degree at Baylor Medical in Houston. My family couldn't pay for my tuition. As a kindness to my wife, Heather's family, the Jenkins, paid all my expenses. Things seemed great at first. We'd see each other on weekends and holidays. But then there was a shift.

"As you probably know with your brother, internship and its long ungodly hours are a requirement. The stress took its toll on our marriage. Soon, Heather and I grew apart. Then one night I woke up to a disturbing phone call. Heather and an associate attorney were in a car accident. Both were killed on impact." He shakes his head. "She was pregnant. I have no idea if she even knew. I'd like to think she didn't. Surely, she would've been more responsible."

Ethan withdraws a long sigh. "Heather's blood-alcohol level was 1.7. She was driving. When I first heard of Heather's pregnancy, for about five seconds, I thought I was a father, until I realized the baby wasn't mine."

I see sadness stirring in his eyes and I instantly push down the knot lodged in my throat. "The baby wasn't-"

"Nope. She was only a few weeks along. We hadn't been sleeping together for several weeks. The father of her child died along with her in the car accident. Dan Atkins was his name. To twist the knife further, Heather was planning to leave me for Dan when she returned. Divorce papers had already been drawn."

"I'm so sorry." I wanted to throw my arms around him. My heart breaks for this man and if I'm not careful, I'm going to fall hard for him.

Ethan takes a deep sip of his coffee. "Heather's death nearly destroyed me. Dealing with her needless death and her affair all at once, I didn't know if I should've mourned over her or been angry."

"My parents were killed in a car accident too. They were driving from a party when a drunk driver swerved into their lane and hit them head-on. I was only eighteen."

"It seems we both have lost loved ones. My dad died of a heart attack. We didn't know he was having problems. His heart attack struck while he was on the tractor and down he went, falling to the ground. He was found dead come supper time. I think he died before he hit the ground. I decided then that I wanted to be a doctor. I was a sophomore in high school.

"It hit my family pretty hard. Mom acted all tough, never breaking down in front of anyone. Though when she was alone, I'd hear her crying every night for months. Then, she healed as much as one can and the new normal settled in."

"My parents were married for more than thirty years. I always thought they were happy, and we were a normal family. I miss them, you know." I sigh softly.

"I miss my dad too." Ethan squeezes my hand.

I shrug. "Why do I get a feeling there is a purpose for you opening up to me?"

Ethan leans forward in his seat and sighs. "I want you to understand and believe me when I say Dr. Rice and I were nothing more than two lonely people helping each other make it through the next day. I have no emotional attachment to Kim other than as a friend. I was a mess and nearly lost my internship. Kim helped me work through my anger issues. I'll admit, my therapy was between the sheets. I'm grateful for Kim's help, but we were each other's itch. She distracted me from grief. Neither one of us wanted a serious relationship."

"I'm curious about something."

"And that is?"

"Why were you not interested in having a serious relationship with Dr. Rice. She's beautiful, career-minded, and smart?"

"True," he shrugs. "But she's an arduous woman. Kim's a lot like Heather. Everything has to be perfect. I can't breathe with that sort of woman. I'm just a man that comes from a farmer's family. I prefer beer over champagne, hot dogs over caviar."

"Oh, my!" I crinkle my nose. "I'd have to draw the line with fish eggs."

"Have you ever eaten it? It's the worst."

"I think I'll take your word for it," I laugh.

"Enough of my past. What about you?"

"Huh, me?" Oh geez! I'll keep it short. "I understand betrayal. Tad, my ex-boyfriend, and I didn't see eye to eye. And the final straw that broke us up was when I caught him in bed with my best friend. So, I left him and came here to stay with Jeff."

"And he's the reason why you're seeing Kim?"

"Tad is part of the reason, though not entirely. I have holes in my childhood memories. We're trying to figure out why."

"I see." Ethan pauses. "Do you still have feelings for Tad?"

"No, I don't think I ever did. When I first met

Tad, he was sweet. But it was only on the surface. Shortly after we moved in together, his whole demeanor changed for the worst. I didn't see it coming. It was like he did a one-eighty overnight." I exhale. "Can we change the subject?"

"Good idea! Enough with the heavy," he smiles. "I do hope you'll continue using Dr. Rice. She's a good doctor. Whatever your problems are, she can help you see a brighter future."

"I plan to continue." I try to smile, but I can't. I think Ethan sees it too as he touches my hand, stroking it with his gentle fingers. A heaviness centers in my chest. I'm not used to a man's kindness. Ethan is too perfect to be real and self-doubt plagues me as to whether I'm deserving of someone like him.

When we return to the apartment, Ethan walks me to my door. "Oh, I almost forgot. Your keys." He pulls them from his jean pocket and hands them to me.

"Thanks," I say as I jiggle the metal in my hand. "Hmm, I had a nice time." I lean against the door pausing. I find myself not wanting to end the night.

"Me too!" His green eyes dance.

"Well, I guess I better call it a night. Good night," I say, wishing he'd kiss me already. The prolonged anticipation is driving me bonkers.

"Yup. I better get some sleep too," he says as he

rocks on his heels with his hands stuffed in his jean pockets.

I open my door, and toss my hair over my shoulder, turning back to Ethan. "Well, see you around," I smile.

"Yeah, nighty-night." Ethan doesn't move but awkwardly clears his throat. "Hmm, there's something I've been wanting to do, but I haven't had the nerve." His velvet voice catches my breath.

"Yes?" I ask, holding my breath.

All at once, Ethan leans in and kisses me. Surprisingly, his lips are gentle and thoughtful. I kiss him back with reckless abandonment.

When he pulls back, his eyes glisten. "I've been wanting to kiss you since the first day I saw you."

Talk about a mixed-up girl. I wanted him to kiss me, but I'm terrified too. What if I fall in love with him and the feelings aren't reciprocated? "I'm not sure I can give you what you want. I'm still trying to pull myself together."

He gathers my chin into his palm. "Annie, I know you're mending. Let me be there for you. That's all I ask."

I close my eyes, fighting back tears. "That might be more than I can give." I force a smile. "Good night."

That night, tears cradle me to sleep as I toss and turn most of the night with dreams haunting me, and the thought of Ethan tormenting my heart.

GIFTS BEYOND

The next morning, the alarm on my phone blasts my brain far too early. I hit the snooze button twice before finally dragging myself out of bed. Since I slept through two snoozes, I wouldn't have time for breakfast but maybe I could manage a quick cup of coffee to pry open my eyes. I rush to the kitchen to start the coffee brewing and then head for the shower, yawning, eyes heavy with sleep.

I glance outside my window. It's overcast today, so I check my phone for the weather. Eighty percent chance of rain. That's a given. In this neck of the woods, rain is often.

After showering and drying my hair, I throw on a beige sweater that hovers just below my butt and tug on a pair of thick leggings with my western boots. It rarely snows or ices here like Dallas, Texas, but it rains a lot more.

When I enter the living room and kitchen area, the smell of coffee awakens my senses. I love its aroma in the morning, with a hardy load of bacon. The best ever. I have to settle for just coffee this morning, though. I pour the dark liquid in my large mug and sweeten it with creamer and Splenda.

I shrug on my raincoat on and grab my umbrella from the coat closet when the door flies open and in steps Jeff. My head snaps up and a smile tugs at the corners of my lips. "Hey, Jeffie! Boy, you must've had a tough night!"

He looks like something the cat dragged in. "Nothing I haven't handled before," he yawns. "Another fatality. Never a good night when you lose a patient."

He goes to the coffee pot and opens the cabinet, pulling down a mug to pour himself a cup. He takes a long sip, and my eyes almost fall out of their sockets.

"Wow! You did have a rough night." I study him as he takes another long drink.

"Stop drinking that before you scald your whole "

"I'm a doctor. I know what it can do," he lashes out. "I never can get used to seeing a person mangled. It thrusts me into oblivion."

"I'm sorry. I know it must be hard for you." I

come to his side and gently squeeze his shoulder. "I wish I could make it all go away. You deserve happiness too."

He looks me in the eye for the first time this morning. "Maybe we both do." He tries to make light, but I know Jeff. He keeps his pain bottled up until it festers.

"Do you want me to call off work and stay home with you?" I need to go in, but my brother is my priority.

Jeff's brow furrows into a scowl. "Hell, no! You need that job. You still owe me for the phone," he then teases.

I smile to myself. "You don't have to go there, ya know!"

"Yes, I do. I'm not supporting your ass 'til retirement."

I stare back at Jeff, knowing there's a little truth to his tease. "*Ooooo-kay*, point taken." I cross my eyes, teasing, but I caught the *T*.

"I'll try and catch you later, after work." I grab my purse by the door, but it slips from my grasp and all my personal items go falling out, scattering all over the floor. My eyes go wide when my pistol slides across the floor, nearly hitting Jeff's foot.

Damn! Damn! Damn!

His gaze drops to the gun, and his eyes bulge like he's in a horror film. "Anna Lee Baker! What the hell are you doing, packing a gun?" He glares at me, filled with anger.

"I bought the gun for protection!" My heart races.

Jeff's expression says it all—face blistered like a red-hot branding iron.

"Ann, if you need protection, get a can of mace. That should bring sweet Tad to his knees long enough for you to escape. But a gun?"

"I didn't have much choice. Tad is dangerous. I was becoming his punching bag."

Jeff's lips pull into a flat line. "Stop with the bullshit, Anna!"

I'm caught off guard by the sudden rage in his voice. "I'm sorry! But mace wouldn't have stopped Tad!" I scream as tears stream down my cheeks.

"I'm tired of worrying about you. Keeping a gun on you is reckless."

Jeff's tone was starting to exasperate me. "It's not like I don't know how to use it."

"You're kidding?" His eyes grow wide. "*You*, of all people, shouldn't be handling a gun!" He glares at me like I'm the village idiot.

I rush to pick the pistol off the floor and double check to make sure it's on safety. I turn my eyes on Jeff and say, "Do you think I got it off some sleazy dude in a dark alley? I went to a firing range and hired an instructor. I'm registered. The gun is legal," I snap.

"Get a can of mace!" he orders. "Get rid of the gun. I don't want it in my home."

"Alright!" I snap again. "I'll get rid of it." I check the time on my phone. "Gotta go! See you tonight." I reach up and kiss Jeff's cheek. "Get that elbow on ice."

"Aye-aye, doctor!" He salutes me.

"Don't be a smartass!" I give him the evil eye.

"Be careful, will you?"

"Don't worry. I'm more than careful," I reassure him as I stuff my gun back into my bag and disappear out the door. Geez! The last thing I want is for Jeff to know I carry a gun. He has such little faith in me that he thinks I'll shoot my toe off. I need to be more careful about hiding it.

I rush through the lobby and out the double-paned, door. I'm late. I hope this doesn't upset May. Apart from me needing this job, I like her and I want her to like me back.

I manage to get to work on time. It's a miracle that I hit all green lights. I must have a guardian angel.

May's counting the money and loading the registers as I enter from the back of the store. I toss my bag in my locker and throw on my apron, tying it in a bow as I rush toward my register. "Good morning!" I smile.

"Good morning, chile!" She hands me my bundle of money. "Here, count this first. We need to be on our toes today. Fridays are busy."

"Okay, I'm right on it!"

I take the bundle and start counting. After I finish, I tuck it in its place in the register and check the aisles and merchandise to make sure everything is in check. I find myself enthralled with the shop and all its peculiarities. I've been going over the catalog, trying to learn about spellcasting and what tools are used. Like candles, for example. Each color has a significant meaning, like red represents the element of fire and promotes passion. Pink promotes self-love. I should buy a whole truckload of pink.

During the day, I tried to focus on my work and keep myself from wondering about Ethan. That mind-blowing kiss still lingers on my lips and sharing his intimate past with me has me reeling. It seems, when it comes to picking partners, Ethan and I could use some help. My heart aches for him. Wow! How he must've felt when he discovered his wife was pregnant by another man? Infidelity is never easy to swallow. I think in my case, my dear friend, Susan, did me a favor.

After work, I plan to visit the local college and, hopefully, get registered. A university is out of the question. My high-school grades are barely passing. But they're good enough for community college, and I can get a degree or vocational training in a field that will give me a leg up. The taunt Jeff gave me this morning wasn't a tease. He meant it. I totally get it. Considering all the years he has been working for his doctorate, I wouldn't want someone mooching off me either.

I do think I'm making progress. It's slow, but I'm steadily working on it. I do have to keep myself in check. My infatuation with Ethan is a prime example. But damn! My heart and body are telling me differently.

The long day comes to an end as I change the sign in the door to "Closed". I start closing out my register and counting money. We'd had a busy day. The bell on the door didn't stop chiming all day. The shop had been packed full and I loved every minute of it. I've never liked a job as much as I like this one. I hope May will keep me.

After closing my register, I head to the office to drop it off and confirm my balance. When I enter, May looks up. "Hey, we had a great day!"

"I don't think I looked up from my register once." I half laugh and ease into a chair in front of May's cluttered desk. "Although I'm gonna need some better shoes," I laugh as I rub my feet.

"You did a good job today. The customers seem to like you too. Even the regulars. And they ain't easy to please."

"Thank you," I sigh. "I love your store, and I enjoy working here."

"Oh, I almost forgot! Your paycheck." May hands an envelope to me.

"Awesome!" I smile and stuff the envelope in my pocket.

"Hey. I'm about done here. You wanna have some tea with me? I'd like to read your tea leaves. This one's on me," May kindly offers.

"A reading? Like fortune-telling?" My breath stalls. "I've never had my fortune read." As interesting as this odd world of magic is, dabbling is something I'm reluctant to try.

"Ah, honey-chile, then this will be a real treat. I've been doing readings since I was twelve years old. Come on now, I haven't got a lot of time! I'm making groceries after I leave here."

"That's grocery shopping, right?"

May laughs. "Chile, I forget you're from 'round her'."

"Yeah, the slang is going to take me a bit to getting used to," I giggle. "Alright, I guess, since it's a quicky."

"Follow me, back here."

May gets up from behind the desk and I follow her to the back of the shop. We pass a bunch of stock stored on shelves and we come to a white door at the very back. I've only been in this area once, but I never noticed the white door.

May turns to me and says, "I use this room for

my special customers." A spark of mischief flickers in the glint.

She holds the door open for me and as I enter the small room, a scent of tea wafts through the air. I notice a pot on a small stove and two cups and saucers laid out on the counter.

"Have a seat while I fix you a cup," May urges.

I hesitate, thinking there are a million and one things I'd rather do right now than sit here and shiver in my shoes. I smile awkwardly and sigh. "Alrighty."

I take a seat at the small round table and glance around the quaint room. It's not a typical room that one would find in the back of a storage space. The color on the walls is a dark purple, and paintings of old people and old mansions decorate one wall. On a wall to the left: bookcase sets with shelving on various subjects related to magic.

I have to say the one book catches my curiosity: a giant black book, thick with jagged pages. I wonder if that's her book of shadows? A book of personal spells. I learned about such things watching *Charmed* on the CW. Of course, the show is fiction and what do I know about real magic or if there even is such a thing?

"Here's your tea, hon." She sets the cup and saucer down in front of me. "Drink it nice and slow. Take your time. No rush," she smiles as she takes a chair next to me.

"Thank you," I smile in return as I take a whiff of the brew. "What kind of tea is this? It smells wonderful." There's a hint of ginger and something else I'm not familiar with.

"It's called Oolong. A traditional Chinese tea. I've been using it for years. Not only is it excellent for reading, but it's also healthy."

"Oh, that's interesting." I blow on mine to cool it.

May sips slowly from her cup, and I follow her lead. She looks up from the brim and asks, "How are you liking Nawlins?"

"I like it, but I haven't had a chance to explore much."

"This city has its strong points and its demons."

Suddenly, I choke on my drink and clear my throat. "What do you mean by *demons*?"

"The city is rich with history and culture, but because of its past, spirits from the beyond cling to this place."

Okay, I'm breathing in and breathing out. It's only a belief. It doesn't mean goblins and vampires are running amok. Fortune-telling is merely entertainment. That's all. "You believe in the afterlife?"

She laughs. "Honey-chile, I believe in a lot of things. In Nawlins, it's best described as a gumbo. From Catholicism to Voodoo, traditions from its smorgasbord of cultures and religions have melded together where you can find all sorts of beliefs and traditions that surround this city. I've seen things with my own eyes that will make your hair stand up."

I take a deep gulp of tea and shrug. "I guess we all have to believe in something."

"What do you believe in?" May doesn't like beating around the bush.

"Hmm … I believe this tea is delicious." I smile as I take a sip. "Since my parents died, I often ask the same question. Though, to be honest, I'd rather not know the answer."

I finish my tea except for a few drops and set my cup in its saucer.

"Well, let's see what your future holds." May reaches for my cup, handling it carefully and places the saucer on top of the cup and flips it over, letting it sit until the remains settle.

After a minute or two, she removes the saucer from the cup and sets it down right side up. I watch in silence as she studies the soggy leaves. "I see one leaf has floated to the top of the cup. That means you're going to have an unexpected visitor." She looks up at me. "Are you expecting company?"

I shake my head. "No. Not a soul. It's just my brother and me."

May nods and moves on. "I see much pain in your past. Obviously, since your parents' death." She holds up the cup, pointing to one side where I can see. "See how the leaves gather?"

"Yes." I have no idea what she's pointing at, but I go along with it.

"This shows that something profound in your life is troubling you. There is someone in your life that isn't truthful. Perhaps this person is hiding a secret from you."

"Huh … I was in a relationship with someone, but we're no longer together."

"Is he deceased? I see a shadow hovering over you."

I suddenly feel uneasy. "No, my ex-boyfriend is still living. It's just that we didn't part on good turns."

"I see." A strange expression spreads over May's face. "Anna, the dark shadow is not your ex-boyfriend. It's more malevolent. I do see you will have better days to come, but before you reach peace, you will have to confront the darkness first."

"Darkness?" I give a nervous laugh. "Leaving an abusive boyfriend and losing my parents is about as dark as you can get." I wring my hands, trying to settle my erratic pulse.

"Bless your heart. You're so young to have lost so much."

"My parents' death changed my life."

"Honey, I'm sorry. I don't mean to scare you, but someone close to you will be impacted by an unexpected event."

I shift in my seat, feeling the weight of disquiet

on my shoulders. "I have made mistakes in my past and I'm trying to correct those errors." I sigh, swimming in regret. "Hey, I gotta go. Thank you for the reading. It's been interesting." I smile, but inside I'm crumbling to my knees.

"Sure, chile! I'll see you tomorrow." She puts her hand on mine and pats it. She smiles, but it doesn't reach her weary eyes.

I grab my bag from my locker and start to head for the back door.

May stops me on the way out. "Listen, I know I scared you and I'm sorry," She smiles faintly. "If you need anyone to talk to, I'm here. No judgment."

I shift my weight as I tuck my bag under my arm. "I appreciate your concern, but I'm okay."

I flash a quick smile as I duck out the door.

ACQUAINTANCE

*R*eneging on my promise, I should be stronger. Nonetheless, after May's reading, the thought of checking out the local college is more than I can handle. I plan to give myself a break, dress up, and go out and paint the town. New Orleans style. I think it'd be a well-deserved break. I have a little money in my pocket. Who knows, I might even have a drink. I haven't had an alcoholic beverage since Mom and Dad's accident. What's one drink? It's better than smoking weed. Besides, I'm in a gloomy mood. Jeff's at work, and if I dare refer to Ethan as my only friend here, he's working tonight too. So, I'm the Lone Ranger. How much trouble can I get into? I'll stay in the crowd and under the streetlight.

I want to feel like a girl tonight. I decide to indulge myself and buy a new dress. A red mini with a low neckline and knee-high, black patent boots to match. The dress is form-fitting and leaves very little to the imagination. Who knows, I might find a dancing partner tonight. Not exactly the right shoes for two-steppin' but I can wing it.

I circle uptown and find this one bar that has the flair of New Orleans, called Le Bon Temps Roule. It looks like I'm in the historic district. It's a neighborhood on Magazine. How cool! A bar in the middle of a family neighborhood.

The homes in this area are aged, as towering oaks line the sidewalk. There's a subtle charm that appeals to me. I have a great feeling about this little adventure.

The closest parking spot I can find is several blocks down from the bar. The joint must be packed tonight. It's not too bad. The street is lined with generous light, giving a quaintness to the old, cracked sidewalk. I park at the corner and kill the engine, grabbing my bag and sliding from the car. I lock up as I take a deep breath.

I've never gone to a bar by myself, but I can't sit home another night alone, chewing my nails and watching mindless television either. I need some good ol' stimulation.

I make my way to the front entrance, but I've discovered that walking in heels in New Orleans is a challenge. The weathered sidewalk is unleveled, and I wobble worse than any drunk. I should've worn my tennis shoes.

As I approach the front, my eyes photograph the establishment. Its rustic condition, old beadboard, and uneven foundation show the telltale signs of a deteriorating building. Yet the tattered condition adds much to its southern charm.

I reach the entrance; two distressed wood doors are open wide for business. I walk past the doors and my eyes slide over the bar. Just as I'd expected. The cozy lit place is packed: people shoulder to shoulder, laughter, country music, the smell of liquor and smoke lingering hard like heavy perfume.

I spot, toward the back, in another section, a band playing. I'm immediately drawn to the music. A nice catchy tune that gets my blood pumping and my feet stomping. Nothing like good ol' country music.

I make my way to the bar and flop down on one of the stools. The bartender approaches me asking, "Wha'd dat be, little lady?" The man rolls his words off his tongue fast; living in the south, though, I'm able to understand most of the slur. His distinctive, deep, throaty accent feels like home.

"I'll have a Po' boy sandwich and a Bud Light,"

I yell over the loud music and the hum of people's aimless chatter. I don't think one beer will kill me.

"No problem! You want it dressed?

"Dressed?"

"You know … lettuce, tomato …"

"Yeah-yeah-yeah! That sounds good."

"Sure thang! I'll put a little lagniappe on da side fer ya. Just have a seat in the back. My boy'll bring it to ya."

"Thank you," I say as I slide off the stool and head to the back. I guess when my order comes out, I'll find out what "lagniappe" means. I shake my head, laughing to myself. I should get out more.

I sit at a table in the far corner, facing the band. I set my bag in the chair next to me, closest to the wall. A girl can never be too careful. The last thing I need is someone stealing my bag. I'm packing my pistol, tucked in a zipped compartment. The pistol's small and doesn't take up much room, but it's very effective.

As I'm waiting for my food and drink, my gaze drifts over the bar. It's larger than I first thought. The music and restaurant area are in the back. Lots of entertainment here. I spy pool tables in one part of the place. Colorful lights of every color dot the ceiling and the bar area like Christmas lights. The neon lights brighten up the rustic walls, making it quaint and busy to the eye.

I glance over the patrons. It's sorta easy to pick

out the locals from the tourists. The locals are casual, at ease, like this bar is their home. The tourists are louder, sport brighter colors, are well dressed, and feelin' the liquor. And then there's me, sitting alone. I think I'm the only one here that doesn't have a plus one or more. It's a little awkward, but I'm fine. It's nice getting a break from my problems ... Ethan, Jeff, the therapist, and now the fortune-teller.

May surprises me. To look at her, you'd think she's just a regular person but, now, after the tea leaf reading, I see a whole different side of her. I still like her. But I'll pass on future tea readings. I fiddle with my hair. I teased it and sprayed the heck out of it. Now it feels like a bird's nest. I release a long, hard sigh. I got to get my mind off of *me*. I could use a distraction.

The waiter brings out my sandwich and the ice-cold Bud. I discover that the "lagniappe" is spicy fries. I'm down with dat! I can't wait to devour my sandwich. At work, we were so busy that I didn't even get a bathroom break. I take a whiff of the delicious aroma, as curls of steam taunt my stomach. I lean over and sink my teeth into the sandwich, and chew slowly, savoring the flavor exploding in my mouth. It's *sooo* good! It melts in my mouth. Gosh! This town is growing on me.

After one beer, it starts to kick in, and I'm about halfway finished eating my sandwich when a light-skinned black man drops down at my table in the chair across from me. I get the impression he has an identity crisis … the dainty man is dressed lavishly as a woman. My gaze hits his face, and my hand goes to my bag. I'm not planning on using my gun. It isn't that sort of alarm. It's more on the lines of whether he's planning to steal it that bothers me.

What an odd creature. I eye him from head to toe. Decked out in a bright pink, form-fitting dress, makeup that might take a week to wash off, thick black eyelashes that bring out his deep blue eyes and a Marilyn Monroe wig. The diamonds dangling from his earlobes, I assume, are fake, along with his inch-long nails. I must admit, with his creamy caramel complexion, he's an attractive she-man.

"Good evening! How ya are this luscious evening?" he smiles, posing a hand like an expensive model.

I glower. "I was enjoying myself until you interrupted." I'm not in the mood to visit with strangers.

"Oh, aren't you a grumpy girl tonight?" The little man flashes straight white teeth; a little residue of red lipstick is stuck to his two front teeth. "I thought I'd introduce myself since you're all by your lonesome. I'm here too by myself, and it never looks cool to sit alone, if you get my drift, boo," he rambles on. "My name is Francis Bon-Ton. My friends call me Franny."

"Hello, Franny." Irritation flavors my tone. "I'm

Anna," Every fiber in my body warns me against him.

He wiggles in his seat and swats the air with his ruby-red manicured nails. "Oh gal, you need to get that stick outta ya ass. I'll buy you a beer," he offers as if we're BFFs. "Hope that'll loosen your stuck-up self." He waves the waiter down.

The young waiter approaches our table, "What can I get you?" he asks.

Franny speaks up, "Get this lady another cold beer and I'll have your fine lovely self!" Franny groans as he drinks in the blond-haired waiter with the dimpled smile. "I'm kiddin'. I'll have what she's having but make my drink an appletini, *STRONG*, *babee*." He twists his nose up at me but is still talking to the waiter. "My company tonight is rather boring."

My mouth drops open. "Oh, really?"

"Yes, really! Miss-Cork-up-her-Butt!" He turns to the waiter and flashes a wide smile. "Please put this on my tab and your telephone number too, sugah!" Franny winks at the waiter as the young man blushes.

"No, problem. I'll get that right out." The waiter spins on his heels and is gone out of sight.

I study my new acquaintance. "You're going to pay for my bill?" I eye him suspiciously. Why would a total stranger offer to pay my tab? What does this guy want?

"I do have my generous moments. But since ya askin' … I need a ride home tonight." He leans back in his chair and fans his face. "My fella got pissed off at me, a d the stupid mutherfuker left me stranded. Someone that looks as good as I do don't need to be walkin' home in the dark. I don't know if you've noticed, but this town is full of weirdos." He keeps fanning himself with his long fingers and even longer nails.

"So, what makes you think I have a ride?" I'm not sure I want to get involved with this man-woman person. How do I know he won't rob me?

"Bitch! You gotta ride! I saw you gettin' out of your damn car." His voice goes up a pitch, full of fire. "Now, will ya help a girl out, or do I have to hustle some stranger for a ride? I could get hurt!"

"Do you always take liberties with folks you don't know?" I stare back at this odd, imposing person. He's getting under my skin.

"Honey-chile, this is Ny-oo-aw-lee-inz, and anythang goes."

"I can see that. We both know you're not female. Not trying to insult you, but I think it's obvious." I arch a brow, waiting for the man to confess.

"*Oooo-kay!* Haven't you ever seen a drag queen?"

"No, you're my first. I don't get out much," I laugh in answer. One thing for sure, this guy, whether female or male, has an attitude. "You're not homeless, are you?"

He drops a look at me that could've killed a platoon. "Honey, do I *look* homeless?"

Oh geez! Now I've offended him. "My bad! I'm just wondering. You said yourself you didn't have a car,.." I smile back as I take a bite of my sandwich.

"I didn't say I was *homeless*." He presses down on that last word. "I said, my friend left me stranded."

"Wait! Are you a prostitute?" Oh, hell to the Nah! This fool needs to move on if that's the case.

"Now, that's the meanest thang anyone has ever said to me. No! I ain't no pro. I have better taste. I got a job. I'm a hairdresser. Do you like my Marylin Monroe do, boo?"

I laugh. "That explains the wig and black dot on your cheek."

"You are not nice! Do you receive me?" He purses his lips. "But I do need a ride home. Help a gurl?"

I inhale. It would be nice to have a conversation with someone not associated with my life. I pause a minute longer, debating on whether I can trust this cat. "Where do you live?"

"Whodie! The ninth ward."

I nearly choked on my sandwich, "The *ninth ward*?"

"Did I s-s-stutter?"

Whatta smartass.

"How about I call you a taxi?" No way am I going to the ninth ward in the middle of the night.

"Do I look like I want to waste my money on a taxi, boo?"

"But you expect *me* to go there?" This she-man is not my problem.

"I expect nothin'! I was just hopin' you might have a kind heart, and since I'm paying the bill, you'd be willing to take me home."

"Alright! I'll take you home." I roll my eyes. Might as well give him a ride. Spending the whole night listening to him yammer about being stranded would put a damper in my night. Besides, I glance over him, how harmful could he be?

"Thank you!" He breaks into a dazzling smile. "C'mon! We need to dance!" Before I protest, he grabs my hand and drags me onto the floor in a jaunty two-step. I'm sure we looked silly. Two girls in heels dancing together. Though Franny seems to have a way of making me forget my troubles and letting loose. I'm sure the alcohol helped as well.

When the bar decides to close, I'm feeling the booze. I had one too many appletinis, and everyone in the place, including the drinks, are swimming.

"Franny, can you drive?"

"You too drunk?"

As we head for the door, I stagger, slurring my words. "Y-y-yep, I think I might be."

"Gurl, I told you to go slow on those appletinis. They'll kick your ass to the moon!" He puts his arm around me to hold me up. "C'mon! I can drive. I'll take you home and bring your car back in the … hell, it's morning now!" He checks my wristband watch. "Don't worry! I'll get you home safely, boo."

With his arm around my waist, we head to my car. The sidewalk's spinning, the street's rocking, and I'm wasted. I start to waddle in the opposite direction of my car, but Franny pulls me back into the embrace of his arm and walks me in the opposite direction.

"Okay, I need to get the key out of your purse." Franny leans me up against the car and soon I hear something jingling. In the next breath, I hear Franny gasp. "Gurl, whatcha doin' with a gun?"

He sounds alarmed. "Ya know what! Never mind. I need to get ya home. I ain't buyin' you no mo alcohol. I should've known better. White gurls can't hold their liquor and ya half cray-cray, carrin' a gun in your damn purse. Lord have mercy! What the hell was I thinkin'?"

He pauses, unlocking the door. "I should've known askin' for a ride was gonna get me in trouble. Now, I gotta sleep in the damn car. Ain't no way in hell is you drivin' me home."

He supports me by putting my right arm around his neck and his other arm around my waist. "C'mon," he moans, lugging my weight.

"I'm gonna put you in the front seat. You haven't told me where your ass lives. And I ain't gonna take you to my place."

All at once, two strangers step out from the brush. I hear a thud and, suddenly, Franny's arm leaves my side. The strangers reach in the car and start tugging at me. I fight, scream and scratch, but I'm in no condition to fend for myself. Suddenly, I start throwing up my cookies and hear a strange male voice yelling, "Yuck!" and a gagging sound follows.

Then I hear a gun blast.

Is that my gun?

I suddenly hear Franny threatening the strangers. "You git your mutherfukin' asses away from her, or I'll shoot ya where ya live! That's right, mutherfukers, I know how to use a gun! This drag queen knows how to hold her own! Get down on your knobby knees. And, no, I don't want no blowjob! Hands, behind your fuckin' backs! *Now!*" he shouts with authority.

Everything is muffled, but I think I hear sirens going off and heavy footsteps all around. Several different male voices float into the cold draft. I try to make sense of it all, but my brain is drowning in booze.

Suddenly, I'm airborne or floating. I can't make out which is what. Cold hands are touching me, and I'm lying flat on a thin cushion. My vision is blurry. I see faceless people in uniforms, male voices encircling me. I recognize Franny's voice and feel his hand patting my head.

"I'm gonna be ridin' with you, honey. You're okay. Nobody's gonna hurt you now." I sense worry in his voice.

"My bag? Where's my bag?" I slide my gaze around, fuzzy faces hovering over me.

Franny gets low to my ear and gently whispers, "I got that taken care of, boo. Your secret is tucked back in your bag." He pats my shoulder.

I feel my body lift, sliding into a cocoon of warmth; a loud humming sound is drowning out the voices. A strong smell of alcohol drifts throughout the closed space—not the kind to drink, but the sterile stuff for cleaning.

I think I'm in an ambulance? The uniforms must be paramedics. Sweet Jesus! They're taking me to the local hospital! I can't go there. I'm in such deep trouble! I start thrashing my head side to side. I frantically grab Franny's shirt. "I ... I ... I can't go there!"

Franny pats my hand again. "Boo, don't ya worry. I got ya!"

"No-no-*noooo!* I have to go home." I try to raise my head, but something is holding me down. I need to rub my temples. A splitting headache is coming on as panic bangs my head like a screen door in a hurricane. "I'm doomed! My brother will kill me. I can't go there!"

"You need to calm the hell down!" Franny pulls loose of my death grip. "We takin' ya to the hospital. Gurl, why didn't you tell me you can't drink none? Don't you know there ain't nothin' worse than a white girl that can't hold her liquor!"

I hear laughter in the background, in addition to Franny's weary voice. I just close my eyes and let the spinning take over. I hear doors open and a rush of cold air hits my face.

Then, a quick brush of warm air encases me. Two male voices are chatting; Franny is one and the other one, I'm assuming, is a paramedic. Another rush of cold hands rub my wrist. Then, I feel the sharp prick. That must be an IV being administered. Ouch! OMG! I'm getting admitted!

CHARITY HOSPITAL

J wake up to bright lights, and an IV stuck in my arm. Oh, geez! I bury myself under the sheet, hoping to avoid the inevitable. I can just hear the gossip circulating the hospital like wildfire. "Did you see Jeff's sister come through the ER? Overdose on alcohol!"

Sweet Jesus! What am I doing? Jeff is going to kick me out! I feel it in my bones. At least my panicking is sobering me up. The last thing I want is to be inebriated in front of Jeff. *Yeah, Jeff, I screwed up ... again!* I might as well practice my confession now.

I keep hearing Franny's voice. Why does he keep hanging around? He doesn't owe me anything. Oh, I forgot! I was supposed to take him home. Is he waiting for me?

My stomach churns, and a quick onset of sickness overcomes me. I feel it surfacing and about to eject like an active volcano. I raise my head, "Oh Jesus! I need a bucket, a trash can, anything!" My words rush together.

I hear Franny in the room. "Lawd, have mercy! What the hell am I supposed to do?"

I hear fast-moving steps stomping across the floor, and then I feel something metallic and cold pressed against my neck and under my chin.

"Gurl, stick a fuckin' finger down your throat, and get that shit out of the way! But you best not projectile on my new outfit or else you buyin' me a new Giorgio Armani. And honey, I don't do cheap, includin' my drawls!"

Lucky for me that I don't have to use a finger. I lift my head and lean over the bed. My body does the rest.

In the background, I hear the echo of someone gagging. Mirroring me. I think it's Franny. Oh, dear! He has a gag reflex problem. Me too, as I went in for round two and three. I'd laugh if everything would stop spinning.

When my stomach settles; I quickly tire. I lay my head back and close my eyes. Soon, I fall into a deep sleep.

I don't know how much time has passed when my eyes pop open to a familiar voice. I feel the weight of someone on the edge of my bed as my eyes slowly open. I spot a white jacket and Ethan's face, smiling broadly. "Looks like you did some party binging."

I notice right off his spicy cologne as it stirs my senses. My eyes flutter and I know I look like hell. I smell alcohol and vomit on my breath.

"I messed up," I smile weakly. The haze of alcohol has eased, but my body and mind haven't caught up. "I guess I had one too many."

"Apparently so," he curtly answers, yet he's smiling as our eyes lock.

Man, I love his green eyes and the feel of his warm palm stroking my back. I want to drink him all up, down to the very last drop. "I'm your doctor today. How's my girl?"

My brows push together. "I feel like I can drink an ocean."

Ethan laughs a deep, thoughtful laugh. "Yeah, I'd expect that much."

I sense his disquiet.

"You had a close call tonight. You were attacked by two men."

"I was attacked?"

"Don't worry. The police got there in time to arrest both men before they hurt you." He pauses, clamping shut his mouth for several seconds. "Apparently, you delayed their endeavors. You'd vomited all over them. The cop who arrested the men gagged and laughed the whole time he was cuffing them."

"Wow! That's disgusting." I bury my face in the cover.

"Yes, but very effective." Ethan's eyes glisten, smiling down at me.

My mind briskly switches to my bag as I glance across the room. "Have I been admitted?"

"Yes, young lady. Just for the night. You need fluids, and we'll see in the morning. Okay?" His eyes are soft and tender.

"I don't suppose I get a say?" I pout.

Ethan laughs. "Nope, you're all mine."

"Have you seen my friend, Franny? He rode with me to the hospital."

"Franny? I don't know anyone by that name, and as far as I know, you came in alone."

My lips tighten.

"You can't miss him. He's a tall skinny black man dressed in drag."

Ethan laughs, shaking his head. "That could be half of New Orleans, doll."

I bite my bottom lip. Ethan called me "doll". "Did you see my bag?"

Ethan looks around the room and then returns to focus on me. "Don't worry your pretty little head. I'll have one of the nurses check with the medic who brought you in. It could've gotten left in his cab. If so, he'll bring it back. Get some rest, and I'll see to it that your bag is found."

"Hmm … have you spoken to Jeff? I'm sure he's furious with me."

"Don't worry about your brother. I'll handle him." Ethan squeezes my hand. "I got you!" he half-whispers. "Gotta go. I'll check on you later." He leans in and kisses my forehead.

I smile back, holding my worry for tomorrow. I watch as Ethan leaves. After he's gone, I stifle the pissed-off sensation. No doubt that Franny took my bag and my whole paycheck, gun and all. I'd cashed my check earlier today. I should've left my money at home. Hell, I should've stayed home too.

I wake up to angry voices. Familiar voices. I spot Jeff and Ethan just outside my door. Jeff starts to walk into my room when Ethan swiftly grasp his arm, halting him. I hear them in the hall as their low voices echo in my room.

"Hey, she's sleeping." Ethan drops Jeff's arm and crosses his arms across his chest and leans in the doorframe, blocking Jeff.

"I'm not allowed to see my own sister?" Jeff smiles, but his whole demeanor changes when his gaze catches mine.

Ethan answers, "Nope, brah. She needs to rest, and you need to let her breathe."

"Breathe?" Jeff snaps.

"That's what I said, my man." Ethan speaks with resigned authority.

Jeff scoffs, "You've got to be kidding me? What, are you her doctor?"

"Yes, sir. I am at the moment, and I've ordered no visitors. Besides, I know you far too well. You'll go in there and rip her apart. This young lady was almost raped tonight. I can't have you upsetting my patient. She's been through enough."

There's a tense pause.

"Do you have any idea what my sister has put me through?" Jeff presses his hands angrily on his hips.

"I get that you have helped her. But that's neither here nor there. Annie's a grown woman. It's time to let go of the past. Not everyone is like you, all perfect, pristine, and never wrong. You live a rigid life. But that's you. Don't expect her to live by your golden rules. So, she got drunk for the first time in how many years? Hell, I've been drunk more times than I care to count. She had a little too much and was nearly raped! Be glad that a hangover is the only thing she ended up with. It could've been detrimental."

"I am fully aware how heinous this situation could've been. But tell me this, brother … how many times do I have to keep cleaning her moronic messes up? She needs to understand the consequences of her poor decisions. Especially when it affects others! A prime example … who's going to pay her medical expenses? *You?*"

"Don't worry about it. We can revisit this tomorrow. In the meantime, you need to simmer down and let the girl sleep. You can't resolve your issues tonight. All you want to do is vent your anger at her. She's been badgered enough."

"Oh, I have badgered her?" Jeff laughs darkly.

"Yes, you are always harping on all the mistakes she's made. Can't you back off one night?"

"*You don't know anything about my sister.*" The words seem to grind from Jeff's mouth and he spins on his heels to leave.

Ethan remains standing in my door. I hear a long sigh as he stares down at the floor. I'd give anything to know what's running through his mind. Then I think of Franny and my bag. I'm in such trouble that I doubt I'll ever dig myself out.

BACK TO NORMAL

A week has passed, and I'm fully recovered and have sworn off alcohol and bars, forever! I promised Jeff. In return, he promised if I ever screwed up again, I'd be out on my ass. Homeless.

I realize more than ever the dangers of getting stupid and the predators lurking in the shadows. Jesus! I was almost raped that night. I couldn't recall every detail, but I'm pretty sure Franny saved my ass from a fatal event that would've marked me for life. I plan to thank him if I ever see him again. He's the strangest creature.

When I returned home from the hospital, my keys and bag with all its content have been left at the desk. My car was parked at the apartment, all squeaky clean. I feel terribly guilty for all the name slashing I'd called Franny. I wish I could take it all back. Glad he didn't hear it.

Nothing makes sense in this crazy city. Franny disappearing like an apparition. Now I see him and now I don't. The man shot my gun and called the police. Ethan gave me his word he spoke to the medic on call that night, and he doesn't recall encountering a drag queen. Is it possible I could've imagined Franny? I *was* naked wasted. I asked the clerk, Fred, at the desk if saw Franny and he claimed he didn't see a drag queen. Chills run down my spine.

I'm at my therapist's office for another session with Dr. Sex. I mean Rice. Even my doctor is odd. I blow out a sigh. Can I ever have anything normal? I'm sitting in her small office on the soft couch, wringing my hands. It seems like I've been waiting for an hour, but it's only been about twenty minutes. I dread this session more than any of the others. Alcoholics Anonymous, here I come.

When Mom and Dad died, I'd stopped drinking with no problems. I was only eighteen, underage. I was lucky to have never craved it, not even a hint of withdrawal or back-sliding, none of the usual for an addict. And then seven years later ... I pick up a drink ... *actually several*. I didn't even realize the drinks were hitting me until the end of the night. Sweet Jesus! What the hell was I thinking?

Ethan is great. He's the best doctor and a treat to

look at too. Though I'd never tell Jeff that Ethan's bedside manner is much better. I'm still stunned over Ethan not letting Jeff in my hospital room. I think he was protecting me. It made me giddy. Yet I hated that Ethan and Jeff argued. I wonder if it will be constant turmoil with Jeff if I do start dating his friend. Will he blow up and insist I dump him? Addled as to how I should handle my brother, I do know Jeff has my best interest at heart. On the flip side of the coin, I don't understand why he's not in favor of me dating his friend. I like Ethan. A lot. I wonder if I will have to pick between the two.

I hear the door creep open and my head jerks up in the same direction. Dr. Rice steps in. As if set in stone, she's wearing that same stiff smile. It never changes. That generic smile. You never know what she's thinking behind it either.

Then my mind slips back to that day at the shop when she came to visit Ethan's mother. I wonder if the doctor had another agenda. Probing for answers, trying to get Ethan back. Maybe she thinks there's more to their fling than there was. Could he be lying? If Ethan says he wasn't in a relationship with her, then I have no other choice but to take his word at face value.

Dr. Rice walks up to me and extends her hand just like the last time. "How have you been, Ann?"

She still hasn't gotten my name correct. I see she is dressed to the hilt: perfect pink lipstick, boldly poured into a form-fitting designer's dress, navy blue, just above the knees. Including, Louboutin strappy heels, crystal-embellished. The doctor's killing it.

I straighten up, shoulders back, "I'm doing as well as expected." Why bother to elaborate? She's going to drag it out of me if she doesn't know already. I know my brother. He'd squeal like a pig going to market.

"I understand this last weekend, you had a relapse."

Unlike the other appointments, the doctor is wearing a pair of black frame glasses. She must wear contacts. Whatta vanity girl. Yet, her glasses aren't what's bothering me. She could at least look at me between scribbling on her notepad.

And before I know it, I lash out. "Relapse! I didn't relapse. I simply had too much to drink. That doesn't make me an alcoholic."

"Do you know the definition of an *alcoholic*?" The doctor emphasizes the word.

"Why don't you give me the clinical meaning?" Attitude intertwines my words.

Now she's eyeballing me dead in the face. "I sense disquietude from you, Ann. Can you tell me why?"

I roll my eyes, not caring if I offend. "My name is Anna. It's sorta an easy and common name."

"I apologize ... Anna." She spreads those hot-pink lips, attempting to smile, but her effort seems more like the North Atlantic winds: bitter and hostile.

I shrug, staring back at her.

"I get your frustration, but you have to be honest with me for me to help you." She flashes her usual cold smile. "If you don't acknowledge your problems, we can't repair the damages."

"I'm gathering my brother has informed you of my recent … *episode*." Why didn't Jeff let lying dogs lie? My chest is tight, breath short from anticipation.

"Yes, he did, but I'd like to hear your side of the story." This time she's not smiling. Creepier than ever.

"I think Jeff covered all the bases."

The doctor stops, lifting her eyes to mine and asks, "Anna, if you don't trust me, how can I help you?" She lays down her glasses and sighs. "Why don't you tell me how you're feeling instead?"

"I feel?" I emphasize. "I feel, I feel … I'm always feeling!" I rush the heated words like I'm trying to erase myself. "I'm so sick and tired trying to live up to everyone's expectations. Why do I keep …"

"You didn't finish your sentence," she observes.

"I meant to say, why do I keep fighting an end-less battle?"

Dr. Rice inhales a deep sigh, "You say you haven't had a drink in seven years. Quite some time. There is a difference between alcohol dependency and alcohol abuse. People who abuse alcohol drink too much on occasion and their drinking habits often result in risky behavior and poor judgment. Alcohol abusers generally aren't dependent on alcohol.

"Alcoholism, on the other hand, means a person needs alcohol to get through their day. That's obviously not in your case. I do think you abuse alcohol, but you needn't worry; you're not dependent. However, since you don't have good control of yourself, I wouldn't recommend drinking. On a brighter note, I am glad to see that you're okay and you didn't get hurt."

"Thank you." I look down at my hands, clasped on my lap. "I'm sorry for my rudeness."

She slaps on that plastic smile. "I understand, and all is forgiven." She pauses. "Your brother, Jeff, had planned to sit in our session today but he declined. He thinks you and I should resolve the elephant in the room issue before we proceed."

Sweet Jesus! What *now?* "Like what?" My pulse kicks up. Sometimes, Jeff can be pushy.

"I understand that you have become quite acquainted with Ethan LaBlanc. Jeff briefed me on your involvement."

Staring into a stoic face, I realize she must despise me. "Yes, we are friends." I hold my voice low. I don't want to sound like I'm on the offensive.

"Then, you two are intimate?"

"Excuse me!" My gaze flies up at her. "Is your probing appropriate, since you and Ethan have a past? I don't mean to offend, but this is now, and you're his past. Sorry, I don't mean to pry, but you did bring it up first."

She smiles, always poise, sitting perfectly like a painting—stiff, lifeless, and cold. "Past? Why would you assume such a thing? Ethan and I are very present."

"You mean as friends?"

Her full lips pulled into a broad smile. "I'm afraid it's *much* more. I'm sorry, but you did ask."

The doctor sucker-punches me in the gut with that last sentence. I glower. It takes restraint not to give her a good old- fashioned Texan-two-step smackdown.

"Come again?" I attempt to hold the surprise in my voice.

"Of course, you don't know the full story," she sings. "Ethan is smooth and charming. He can tame a vicious lion. And he can also lie better than any politician."

"What are you trying to say?"

"I'm saying that Ethan and I have been together as a couple for many years. He lost his wife and … well, he needed consoling. Our friendship blos-somed into something much more, and later into an engagement.

"We were to be married until he came to me a couple of weeks ago." She smiles without it reaching her brown eyes. "He broke up with me, claiming he'd fallen for a younger woman. I didn't know who he was referring to until your brother, Jeff, enlightened me."

"My brother *told* you?" My eyebrows arch almost to my hairline.

"Jeff and I are close friends." The corners of her mouth tip faintly. "He's against you seeing Ethan. I told Jeff not to worry. I know Ethan better than anyone. He'll lose interest after a while. Don't get me wrong. Ethan has his good points. It's just, he becomes bored with simpletons. He likes his women with more … *dimension*. Sorry, dear. I don't mean to be cruel."

"You think I'm a-"

"Ann, you're in no condition to be starting a serious relationship. Ethan deserves someone who can give him stability. Someone who is reliable, constant."

"You mean someone like you?" I scoff. "A woman who is stiff and inflexible like yourself?" I shouldn't have said that, but she'd pushed me.

"I'd describe myself as focused, successful. You hardly have a high school diploma," Dr. Rice sighs. "Do you get my point?"

My lips clamp down as I snatch up my bag and spring from the couch. "I think this session is over.

Since our patient-doctor relationship is a conflict of interest, I won't be returning," I say with conviction and launch for the door.

When my fingers touch the knob, Dr. Rice calls out, halting me. "Ann, before you leave, you must know that Ethan and I are back together. I think after he saw how pixilated you were at the hospital, he decided you were too unstable. I'm sorry to have to be the bearer of bad news, but both your brother and Ethan wanted me to tell you."

I can no longer face the bitch. Seeing her sardonic smirk would push me over the ledge. Without uttering a word to her barbed confession, I swing open the door and fly out, past the lobby.

I don't stop until I reach my car. I fumble in my bag and find my keys at the bottom. The dangling noise is like music to my ears. I unlock my car and slide inside, shutting the door behind me. After locking the door, I stick the key in the ignition and turn it. Hearing the purr of the engine feels like fine red wine slipping down my throat. I can breathe now. I turn the radio on and lean back a minute, shutting my eyes. I don't want to think about Dr. Rice, Jeff, Tad, my ex-best friend, and especially Ethan. *GRRRR!* That bitch! Dr. Rice makes me so mad that I could spit nails.

Did she cross the doctor's code of ethics? What good comes from her telling me about Ethan and her little love nest? Could she be trying to push me over the edge?

Screw that bitch and her damn practice! I'm done! I am so pissed at Jeff, I could spit nails again. He let me walk into the lion's den without warning. There has to be a line drawn between Jeff and me. He can't dictate who I can and cannot like. I'm past the age of twenty-one.

Then Ethan comes to mind, and a sharp pain rips my insides out. What if Dr. Rice is telling the truth? I can't fathom her jeopardizing her career. Would she be willing to throw everything away, just to get Ethan back? I bury my face in my palms. I hate losing control, but I let myself become racked with sobs.

About thirty minutes pass, and my tears dry. I find a clean napkin in the glove compartment and wipe my tear-stained cheeks. Checking my phone, I realize I have to get moving, or else I'll be late for work. I put the car in gear, punching the gas.

Work is busy today, and I bask in its constant hum. The continual pace, customer service, stocking, ordering; it keeps my mind cluttered rather than on thoughts about my brother, Dr. Rice, and the charming Ethan LaBlanc. I'm grateful for small favors.

I roll up to the apartment a little after six and kill the engine. Gathering my bag and keys, I slide out of the car and head to the front entrance, when I spot a familiar face.

He's leaning against the glass pane, grinning as if he's the canary that played a fat joke on the cat. I stop in my tracks, gaping. "Oh, my God! Where have you been? I owe you big time, dude!" I run to Franny and throw my arms around him.

"F'sure! But git your damn hands off me." He steps back as if I've robbed his virginity. "Since you're so grateful, you can feed me. I've been out her' waitin' for you so long that I'm about to pass out. My belly and ribs are rubbin' together," Franny grumbles.

The attitude I recall quite vividly, but this Franny looks more male than the other night. He's still wearing his fuchsia lipstick and mascara, but I'm getting a glimpse of the man inside the woman. He's dressed casually, wearing designer jeans, and a beige sweater and brown boots with a low heel.

"I'll pay if you drive." My energy is spent for the day.

"You gotta deal! Give me them damn keys." He opens his long slender hand, and I drop my keys into his palm as we head for my car.

A few miles down the street, we turn onto Mazant Street and take a sharp turn into the parking lot of a diner called The Joint.

At first, I hesitate. The neighborhood homes appear rickety and folks are congregating at the corner, chatting. The word sketchy flutters through my mind. Yet I wouldn't change a thing. It's the essence of this classy city and with each day that passes, I become more in awe.

The establishment sits right smack-dab on the corner. Front and center. Taking up the entire corner, bright yellow stripes embellish the outside and teal doors greet us for service. Whatta interesting place, I draw in conclusion as my gaze roams the area.

When we park, my mouth begins to water. The smell of barbecue ribs wafts through the air. We jump out of the car and Franny begins to head inside as I pause for a minute, savoring the delicious aroma.

He tosses over his shoulder, "C'mon! Don't you know skinny folk gits crabby when they don't eat?"

I snap my head up in the direction of my new friend and say, "You must be hungry all the darn time."

"Oh, now that's just tacky!" He wags a finger at me as if I've revealed his deepest, darkest secrets. His grumbling doesn't stop until we take seats at a small round table close to the bar.

My eyes wash over the place. No argument t... they sell alcohol here. Perhaps, I'm reneging on my promise. I swore off bars, but it's not the bar's fault that I had too much to drink. It was mine, and I have no problem saying no to alcohol and giving Jeff a reason to throw me out.

The atmosphere, dim with low, colorful lights feels quaint. Nothing fancy. Rustic, ordinary tables. An uneven concrete floor. Glass is clanking faintly in the background, and the aroma of all sorts of spices taunts my senses. Hands down, it definitely has the bar vibe, but I love the rugged uniqueness. I lean into Franny's shoulder and say, "No alcohol for me!" I can't afford another relapse. My confrontation with Dr. Rice digs into my brain as I reflect.

Franny looks at me with a sour lemon face. "Is dat your attempt of a joke, gurl?" he huffs. "I might be eccentric, but I ain't cray-cray! The last thing I want is Ethan whoopin' my lovely ass."

"Ethan?" My mouth drops open. "You know him?"

"That's what I said."

Taken aback, my voice elevates. "Ethan, the doctor?"

"Is there another?"

"I asked Ethan about you, and he had no clue. He didn't see you at the hospital. In fact, no one saw you that night." I stare at Franny, panic rising from my gut.

"There are a thousand and one medics that come and go from this hospital."

"Did you talk to Ethan?"

"Gurl, bye! Once I knew you were alive and kickin'. I returned your old raggedy car and got my own ride home. You were more shit-faced than Dean Martin could ever be."

"I was drunk that night," I blush.

"Any oh hoot, I shouldn't have got you drunk! My bad."

"You didn't pour the alcohol down my throat."

"Gurl, go on! I was the devil on your shoulder." He purses his lips.

"Whatever! Since you know Ethan, tell me what he's like," I ask a little too eagerly.

"If I give out all his childhood secrets, he'll whoop my ass." Fran gives me a tart look.

I burst into laughter. "Yeah, right?" Then my mood swings darkly. I almost tear. "Don't worry about it. Ethan's back with his doctor friend, Rice."

"What you talkin' 'bout? Ethan and I go way back, boo. Doctor Kim Rice ain't his type. Sure, he slept with da bitch, but that's a man thang."

"A man thing?" I raise an eyebrow.

"Don't you know nothin'?"

"I know more than you! Doctor Kim Rice herself told me that she and Ethan are back together."

"How da hell do you know that bitch?" A look of doubt strikes Fran's face.

The waiter comes up to take our order and immediately halts our conversation. Franny asks for fried oysters with hot sauce and a beer and water. The water is mine.

As soon as the coast is clear, I answer him. "Until today, she was my *therapist*."

"No way!" He nearly drops his chin to the floor.

"Way times a million." I'm hoping he might shine a light on this whole debacle.

As he crosses his legs and leans back in his chair, Franny stares at me like I've lost my mind. "Wait a damn minute! Dr. Rice told you this during your therapy session on *your* damn dime?"

"To be honest, it's Jeff's dime, my brother."

"Boo, I'd first go tell Ethan what that bitch said. No, wait! First, I'd go whoop that bitch's ass for lyin'!"

"Don't be ridiculous. Dr. Rice is a friend of my brother's." Even I know my excuse is lame. She was warning me to stay away from her man. Duly noted.

"A doctor should never talk to you like that!" Franny's words roll out angrily. "Hell, I want to whoop her ass myself!"

"I think I should let it go. It seems too many people are against Ethan and me becoming a couple, or even hanging out. My brother is a prime example." I shrug, swallowing the knot lodged in my throat.

"I say the bitch is yankin' ya strings, boo."

I fiddle with my straw. "Maybe."

"Why are you takin' this ho's word fer it?"

"Why wouldn't he take her back? The woman is the epitome of sex. She's hot!"

We pause when the waiter brings our food in red plastic baskets with red checkered paper. "Will there be anything else I can get for you?" he smiles, eyeing Franny.

"We good, sweetie. I might catch you later, though," Franny smiles.

The waiter grins and is off to his next table.

"Can you refrain from hitting on at least one waiter, for Pete's sake?"

Franny pulls one of his cigarettes from a diamond-gemmed pouch and lights it, blowing smoke into the thick atmosphere. "Ethan and I come from modest backgrounds. We used to hang out at the same corner. He'd protect me from the neighborhood bullies. Hell, he knew I was gay before I knew it.

"Anyway, Ethan isn't about the bright lights and living it high on the hog. Nope, that man wants to help people. He volunteers at the health clinic twice a month. The man is nearly a saint."

"A saint doesn't make him resistant to the gorgeous Dr. Rice."

"I'm telling you that Ethan doesn't like all that glamour and poop. When he was married, his wife was a very highfalutin' attorney. Ethan was never about money. His wife's family was all about plantations and big corporate business. Cuz of the ex-treme *raison d'être*, her family didn't like Ethan."

I laugh. "You're kidding? Ethan's a surgeon."

"That don't mean a thang. His deceased wife's family owns Nawlins and every thang around it."

"Yeah, you right! That doesn't seem like Ethan at all."

"Her thirst for success and his interest in the common folk drew a line in the sand. His wife started having an affair. When she found out that she was pregnant with the boyfriend's baby, a col-league from her office, she was going to slap Ethan with divorce papers."

"Wait! How do you know all this?"

"It's in the street, boo. Ethan's a local in my neighborhood. May, his mama, gives me the low-down. She's my second mom."

"Oh. That makes sense."

"Anyhow, Heather didn't finish filing the di-vorce papers. She and the boyfriend were killed in a head-on collision. It turned out that Heather had had one too many and hit a tree."

"Ethan told me some of this," I say. "How did Ethan learn about his wife's infidelity and child?"

"His sweet father-in-law filled him in on the gory details. It was like a twisted knife in the gut. Ethan was hurt, really hurt."

"I bet," I take in a sharp breath. "How did Ethan react to the news and loss?"

"He hit rock bottom. It damn near killed him. That's when the good doctor wormed her way into his life. I think he just needed someone to focus his attention on until the pain eased."

"What a terrible story." Tears start to well.

Franny pauses as he studies me for a minute. "I got an idea. Why don't you come with me on Saturday night? Yours truly is in a drag queen contest. I'll be the one with the winning ribbon." He frames his face with his long hot-pink fingernails.

I laugh. "I better just stick to work and staying out of trouble."

"Don't be silly! Boo, you can't hide up in your bedroom and let life pass you up. Live a little!" He grabs my hand and squeezes.

"This Saturday?" I release a breath of dread. It does sound like fun, but I can't slip up again. Jeff will disown me.

"Meet me at the club. I'll have a seat reserved for you and my friends."

I bite my bottom lip a little too hard. Gosh, I want to go. "Where?" I dare ask.

"Bourbon Pub! Where else, boo?"

THINGS THAT GO BUMP IN THE NIGHT

I left Franny at The Joint. He had friends meeting up with him. For a man who doesn't have a ride, he is quite a resourceful fellow.

I take the elevator to my apartment. I check the time, eight p.m. sharp. That means Jeff's at the hospital and I have a little time to myself. I'm dreading our next talk, but there's no way around it. Boundaries must be set. Starting with me seeing Dr. Rice. I can't go back to her. Jeff will have to accept my decision, regardless of how angry he gets. I'll go see another doctor, any doctor ... but *not* her.

I step off the elevator and almost collide with Ethan. He must be leaving.

"Hey, sleeping beauty! I haven't seen you since you were released from the hospital. You look great!" He drops that lopsided grin that will melt any iceberg.

"Yep, I'm back." I shuffle in my feet, hoping to evade this conversation right now. "I see you're headed out. I'll catch you later," I force a smile and move past.

Ethan's brow furrows. "What's wrong? Are you okay?"

I can't look him in the eyes. He'd see right through me. "I'm fine. Long day is all." My mouth pulls into a vague smile.

Ethan reaches for my arm and gently catches me, drawing me back to him. "Why do I get the impression that you're avoiding me?"

Jesus! Transparent much? "Ethan, I know about Dr. Rice and you," I blurt out. "She broke the news to me during our session today. She was very clear that you wanted her to tell me that the two of you are back together."

"Kim said *what*?" His eyebrows knot.

"Dr. Rice told me everything." I choke back a sob.

"What the hell are you talking about?" His shoulders stiffen and the anger in his eyes could've burned a hole through me.

"Stop with the pretense." I stare at the floor.

"Excuse me!"

I roll my eyes. "How many times do I have to

repeat myself? Your girlfriend relayed the message to me that you're back with her."

"Why would she go to such extremes to tell you such a stretch? I'm not back with Kim."

"According to her, you are. And I don't appreciate being your distraction either."

"Hmm ... firstly, you are not a distraction and, secondly, I haven't spoken to Kim in weeks. I didn't lie to you, Annie!" Ethan's words have a ring of truth. "Why do we keep coming back to my nonexistent relationship with Kim?"

"It came straight from the horse's mouth that the two of you are a couple!" I yell.

Ethan steps up, almost touching me, and whispers, "I'm telling you the truth." His pools of green soften.

My breath stalls. I step back. "I can't do this right now." I barely manage to choke out the words. And before Ethan can say another word, I'm down the hall and inside my apartment.

I lean against the door and gather my breathless thoughts. I feel like a whiny female, clingy, and insecure.

After a minute of self-loathing, I take a good look at the apartment and see that cleaning is overdue. I go looking under the sink and get to work.

Jeff's been the neat freak, and I've been the slob. The mess in this apartment has my name all over it, and Jeff's not complained once. I start by gathering my dishes from the living room and doing the dishes.

After I finish with the living room, I head for the bathrooms. When I finish up, I throw a pile of clothes in the wash. I check the time and it's 11 p.m. No wonder I'm drained. I finish up and head for bed.

At least when Jeff comes home, it'll be clean and he'll have one less thing to complain about. I finish my shower and crawl into bed. I'm so tired. As soon as my head hits the pillow, I'm deep in slumber.

At six the next morning, I jolt upright in bed, hearing the door slam, vibrating the walls. Footsteps stomping. Hazy minded, I realize Jeff's home and in one of his foul moods. He's always been broody, but I've only seen him angry a few times in my life. Whatever it is, he sounds upset.

Despite his anger, I can't lie in bed listening to him suffer. With a long-dreaded sigh, I throw off the covers and leave the comforts of my bed and head for the kitchen.

"Good morning!" I say as I approach him sitting at the island with coffee.

"I'm not really in the mood for conversation. If you don't mind." There's a sharpness to Jeff's voice. Not a good sign.

"Yeah, I sorta got that when you woke me up from a dead sleep." I study Jeff when he doesn't bother looking up from his coffee mug. "What's up?" Tension saturated the already heavy air.

"Kim told me you walked out of the middle of your session."

"That woman doesn't waste any time."

"Kim said you refused to face your drinking problems and you lost your temper." His eyes narrow. "I can't take much more of you."

"Whoa! That's not the reason why I walked out!"

"Then what is it?" Jeff snaps.

"First, I'm not an alcoholic!" Hurt rips at my heart. "And, as for your friend, Dr. Rice, she's lying."

"Anna, Dr. Rice was helping you, and I guess you blew that too!"

"I walked out because she basically told me I was a loser and to leave her man alone." I cross my arms as anger stiffens my shoulders.

"That's absurd! Behavior as such is unethical. Rice would never compromise her profession."

My hands fly to my hips. "Obviously, Dr. Rice's practice must not mean as much to her as you think. I know what I heard."

"Are you sure you didn't misunderstand her?"

"No! I heard her perfectly."

"Anna, I can't believe Rice would speak to you about her personal life. Considering your circumstances, you should have some test run; you might have an underlying problem that would explain your illusiveness."

"Illusiveness?" My brain clings to that word. "I'm not insane!"

"I believe *you* believe what you're telling me. Despite what you say, it sounds preposterous."

"Preposterous! I saw her come into my work and speak with Ethan's mother. Sh-sh-she carried on about how much she cared for Ethan and spoke of their previous relationship. I was there. I didn't imagine it!"

"Look, let's get you an MRI and go from there. And if I'm wrong, I'll be the first to say it."

I stand there with my mouth in the shape of a large O. Did I just hear him correctly? Does he think I'm schizophrenic? "Alright! Fine!" I throw my arms in the air.

"I've gotta get ready for work." I spin on my heels and storm off to my bedroom.

I can't believe Jeff is taking Dr. Rice's word over mine and, now, he thinks I'm insane. I am so angry, but most of all, I'm hurt. Tears tighten my throat.

Work is as usual. Customers have been pouring in all day long. No complaint here. It keeps my mind off my troubles.

May says at this time of the year tourists begin

to thicken, and to expect crowds as it gets closer to the Mardi Gras. The festive fervor is contagious. It's exciting to feel the rush of energy growing as time moves closer to the big event. I hope to attend.

When it comes time for closing, May and I get a break. Questions about Rice surfaces and keeps itching on my tongue. Surely, I didn't imagine their conversation too. I have to find out before I implode. May comes up from the back when I spring my dilemma on her. "Can I ask you a question?"

"Sure, hun! Let me take care of the door."

She goes up front and flips the sign to "Closed" and locks the door, and then heads back to the counter where I stand. "Why don't we take a load off in my office?" she smiles.

"Okay." I follow her to the back.

May sits at her desk and unconsciously pushes aside a stack of papers and I take my usual chair.

May groans as she sits, looking up at me. "What's on your mind?"

"I hope you don't mind me asking, but it's sorta personal about Ethan and Dr. Rice." I hold my breath, knowing I'm putting May on the spot.

"I'll tell you what I can. I don't know much. I keep my nose out of Ethan's personal life."

"Of course," I say, exhaling deeply. "This is mostly concerning Dr. Rice."

"Kim Rice? Oh, Lord, I don't know if I can help you out there but ask away."

"Thank you." I lick my lips. "Have you ever found Dr. Rice to be deceptive at times?"

May gives a curt laugh. "Don't we all from time to time?"

I shift in my chair and tuck a loose strand of hair behind my ear. "Yeah, I guess."

"Why do you ask?"

I shake my head. "I overheard your conversation with Dr. Rice. It was my first day here. I got the feeling that she was trying to get information from you about Ethan."

A line deepens between May's soft gray eyebrows. "What conversation?"

I nearly choke on my breath. "My first day on the job, Dr. Rice came by and spoke to you about Ethan. You had me get her a candle and ring it up. I'm sorry. I didn't mean to eavesdrop but-"

"Honey, my mind doesn't work like it used to. I'm sorry, but I don't remember Dr. Rice coming by. That woman is not the type to be slumming around these parts."

"I'm sorry. What must I be thinking? You're right." I extend a smile, but I'm freaking out on the inside. "I best get going." I suddenly feel stifled. "Do you have anything for me to do before I leave?"

"Nope! You go on. I'll clear your register for you. Then I'm leaving too," she smiles.

"Okay, I'll see you on Monday." My pulse is

bouncing along my throat, and it takes everything in me not to collapse. I'm out the door in seconds and inside my car, speeding off as fast as I can.

I don't understand. Am I imagining things? I remember Dr. Rice visiting the store like it was yesterday. It happened!

Or could I be mistaken? Is Jeff right after all? Am I schizo? Jesus!

EYE SPY

I almost decided not to go tonight. Then I think about how hurt Franny would be if I weren't there, cheering him on as he struts his drag-queen-self down the catwalk. This contest means so much to him, and I hate the idea of disappointing him. I slap a smile on my face, reassuring myself it will be fun.

I stare back at myself in the mirror, examining my straight black hair, which hangs to my waist. It shimmers in the light and makes my tawny face pop. I have never liked a lot of glamour. My lashes are long enough and thick enough to capture the vibrancy of my hazel eyes. Dr. Rice was right about one thing … I am a simple girl … and damn proud of it too!

I'm wearing my ripped jeans, western boots,

and a white blouse with my black leather jacket. I swiped it from Tad. It's cool with the Harley Davidson patch on the back.

I snatch my bag and hesitate to leave Jeff a note. Chances are if Jeff finds out that I've been consorting with a drag queen, he's going to hit the roof. It seems ironic since Jeff is gay. Sometimes, Jeff's reasoning isn't always fair. Despite his protest, I'm going. I promised Franny I'd be there. I'll just beat Jeff home and throw the note away. He'll never know.

Grabbing a Post-it, I jot a vague note: *Out for a while. Call me if you're reading this note. Love, sis.*

This way I'll have back up if I do disappear. At least Jeff can alert the authorities.

By the time my car heater heats, I'm parking to the side of the building. When I reach the front doors, I look at the sign that reads Golden Lantern. Taking a deep breath, I pause just inside the door for a minute.

The ceiling is dotted with illuminating lanterns. It takes a minute for my eyes to adjust to the faint lighting. The music is loud, and the place is packed. Lots of men in drag, dressed to the hilt. A sea of Stilettos, boobs, and big blonde wigs.

As I wade through the throng of people, the smoke and heavy perfume, I see Franny waving a long arm at me. I instantly smile as a rush of relief surges over me. The last thing I need is for my crushed ego to get stood up.

I trudge toward Franny. He would have to pick a table in the far back by the stage. It's just like him to be front and center. In plain sight, for everyone to admire his performance.

"Gurl, you made it! I was afraid you wouldn't come." He hugs me.

"I wouldn't miss this for the world!" My gaze roams over him. "Wow! You look great! Marilyn Monroe?"

"You know it!" Franny does a sexy twirl.

I have to admit, he makes a beautiful black Marilyn. I gasp at his undeniable beauty. "You're *stunning!*"

"Make yourself comfortable. I gotta go back and do some touches. Order a drink on me, boo!"

"Oh, okay." I hug him once again for good luck. "I'm rooting for you!"

"Gurl, I got this!" He twirls off, swaying his hips side to side.

I laugh to myself. It has to be fun getting all dressed up and becoming someone else for a night. Franny must be onto something. Glancing at the table, there's no one here but me. It's still early. I sit down, and my eyes take in the joint. Laughter clutters my ears, but I wouldn't have it any other way.

The waiter comes up and yells in my ear asking, "Whatcha havin', honey?"

"Coke, please." I'd love one of those sweet drinks like a piña colada, but it's not the same without the rum. A Coke is fine.

After about thirty minutes pass, the spotlight comes on, and the host walks out. I swear he's the spitting image of Dolly Parton. How fascinating! I couldn't peel my eyes away from him. He begins his introduction, and I am totally soaking in his stage presence.

All at once, from the corner of my eye, I catch a familiar face. I jerk up my head, looking about, and notice the back of a tall light brown head a few paces away. The man's back is to me. I freeze. Oh my God!

Surely that's not … I crane my neck and extend my gaze. I spy a silhouette, towering over most of the others in here, walking toward the front door.

Catching him consumes me. I jump up, pushing my way through the throng of people, keeping my eyes on his too familiar back. I can't move fast enough, shoving through the sea of blonde wigs. A few dirty looks come my way, but I just ignore them as I weave through the swarm of faces.

Finally, I reach the front entrance door and I catch sight of Tad ducking out. I quickly follow; I'm right on his heels.

When I step outside, I look both ways and see no sign of him. It's like he's vanished into thin air.

Not a trace of him. I stand there puzzled. Could I have imagined him?

I shake my head as my paranoia kicks into overdrive. I *have* to catch him. I refuse to let him become my stalker.

I twirl on my heels, heading down the sidewalk. Feverish with fear, I push past a host of people, bumping into shoulders and nearly knocking down a couple. After several bars down the street, I still see no sign of him. I stop on the edge of the curb, raking my fingers through my hair; my heart pounds heavily in my chest and sweat beads my forehead. I stare in both directions and I see nothing but strangers.

I can't stay here. I have to get out of this place. My head is swimming, and I feel like I'm losing my mind. I break into a run and head for the safety of my car. I can't stay. I'll apologize to Franny later. But if Tad is stalking me, he's here to hurt me. I can't tell the police. They'll think I'm crazy. Hell, maybe I am.

I reach my car, desperately checking over my shoulder. I rush to unlock it, but my hands are trembling. After several attempts, I manage to steady my fingers and get my door unlocked. I swing open the door and jump inside, shutting the door behind me and locking it. I clutch my chest. The drumming of my heart is loud against my ears. I watch a minute as people pass my car.

When my hands still and my heart calms, I start my car and drive off. I know I've disappointed Franny and I owe him a huge apology. But I can't do this. If Tad is here, I can only imagine what he will do to me if he catches me.

I'm heading back to the apartment. Apart from the police station, I'm safer there. Tad would have to get past the guard. At least he'd be seen if he tried to find me.

As soon as I enter the apartment, I lock the door, clenching my chest. My breath comes out in puffs. No doubt, if Tad is stalking me, it's not from curiosity. He plans to finish me off.

I drag in a large dose of oxygen. I'm safe now. My erratic pulse has lessened. Beer comes to mind. It would settle my nerves. Sometimes Jeff keeps it.

I look in the fridge and spot three. I don't think one will hurt me. I grab the long neck Bud and pop the top. I throw my neck back and turn the bottle upside and take a long swig. Its soothing chill slides down my throat.

Before I know it, I've finished the bottle. I want a second, but one is enough. Self-control is the key. In any event, getting Jeff riled is off-limits. I toss the bottle in the trash and grab a Coke. Just the perfect combination: caffeine and alcohol.

The evening is still young. I decide to make a night of binge-watching and snacking on chips and dip. I'm feeling pretty silly, letting my imagination run like a madman's.

After watching several episodes of *The Brave*, I decide to head to bed. I drag myself off the couch and make my way to my room. I sigh, heavy-hearted. Tomorrow, I plan to find Franny and apologize. He'll be upset, but hopefully, he'll understand.

My eyes flutter open to the doorbell blowing off its hinges. I check my watch and the time reads seven a.m. Who comes to visit at this early hour on Sunday? For Christ's sake!

I shuffle my feet to the door and swing it open, giving little thought to whom is on the other side. My brain's still foggy with sleep. When my gaze lifts, it collides with Dr. Rice. I nearly choke, eyeballing her synthetic, cherry-red smile. The last person I expected.

"What are you doing here?" Alarm jabs my gut as I stand in the door. I make a point not to extend an invitation. I don't have any desire to be in the same room with her.

"I know this is unexpected, but I'd like to speak with you about our last session." The doctor pauses. "May I come in?"

Dressed to impress, she stands there poised, stiff like a wax mummy. As usual, her clothing is impeccable. It's not your typical Sunday duds for church, though, unless you call topless appropriate. Well, she's not entirely topless but damn near. Boobs spilling out from the top of a skintight top. A high-dollar hooker in a scarlet-red dress, molded to fit every inch and curve of her body. Her deep brown hair nicely tucked in a perfect bun. She is everything I am not: elegant and sophisticated.

I stand there, feet cemented to the floor. Then, irritation splatters me like a bucket of mud. "I think we covered it during our last session."

"Anna, please," she purrs like a stray cat. "I won't take but a minute. I've spoken to Ethan, and he's concerned for you." Her lips attempt a smile.

"Alright, make it snappy!"

She walks past me and turns on her heels, facing me. "Since we didn't get to finish our conversation, I think it's vital to your recovery that we discuss our grievances."

She takes a seat on the living room couch. Holding a breath, I join her, sitting in the farthest chair from her.

"Say what you must and please leave," I snap.

The corner of the doctor's lips twitch, suggesting a smirk, but she catches herself and smiles patiently. "Anna, in my professional opinion, I think you're having delusions."

I catch that she gets my name correct as I cross

my legs and glower. "Dr. Rice, I think you made yourself perfectly clear in your office."

"Perhaps, but I think you're confused between reality and fantasy." She pauses. "For you to get better, you need to confront reality. I discussed this with Jeff, and we both agree it is imperative for your recovery. If you would allow me, I'd like to replay our conversation from our last session."

"What? You recorded me?" A soft gasp escapes my lips.

"Of course. It's standard procedure." Dr. Rice stares at me. "I thought you were aware of that?"

I mull it around in my head, recalling our appointments. I don't recall seeing a tape recorder. "Why wasn't I told this? I had no idea our sessions were being recorded." I shake my head, bewildered.

"I apologize. I don't mean to startle you, but you signed a form of consent. Now, may I show you the recording?"

I detect a hint of ire in the doctor's voice. It's faint, but it's there. I pause and sigh. "Show me," I say, hoping she'll leave afterward.

Dr. Rice pulls a recorder from her bag and says, "I've recorded all our sessions." She places the recorder on the coffee table and pushes play.

I listen, until the recording finishes. Instantly, I know that she tampered with our session. Except for the part where I get up and storm out. "What sort of game are you playing here?"

"Pardon me?" she gapes. "I simply want to help you." She stuffs the recorder back in her bag and lays it beside her. "Ethan came to me, worried that your condition is getting worse."

"What?" I spring to my feet.

"He said you made accusations that I'd made up an elaborate story and that Ethan and I were together."

"I didn't make up any story and what freakin' *condition*?" The fine hairs on my neck suddenly bristle.

"Anna, you're a very ill person. You're suffering from psychosis."

"What the hell is that?" A brain tumor?

"It's a mental disorder where a person hallucinates. He or she perceives things that are delusions rather than reality."

"We've had only a few sessions! Aren't you jumping the gun on my diagnosis?" I narrow my eyes.

"As a doctor practicing for over a decade, I recognize the disorder."

"A doctor!" I burst into blatant laughter, springing to my feet. "More like a quack."

"Anna, please sit back down. This isn't the end for you. Your Schizoaffective Disorder is treatable, with the proper medication." She clasps her hands together and begins asking a multitude of questions. "Tell me, do you ever feel like someone is following you?"

I stiffen. Can the good doctor read minds too? No way in hell will I tell her about last night. "No, I'm fine."

That smug smile appears, as if she knows I'm lying. "Anna, if you don't continue our sessions, you should at least see another doctor. You're not well."

"Dr. Rice, I think it's time for you to leave." I move to the door and open it.

The doctor gathers to her feet. She straps the bag over her shoulder and saunters to the entrance, where she stops. "I realize how you feel about Ethan, but he will never want a girl as damaged as you. Even if you're on medication." She smiles wickedly.

"What did you just say to me?" I stare at her, ready to throttle her.

"I mentioned that I hope you seek professional help and that I will be speaking to your brother about our conversation today."

That's not what she said, but I have to pick my battles carefully. "I don't understand. I am well past the age of a minor. Shouldn't our meetings be under the patient-doctor confidentiality clause?"

"Yes, of course, but you signed a waiver for me

to report to your brother. He is your primary doctor."

"I didn't sign any such thing!" I shrill.

"Anna, you signed the waiver in my office on the first day, before we started your therapy."

I hate her smile.

"I want to see the form," I insist.

"Of course. You'll need to come to my office though. I'm afraid I didn't bring it."

How convenient. "Fine!" I glare at the doctor.

"You're upset. I'm sorry, but unless you seek medical treatment, your psychotic episodes will increase."

"Good day, doctor," I say through gritted teeth.

The doctor casts a coy smile, "Anna, whether you want to believe me or not, Jeff and I do have your best interest at heart."

She walks out and I quickly shut the door and lock it. Contrary to Jeff's opinion, I don't trust her. Something is off with her. Even a delusional person could see right through her pretense.

CRAY-CRAY

*L*ater that morning, when Jeff makes it home, I have breakfast ready. I made burritos filled with egg, hash browns, a little onion, and green chili peppers. I'd also cut up strawberries and cantaloupe, and placed both on a pretty platter, along with a pot of fresh coffee and cold OJ.

"Hey, Jeffie!" I smile.

"Did you make this for me?" His surprised gaze washes over the spread.

"Oh, no!" Disappointment sweeps over me. "Did you eat at the hospital?"

"I'm sorry, sis," he sighs, looking like I've stomped on his favorite toy.

"It's okay. I'll see if Ethan's hungry. No biggie. Really," I shrug and reach in the top cabinet for food containers.

"Hey, why don't you store the food later and join me with a cup of coffee. We need to talk."

I set down the container that's in my hand and look at Jeff for a minute with a stupid blank stare. By his mannerism, I can tell that he knows about Dr. Rice's unexpected visit. That means he knows the rest.

"Uh, sure!" I wipe my hands on a dishtowel and pour us two hot mugs of coffee. I leave Jeff's cup black and finish doctoring mine with the usual. I join him at the island, hopping on a stool next to him, "Okay, shoot."

"Why have you not told me about your meltdown?"

"Meltdown?"

"Don't toy with me." His vexation is evident.

"I haven't had a chance. You've been at the hospital."

"When something of this magnitude happens, I need to be informed immediately."

I notice Jeff white-knuckling his cup. "I honestly thought your devoted friend, Dr. Rice, would've informed you by now," I snap. "She told you, didn't she?"

Jeff takes a quick sip of his coffee. "That's not the point."

"What's the point, then? Dr. Rice bragging to me about how she and Ethan are together?"

"What does Ethan have to do with this?" he

scoffs. "I'm angry because you stomped out in the middle of therapy." Jeff's voice seems to stab the air; it's filled with intense anger. "Do you know how this makes me look?"

"Makes *you* look?" My brother doesn't seem to understand my stance. "Whose side are you on?"

My eyebrows shoot up in ire. "I walked out because of her unethical comment!" Exasperation is only the tip of the iceberg of what I'm feeling for my brother right now.

"What comment?"

"Your friend, the good doctor, Rice, took her passive aggression a step further, visiting me this morning, telling me how unstable I am for Ethan and-"

"Anna, you are too unstable to be in any sort of relationship and especially with Ethan."

"What do you have against Ethan? I thought he was your friend!"

"He *is* my friend!" Jeff's declares, vexed. "I rather he not be yours."

I gape. "Why? Because I'm unstable?"

"Because, before you go jump into bed with another man, you need to focus on getting yourself well." Jeff starts ticking off his fingers. "One, go to therapy. Two, get the appropriate meds you need. Three, go to college, get a skill in something so you can support yourself. And last, but not least, have some damn self-respect."

"Enough! I get it, already," I shout. "Look! No matter how much you defend Dr. Rice, she has no right to attack my character."

"Character? Really?" Jeff scoffs. "It was not only but a few weeks ago that your posse consisted of drug dealers and whores."

Tears fill my eyes. "I can't believe you just said that to me."

"Am I right or wrong?"

I glance away, unable to look Jeff in the eyes. "You're right that I didn't have the best circle of friends." I direct my gaze back to him. "Despite my past mistakes, big brother, I had no clue as to Tad's criminal activities. Nor did I know about his affair with my best friend until the end."

"I can't see how you didn't know." Jeff's tone says it all. He blames me for Tad's infidelity.

I gape, racked with shock. "You're my brother! You are supposed to have my back."

"Anna, regardless of what you think, I do have your back."

"You have no idea how much I needed to hear you say that." I pause for a minute, gathering my composure. Jeff's words hurt more than Tad striking me with his fist. I answer, "I realize you care. Still, I think your friend is playing with my head. The doctor came by early this morning; she played a recording, claiming it was our last session. Dr. Rice lied, trying to convince me otherwise."

"I'm not sure I'm following you."

"I'm trying to tell you she's scheming against me. Your friend has it out for me."

"Apart from your outrageous pessimism, your paranoia is too much." His lips tighten into a thin line. "Why would Rice go to such extremes?"

"Because she wants Ethan for herself!"

Jeff laughs. "I've known Kim since I started my residency at the hospital. She's my best friend. I see her every day. You're thinking that Kim is playing some head game with you is preposterous. Besides, have you given any thought that maybe she and Ethan are more involved than he's letting on?" Anger crosses his face. "I resent the things you're saying about her. Kim has nothing but your best interest at heart. Cut out the paranoia, sis!"

"How can she have my best interest when Dr. Rice is lying? Why can't you see that?"

"The question is not a matter of accepting. It is a matter of you moving on and getting well. I need you back in therapy."

I release an exasperated sigh. "I'm willing to go to therapy, but I refuse to see Dr. Rice. I just can't, and if that means me being homeless, then so be it."

"I can respect that. I won't make you return to Kim's care. I have set up arrangements for you to see a new doctor. His recommendations are quite impressive." Jeff smiles but it doesn't reach his eyes.

"What's his name?"

"Dr. Henry Hunter. He's in his fifties, bald, and wears bright-colored bow ties. You'll like him. From what I'm told, he's an oddball."

"That's not nice!"

"True," he grins.

"You've met my new friend, Franny?"

"You made a friend?" Jeff seems taken aback.

"Yeah, he saved my life that night."

Jeff's brows furrow. "Anna, what am I'm going to do with you? When you were attacked, you were alone. You fought off those men … kicked one guy in the crotch and shot the other guy in the shoulder."

My mouth morphs into an O. "Jeff, I was in no condition to swat a fly, much less shoot an attacker." How could I be mistaken? Fear shoots down my spine.

"It's on the police report."

"Wait! Did I talk to the police?"

"Yes, I was with you when you gave the report that night." Jeff stares at me as if I've lost my mind.

No wonder he doesn't believe me.

I cover my mouth with my hand. I'm beginning to think that maybe I do have a mental disorder. I remember vividly Franny staying by my side throughout the whole night. But Ethan didn't see him either. Did I imagine Franny, like I've imagined Doctor Rice?

My gaze lingers on Jeff's tense face. "Maybe you're right. When can you schedule that MRI?"

A faint smile toys with the corners of his mouth. "Absolutely, I'll make an appointment for you. Don't worry, sis. I'll be there with you. You're doing the right thing." He reaches up and rubs my shoulder.

I nod. "Thanks, Jeff."

The shock of discovery slams full-force into me, making me tremble.

NEW DOCTOR

*H*ere I am at Dr. Henry Hunter's office, straight up at eight o'clock, staring down another feast of paperwork. This time, I read everything before I sign. I go ahead and give Jeff full access to my medical records. Considering that he's paying for the visits. If I can't trust my own brother, then who can I trust?

When the receptionist ushers me into the room, I see that it's different than Dr. Rice's office. This doctor has two wingback chairs and a desk. Eh, nothing special. The room is cluttered with tons of dusty books and a couple of framed degrees on the plain white wall. Through the rubble of files on his desk, I spot a picture of his family. Two kids, a boy and a girl. The girl looks like she's in elementary school, the boy looks old enough to be in middle school, and the dark-haired wife must be in her early forties. A nice all-American family. They remind me of mine when Mom and Dad were alive.

I sigh, missing them. The holidays were the toughest. Mom baked her famous pumpkin bread, and Dad was ridiculously anal when it came to carving the turkey. I laugh to myself but sadness tugs at my heart, too. I wish they were still alive. I wonder why Jeff never speaks about them. I guess it's too painful for him.

I hear the door open and in steps the doctor. He approaches me with his hand reaching out. "Hello, I'm Dr. Hunter."

I shake his hand. "Hi, I'm Anna," I smile curtly.

He appears to be more casual, dressed in jeans, an Oxford-blue sweater, a white shirt underneath, and a bow tie. Not a speck of hair on his head and he's mid-height and a little heavy set. Judging by his appearance, I'd say he's mid-forties, early fifties.

"It's a pleasure meeting you, Anna! Our first visit today won't be too long. I like to get acquainted with my patients before we start diving into the hard stuff," he smiles. "Have a seat and let's talk."

"Okay," I smile in return and take one of the wingback chairs.

"Tell me why you're here." He makes his way behind his desk and seats himself.

"Uh … to start with, I'm having trouble remembering my childhood before I was twelve. My mind is cloudy, and lately, I've imagined things that aren't there." I rake in a sharp breath, worried that he'll assign me to the mental ward.

"I see on your medical records that you were seeing another therapist. Did she prescribe any medication for your condition?"

"Condition?" My brow raises.

"Yes, I see where she's diagnosed you with Schizoaffective Disorder."

"She mentioned something of that nature, but I wasn't aware she'd stuck me with that sticker."

"Anna, you're not a car." His smile reaches his blue eyes. I instantly like him. "You said Dr. Rice didn't prescribe anything for you?"

"Yes, that's correct," I answer. "The doctor did address my hallucinations."

"How interesting."

"Can you explain what Schiz-"

I struggle remembering the entire word.

The doctor finishes my sentence. "Schizoaffective Disorder?"

"Yes."

"Certainly." He shifts in his seat. "The term schizoaffective implies a combination of schizophrenia and an affective, or mood, disorder, which is accurate. Symptoms include those for schizophrenia, as well as a Major Depressive Disorder, manic, or mixed episode.

"For example?"

"This disorder usually displays a disturbance in mood. In other words, an inappropriate, exaggerated, or limited range of feelings. Everybody can have a bad day, and everybody experiences a sense of excitement and emotional pleasure. To be diagnosed with a mood disorder, your feelings must be to the extreme. Such as crying, or feeling depressed, and in more severe cases, suicidal thoughts. Or, the opposite extreme, having excessive energy where sleep is not needed for days at a time and, during this time, the decision-making process is significantly hindered."

My mouth suddenly dries as small goosebumps arise alog my spine. "Do ... do you think that's me?"

"I don't know yet. First, we need to get to the source of your ailment. Once we understand more, I'll be able to prescribe the proper medication for you," Dr. Hunter smiles.

Freaked-out doesn't begin to explain my concerns. I sit in my chair breathless. "Okay, what's next?"

"I'm trying to make sense of Dr. Rice's theory. Tell me, do you have a hard time discerning from reality and fantasy?"

I wince involuntarily. "I'm not sure." I grab a deep breath, calming my irregular pulse. "The other night, I thought I saw my ex-boyfriend. I chased after him, or at least I thought it was him, but he disappeared. I ended my night, panicking."

Dr. Hunter keeps his expression light. "Why panic at the sight of your ex?"

I don't wish to rehash my memories of Tad. I want to bury them, but I know I have to confront them to get well. "I'm afraid he'll hurt me."

"Is there a reason for your fear?" Dr. Hunter asks.

"Tad didn't have a problem putting his hands on me."

"And you think he's following you?"

"Possibly," I shrug.

"How long have you had these feelings?"

"A couple of times," I say. "Recently, I was at an event …" I pause. I'm not ready to mention Franny just yet. "Anyway, I thought I caught sight of Tad. I tried following him, but it was too crowded."

"How far did he go hurting you?"

"Uh … he put me in the hospital … *two broken ribs*."

"Did you have any head trauma?"

"Not sure, though I do seem to recollect he liked banging my head on the floor," I shrug.

"I'm glad you are no longer with this guy. Do you think there is any chance you might go back to him?"

"No, I know what will happen if I go back. He'll

kill me. The last time I saw Tad, I'd pulled a gun on him. It was self-defense."

"That's a very traumatic experience. Thankfully, you're safe now." He clears his throat. "I think, with the head injuries you've suffered, we should look into that a little further. I'm going to order tests."

"Hmm … my brother has arranged for an MRI."

"That's great. When is your appointment?" Dr. Hunter asks in a calming tone.

I feel less stiff and more at ease. "I'm not sure. My brother is setting up the appointment."

"Will you bring in the results at our next meeting?"

"Yes, of course." I sigh. I just want to be normal. Is that too much to ask?

"I'd like to see you twice a week. You can schedule your appointments with my receptionist." The doctor opens a drawer and pulls out a form. He swipes a pen from his cupholder and starts jotting.

I sit quiet, fretting over what could possibly be next.

Dr. Hunter clears his throat and hands me the form. "Before you leave, I need you to take this to our lab here. I'm ordering blood work. Just a cautionary measure I like to take with all my patients. Did your previous doctor order any work-ups on you?"

"Uh," I shake my head. "No, none."

His graying, bushy eyebrows dip down. "That's

strange. It's standard procedure." He sighs. "No worries. We'll get that done."

He gathers to his feet and comes around his desk and opens the door. "I will see you next week." He hands me the signed form. "Just hand this to the lab. They'll take care of you."

"Thank you," I say and leave, following the arrows leading to the lab. Afterward, I schedule my appointments for Tuesdays and Thursdays with Dr. Hunter's receptionist. She pencils me in for mornings, before work.

Asking May for a later shift would not fly. Besides, I'd rather keep my therapy a secret. I'm terrified she'll think I'm a wacko. Then again ... I might be.

I check my watch and see that I have about fifteen minutes to get to work before I'm late. It'll be a close call, but I should make it on time.

By the time we flip the "Closed" sign on the door, the sun has dipped behind the trees and buildings. Dragging my feet from a busy day, my sight is set for home. I step outside, and I'm smacked with a frosty bitter bite. I tighten my thin sweater over my chest and crane my neck back, studying the ominous clouds. An ice storm is approaching fast.

When my car comes into sight, I spot an unexpected friend leaning against the hood, pursing his lips and arms crossed over his chest. Yep, he's pissed. I meander to my car and flinch upon hearing Franny's heated words.

"Well, I was wonderin' if you ran back to Texas." His voice is sour as a lemon. "Bitch, why have you not called me?" Franny's hands fly to his hips.

Today, he's dressed more like a man, no make-up, wearing a thick black hoodie.

"I don't have your number!" I unlock my car door.

"Why did you leave the other night? You didn't even get to see me strut my beautiful self."

I lean against the car, dangling my keys in my hand. "I'm sorry, Franny. I had to leave."

"What do you mean? Did some guy come at you?"

"No, nothing like that." I blow a noodle of hair out of my eyes.

"Then what in the hell was it?"

"I thought I saw Tad, my ex-boyfriend. It freaked me out!"

"Shit, gurl! You're a hot phukin' mess."

"Yeah, you right!" I know that better than anyone. "I'm seeing a new doctor ..." I stop and eye him curiously. "Hey, how did you find me? I didn't tell you where I work."

"Gurl, I got friends with eyes in the back of their head. New Orleans ain't that big."

I study him suspiciously. "Come to think about it, do you even own a car? Or do you walk everywhere?"

"Chile, bye! Do I look like I walk? My lovely feet are too fine to be puttin' through torture."

"Then, how do you get around?" Mistrust rolls over me. "Are you *real*?" I reach over and pinch Franny's arm. I have to know if he's real.

He jumps back, squealing. "Gurl!" Shock covers his face. "Ouch! Are you cray-cray? That hurt!" He rubs his upper arm, staring at me like I'm tied in a white jacket.

"Sorry, I've gone cuckoo," I shake my head. "Lately, I can't tell the difference between what's real and what's not."

"That's just muthaphuckkin' crazy talk, gurl!"

"Really? My brother thinks you're a figment of my imagination."

"Don't pay no mind to your brother. What does he know?"

"I guess, but how do you get around?"

"Let's just say, I'm resourceful." An impish grin crosses his lips.

"Whatever!" I half-laugh. "I gotta get home." I start to slide into my car.

"Oh, wait! I need a ride downtown. Can you

drop me off?" Franny switches his lemon tone to sugar.

"Do I have a choice?" I give Franny a good old-fashioned evil-eye.

"No! And you best not be rollin' your eyes at me. I ain't sure I'm forgivin' you for standing me up."

"I didn't stand you up. I simply left early." I roll my eyes. "I'm sorry for skipping out on you." I slip in the driver's seat and lean over to unlock the door.

Franny jumps in on the passenger's side. "Take me to Bourbon Street."

"I'm not taking you to Bourbon. I'll drop you off a couple of blocks away. There's too much traffic at this time of the day."

"*Ooo-kay!* Can you please hurry? I gotta date. He might be thinkin' I'm standin' him up."

"You're going out with someone? Why don't you make him pick you up?"

"Chile, it ain't that kind of date."

I laugh. "That's more than I need to know."

"That's fine with me. Can we get to steppin', please?"

THE ONE

$\mathcal{I}$ drop Franny off on Jackson Square. We exchange digits and promise to hit each other's phones. It makes me more at ease, having a tangible item to remind me that he's real. No one can disprove his existence. I have proof now.

I arrive at the apartment building and slip out of my car. A sudden sweep of frigid air whips my face and hair. I tremble, shouldering my bag and tightening my light coat. The temperature has been dropping fast since I left work. Snow is falling and starting to stick, swathing the ground.

I head inside the lobby and onto the elevator. Once it reaches the sixth floor, the bell dings and the door slides open. I step off onto my floor and head for Jeff's apartment. It's hard for me to call it home. I'm a guest, and sometimes, I feel like an unwelcome one. But, for now, I have to endure. Eventually, I need to stand on my own two feet.

Getting a degree will give me a sense of independence and Jeff a break. It'd be nice having my own space. Jeff doesn't complain, and I'm grateful for all the things he's done on my behalf. Even still, it's tough living under my brother's rule of thumb. This little bird needs to fly the coop.

Once I get into the apartment, I head for the fridge. I'm salivating for a glass of sweet tea and a turkey sandwich. I look inside the refrigerator and don't find any lunch meat, no tea either. I'll make a pitcher for later. I swear Jeff leaves all the household duties to me. I shouldn't complain. I'm staying here rent-free.

I spy the Cheerios on top of the fridge and decide that cereal will do. I grab the box and snatch the milk. I climb up on one of the stools when the doorbell rings. "Crap!" It better not be Rice. I'm so not in the mood for any of her bullshit.

I stomp to the door in a huff. Uninvited company chaps my butt. I jiggle the chain lock. I don't know why I bother. Breaking one is nothing. I know personally. I discovered that from Tad.

I crack the door open only a few inches and leave the chain latched. That very minute, I stand with my mouth open, catching flies. "Oh, Ethan!"

I compose myself hastily. Unsure if Rice was telling the truth, I'm not sure seeing him is a good idea. "Hold on," I say as I close the door to unlatch the chain.

I crack the door open a little more. "What's up?" I don't smile.

"Oh, I wanted to visit my favorite doll. I haven't seen you in the last few days."

"Yeah, a lot has happened."

"I heard." He flashes a lazy smile, stuffing his hands in his jean pockets. "You feel like company?"

"Hmm." I bite my bottom lip, hesitating. Every minute I get with Ethan, I cherish. Even with the question of Dr. Rice hovering in the air doesn't waver the thrill I have when he comes around. "Sure," I cave. "I'm having cereal for supper. You want some?"

"Gosh, I can't remember the last time I'd eaten cereal. What kind?"

"Cheerios," I giggle softly.

"Sounds good. Why not!" His green eyes dance.

I smile, stepping back, opening the door. Ethan steps in, and the scent of the outdoors engulfs me. Oh, man! How I love the way he smells. It reminds me of summer rain. It's intoxicating.

I make Ethan a bowl and slide it over to him. He takes the stool next to mine. Our thighs touch briefly, and a little shiver runs through me.

My thoughts linger on the idea that he and I are alone in this spacious apartment, and it's been a while since I've had sex. Just thinking about him between the sheets sends a delicious warmth in parts of my body that I haven't thought about in a long while.

Swirling my spoon in my cereal, I ask, "So, what brings you here today?" I look up from my bowl, catching his green eyes. The last time we spoke, I was a total bitch to him. An apology is in order.

"I understand you're seeing a new therapist."

"Boy, rumor travels fast," I scoff.

"Well, I heard it straight from Kim. She claimed she was resigning as your doctor and suggested that Jeff refer another psychiatrist to you."

"Really?" Ire pushes the edge of my limits. "Dr. Rice is lying." I swallow a slew of curses. "*I* ended *her* services. We had a conflict of interest."

I pause for a second, letting my simmering temper dissipate. "By the way, I owe you an apology. I overreacted. I should've asked you instead of assuming." I avert my eyes to gain composure and then look back at Ethan. "It was stupid-"

"Stop! It wasn't stupid. I think you have too many people whispering in your ear." His green eyes glisten with tenderness.

"I think Dr. Rice is trying to get Jeff to have me declared insane!" I half whisper. "Jeff clings to every word she says."

"Like what?" he asks.

"Like I'm imagining people saying things when it's not real." I pause. "That day we ran into each other on the elevator, and I was angry at you, I'd just came from Dr. Rice's office. I stormed out because I couldn't take another word from her. She said I was too simple for you and that you'd never be happy with the likes of me." I lift my gaze to Ethan. "At that moment, Dr. Rice stopped acting as my doctor. She became a jilted lover and was attacking my character. I was incensed by her insults."

"No wonder you were upset. Kim should've never crossed the line."

A rush of thrill pushes through me. Ethan believes me.

"Dr. Rice has a problem owning her own crap."

"Kim's a woman of hubris," Ethan sighs. "She's the classic perfectionist."

"You can stick liar on that list of hers too," I sneer. "She came by here the other morning to clear the air. But the truth is … she came to cover her ass."

"I believe I'm the one that sparked her visit," Ethan confesses.

"You asked her to see me?" I'm taken aback.

"Not exactly. I confronted Kim, asking if you were telling the truth." His lips tighten. "I told her if so, I was reporting her to the board if I heard anything else of such conduct. Naturally, Kim refutably denied it."

"Can't you see that she's jealous of our friendship? Dr. Rice thinks we're lovers. She straight up asked me. I'm telling you, she is playing with my head." I swallow the shards in my throat.

"Anna, are you positive? Those are pretty strong allegations. I've known Kim for years. She has always been ethical."

"You don't believe me either!" Ethan's skepticism cuts down to my inner core.

"Not true. I believe you," he speaks softly, taking my chin into his palm, forcing me to look at him. "Annie, you have to be honest with yourself. It's easy to misconstrue someone's words when your emotions are running high."

"Ethan, I know what I heard." His words singe as I push away from him.

"As bizarre as it sounds, I believe you."

"Can I ask you a question?" If I can't make sense of Dr. Rice's intent, maybe another uncertainty can be laid to rest.

"Shoot. I'm an open book."

"That night when I came through the ER, you said I was alone. Do you recall seeing a man dressed in drag?"

"A drag-queen?" His eyebrows arch.

"Yeah, a big blonde wig, loads of make-up, the Marilyn Monroe type, only he's black."

He scratches his bristled chin. "I can't say. The ER is a revolving door. It often gets crazy."

I hug my waist, feeling a meltdown coming on.

Could things get any worse than they already are? I capture Ethan's gaze. "Franny knows you. He said you guys were neighbors and you saved him from a couple of bullies."

"This guy knows *me*?" He looks surprised.

"You don't remember him?" Is anything in my life real? I sigh. "Wait! I have his number. Maybe it'll come back to you if you hear his voice.

I grab my phone from my bag and scroll through my list of contacts. I have only a few. I come to the last name and I don't see Franny. I scroll up, and it's not listed. My gaze catches Ethan's face. I'm lost for words.

"Annie, you look like you've seen a ghost." Ethan slips off the stool and leans over me, placing his palm to my chest. He moves his hand to my heated, flushed cheeks. "Your heart is slightly erratic."

I see why he's a doctor. He cares about people. All the more reason why I like him. "Hold on, I need to get my bag and take a look at you."

"No, I'm all right. I feel fine." I press my palm against his chest.

"I don't know. You're looking pale." His eyes seem to be drilling a hole through me.

"I'm fine," I lash out and in the heat of anger, I toss my phone across the island.

"Hey, come here." He reaches for my arm and

gently pulls me into his consoling arms, and kisses me on the cheek and forehead.

I melt into him, burying my face against his throat. When I lift my head, Ethan takes my chin into his large palm and kisses me tenderly. I give myself freely to him. I groan softly. This is precisely what I need … *him*.

Not long after, our kisses deepen, and I know where this is leading. My hands lock around his neck, and I press my body against his lean one. My whole being fills with hunger. I need to feel him, every greedy inch.

His velvet hands find my bare skin and I tremble under his touch. I don't want him to stop, not ever.

"Baby, are you sure this is what you want?" He pulls back, catching my gaze, his breathing labored.

"I've never been more positive," I whisper.

He gently strokes my hair. "I'm attracted to you too. But I don't want to hurt you either. I can't make any promises."

"I'm not in any position to demand anything from anyone."

He holds my face consolingly with his palms. "Hey, I think we need to take it slow. Starting first with a date."

I draw in a deep breath. "Okay, I'm game."

Joy shines in Ethan's eyes. "I'm off on Sunday. Let's go sightseeing."

"Hmm … that sounds perfect. What time?" I'm half tempted to pinch myself. Could this be an illusion too?

"Let's have lunch. Noon works for me."

"Alright, noon it is." I bite my bottom lip, holding back the bubbling excitement.

"That sounds like a plan, my sweet lady." He reaches over and gently caresses my cheek. "I gotta go."

He takes my hand and pulls me up; we stroll to the door. He stops right before leaving and kisses me. Lightly, he taps the tip of my nose with his forefinger. "Behave," he smiles.

"I'll do my best," I promise, smiling back.

Ethan leaves, and I take a moment to collect my thoughts. I think I'm over my head, but I don't care. Nothing's wrong with a little eye candy. Still, I need to guard my heart. But what if he *is* involved with Rice? Should I dare let myself fall in love with him? A reality, I fear, but I can't stop myself. Ethan's an addictive drug and I'm falling headfirst.

PARANOIA

*J*ust like Dallas, New Orleans offers the same smog and bumper-to-bumper traffic. Nonetheless, this city shines with a beautiful flare of culture and style like no other. With all its oddities, this city has me spellbound. Even though, in the beginning, my moving here was to get away from Tad, I'm glad to be here. I can't imagine living anywhere else.

I decide to take steps in a positive direction. I'm pulling into the parking lot of the local college, Delgado Community College. I think I'll begin by applying for a student loan and registering. Starting with the basics will be a solid start. Picking a major is not as simple.

I used to write romance. I remember as a teenager, spending hours in my room, writing about adventure and strong heroes. Maybe I'll get an English degree. I haven't figured out all the details yet. I'll wing it as I go.

The snow has melted and has left the ground wet. The chilly breeze tousles my hair as I trot up the steps, two at a time, and enter the main building. Financial aid is the first hurdle to tackle. If I get approved for assistance, then I won't have to ask Jeff for help. He's done enough for me to last a lifetime.

I find a sign giving a list of each department and its floor. I spy Financial Aid on the second floor and head for the elevator.

In minutes, I'm following the arrow to the left that points to Financial Aid. Walking down the long corridor, I push through the swarm of students when a strange sensation bristles the fine hairs on my neck. I glance over my shoulder, and my eyes collide with two very familiar black eyes … *Tad!*

I can pick him out from any crowd. He towers over most and totes a massive biker's vibe. I freeze in my steps. Sweat dots my forehead and my palms are wet. What do I do? Should I go after him and warn him to leave me alone?

Suddenly he ducks out of sight around the corner, and an urge to confront him seizes me. I have to warn him to keep away or else I'm reporting him to the police.

I dart after him, shoving my way through the

crowd. I nearly trip a guy as I rush past. He shouts obscenities at me, but I ignore him, not taking my eyes off Tad.

I reach the stairs and pirouette on my heels, taking in my surroundings. Nothing. Tad's nowhere in sight. I exhale.

"Not again," I mumble.

I sprint down the stairwell, bumping into others. Dirty looks target my back, but I have one goal … finding Tad and stopping this madness.

I dive past the front entrance, hoping to spot him, but to no avail. My eyes scan the premises as far as I can see, but I find *nada*. Just like before, he disappears.

"Jesus! Will this ever end?" I murmur to myself, swallowing a painful laceration of panic and anger.

Chills whip through me like bitter ice as I become conscious of eyes staring at me. My breath feels like it's stuck in my chest; my head's throbbing. I gotta get out of here. How stupid to have come here alone.

I dart to my car. It's my safe haven, my escape, a quick getaway. I hurl myself into the driver's seat and swiftly lock the doors, and sit there gasping. I wipe the sweat off my forehead with the back of my sleeve. My eyes stay alert as I calm my breathing.

Startled when my phone lights up, I reach for it in my purse, and glance at the screen. It's Dr.

Hunter calling. Jesus! He's probably gotten the lab report back.

I can't hear about how crazy I am. I already know. Swirling frustration overwhelms me. I decline the call and turn the phone off before tossing it back into my bag. I'll call him tomorrow or the next day.

I need a couple of days to prepare myself for the inevitable.

THE DATE

*S*unday morning arrives, and the sun is shining. The clock strikes noon, and I hear the doorbell. Talk about punctuality. I open the door, and there stands my date, looking like a million bucks and smelling like a field of wildflowers, flashing his dazzling signature smile.

"Hey, you look nice!" he says, grinning.

"Thanks! You look great yourself!"

Dressed in jeans and a light green sweater and a jean jacket. Dang, he never looked so delicious. I inhale a little thrill.

"Hope you're hungry." He steps into the doorframe. "Where's your brother?"

"Jeff's sleeping," I say.

"Well, lovely girl, grab your things. I have a special place to take you."

"Oh, I'm starving. You notice the junk in my trunk?" I tease.

"Uh-hmm … I certainly have." An impish grin toys with the corner of his mouth.

I slug him. "Hey, no checking my ass out," I laugh.

Ethan ducks as if he feared my punch and chuckles.

I love his teasing. I inhale deeply, diving into his glistening green eyes. I do like him. "So, where is this special restaurant?"

"You'll see!" he smiles, keeping an air of mystery.

The day is unusually warm, in the mid-70s, unlike the frosty weather a few days ago. The weather here in the south is usually mild, but it can change at any minute. A perfect day to take the Harley.

We end up at Café Amelie. It's a charming diner with all the bells and whistles of New Orleans. We take a table in the courtyard, under a shady tree.

"This place has amazing food."

"Sounds like you're a regular," I smile. My gaze keeps stalling on Ethan's chiseled chin, a little more bristled than usual, giving him a mysterious appeal, and sending a shiver of pleasure to my core.

"Possibly. I don't cook, and my girlfriend can't cook anything but potpies." Mirth paints his face.

I gape, "Keep talking, buddy. See if you get any more potpies!" I nudge him with my elbow, but inside, I'm break-dancing. He called me his girlfriend. I bite my bottom lip, cheeks flushing.

"Since you refuse to cook your potpies, I suppose we'll be forced to eat here every night. Such hardships," he teases with a deeply dimpled grin.

"You poor thing. Life isn't fair, is it?" I tease back. I'm digging his teasing a lot. What girl wouldn't? Look at him! He's not only gorgeous, but he's sweet. You don't see that combination very often. Ethan is a total catch. And today, I have his undivided attention.

He laughs and starts to lean in to steal a kiss. I'm holding my breath, anticipating his soft plump lips. Then abruptly, a smooth female's voice seems to drop on the back of my neck. Totally killing the moment.

"Ethan!" she purrs. "How pleasant it is to see you here."

Dr. Rice curls an arm around his chest and pauses as she bends over, kissing him on the lips. Her ass is in my face. And all I can think about is how much I want to put my shoe up that bitch's butt.

She makes herself at home, taking the seat next to Ethan, still ignoring me. I sit there quietly, watching, and fuming.

"Doesn't this place bring back memories?" She almost curls up in his lap.

"Memories?" Ethan's eyebrows furrow.

"Oh, Ethan!" She leans forward, flashing a vixen's smile as her boobs spill out of her low-cut blouse. "Don't dismiss what we had, darling."

"Kim, what are you doing?" Ethan stares at her with confusion.

"What *ever* do you mean? I'm simply having a chat with my longtime friend." She takes his chin with manicured fingers. "I adore you, and I miss us, terribly. Call me," she urges as she gathers to her feet and slinks off.

Talk about a bitch! I sit there with my arms folded across my waist. I'm debating whether I should call this date off.

Silence envelops us as we watch the brilliant doctor sashay out of sight. Shy of a high-dollar model, wearing a tight white dress that leaves nothing to the imagination. My mind and whole being is drowning in chafe.

Ethan jars my attention, his eyes filled with shock. "I'm sorry. I have no idea what brought that on or how she knew where we were."

"It's odd that she drops in on us out of the blue. How did she know where to find you?"

"I haven't a clue." Ethan stares off in the direction the doctor exited the courtyard.

"What did she mean about memories?" Disconcerted, I pointedly glare at him. "Have you brought her here before?"

"No! Well, I don't recall. Look, I understand

why you're upset, but I didn't invite her to our table. Kim took it upon herself to intrude." His jaw twitches. He's angry at me.

I sit back, taking in a long breath. "I'm sorry. Of course, you're right. I don't want to argue over Rice. She just wants her possession back, meaning you." The doctor is transparent as glass. She wants Ethan.

"Kim doesn't do anything by accident. She's very precise, never makes errors. I don't know what that was all about. We merely saw each other on different occasions."

"Duh! I think it's pretty clear that she wants you back." Why can't Ethan be honest about their past relationship? Either way, I prefer to drop this conversation and have a nice time. This is our first date. I want it to be filled with nothing more than fond memories.

"Annie, she doesn't want me back. She never had me in the first place. A woman like that is not a life partner."

"Why do you say that?"

"Kim's not the warm, fuzzy type. She's cold and unattached."

"You mean she's cold, like an ice queen in heat with dogs lined up from Timbuctoo," I mock.

Ethan throws his head back and bursts into laughter; his shoulders shake. "You do have a way with words."

"I have my moments." I force a smile.

All of a sudden, the waiter interrupts our conversation. Ethan takes the liberty to order on my behalf. At this point, I've lost my appetite. But I'll put on a happy face and not let Dr. Rice ruin my day.

Ethan continues to order baked oysters for an appetizer and entrée Number 26, oven-roasted salmon. It looks too tempting, and confusing, as to what to order. And my feelings are too shaken to make even the simplest decision. Besides, it's nice handing the wheel over to Ethan.

Soon, we get our food and I begin to probe a little about Ethan's childhood. "What was a typical day for you when you were a boy?"

"Hmm ... not much different than any other kid. I lived on my bike, played baseball with friends in the neighborhood. We didn't have a lot of money. Vacations were spent fishing off the bayou."

"Do people eat gator?"

"Yeah, you have to try it. It tastes something like fish and chicken. White meat."

I nearly gasp. "Did you ever catch one?"

"Oh, yeah, plenty of times." He takes a bite of his salmon. "We'd barbecue and have a bunch over. After Dad died, Mom was no longer interested in entertaining. I never have time to breathe, trying to finish my residency."

"I like your mom." I sip my water.

"Mom likes you too. She says you're a hard worker."

"I try. It seems I have enough people in my life that I disappoint. It's nice to know I'm doing something right," I shrug.

"Annie, I think you're too hard on yourself. And I know you love your brother, but I think he should ease up."

"Jeff's trying to protect me. He has good intentions."

"I'm sure he does. He's a cool guy, but I think he needs to let you breathe."

"I know at times he feels more like a parent than my brother, but that's just him. He does everything right. Me, I'm a screw-up."

"Don't say that. You picked the wrong guy is all. And you were smart enough to know to get out. I can't tell you how many times I've seen women come through the ER, all banged up from their spouses. The excuses are endless why they stay. There are times I want to shake them to their senses, but no matter what I say, they still feel like they provoked their men into hitting them."

"That must be frustrating to see."

"It is. No man has the right to put his hands on any woman."

"Your mom did a good job raising you."

He smiles and takes my hand. "My dad had a part in it too. He never raised his hand to my mom.

I don't even remember them ever arguing. My parents loved each other. The kind of love they had is the kind of love I want."

"That sounds nice. My mom and dad loved each other too. But they argued from time to time. They took their discussion to the garage. It's funny," I giggle. "The garage echoed."

Ethan and I laugh.

"I don't remember a lot about my parents. When I became a teenager, I was more interested in my friends and the latest music. Teenager rebellion," I shrug.

"I remember having a teenager's moment or two." Ethan smiles, but it doesn't reach his eyes. "I didn't have that sort of relationship with my deceased wife. We were so different, but I was in for life. I thought we could work through our differences. Clearly, I was wrong."

"Now, listen to yourself." I squeeze his hand. "Some marriages aren't meant to last."

"I suppose you're right," Ethan frowns. "The marriage was over before Heather was killed in the car accident. I hated that her life ended so abruptly." He pauses, staring off into nothingness.

"Ethan, it wasn't your fault."

"I know it wasn't, but no matter what, there is always that self-doubt. You know, what could I have done differently? If only I'd been a better husband."

"You have to be true to yourself. If you had pretended to be someone you're not, it wouldn't have made her any happier." My heart ached for him.

"I know you're right. Still, it took me a while to get myself back, after several weeks of drinking, not knowing how I made it home at times. But I dug myself out of the hole." Sadness lingers in his gaze.

"When my parents died, I straightened up. Stopped drinking and smoking pot. I even finished high school. Then, a few years later, I met Tad Taylor. Of all places, the ice rink. At first, I didn't like him. He didn't, though, let my distaste stop him from pursuing me. Tad was persistent. My best friend, Susan, introduced us. I finally caved and went out with him."

I pull in a sharp breath. "It wasn't long after we started living together that he showed a whole different side. I tried to hide it, but you can't keep abuse a secret forever."

Ethan raises my hand to his lips and kisses it. "I'm glad you're safe now."

I smile, ignoring the knot in my throat. "Me too."

After we finished eating, Ethan and I rent bikes. We go to all the hot spots, starting with Bourbon Street. It stretches for thirteen blocks, from Canal Street to Esplanade Avenue. I understand why this area is a magnet for tourists. Bright colors of orange and green, Spanish and French influences line the street with decorative wrought-iron balconies, and huge bushy ferns swaying in the gentle breeze.

New Orleans certainly knows how to roll out the Southern-charm carpet. As we roll by, I spy a short man dressed as a leprechaun and a group of others join him, dressed in bright purple and green.

We bike to Jackson Square and then ride through the prestigious neighborhood of the Garden District. I can't close my mouth, mesmerized by the Victorian homes. Simply breathtaking. I wonder what it might be like to wake up every day in such a beautiful home, walking to your favorite diner or riding the trolley to town? It must be amazing.

On our final adventure, we head to the French Court, stopping at one of the quaint restaurants to have dinner and topping off a wonderful meal with a fancy coffee that tastes sweet and caramelly.

When the night is over, Ethan walks me to my door, our helmets in hand. I hate ending the night, despite Dr. Rice's unanticipated intrusion.

Ethan has his arm around my waist and gathers me closer; I feel his warm hand splayed against the small of my back as he holds my gaze. "I had a great time tonight." He leans in and kisses me softly.

"Me too," I say, coming up for air, my palms flat against his chest.

Ethan's hands slide to my hips and chills flutter

through me. Before I can breathe, I hear the helmets drop with quick thuds to the floor. Ethan backs me into the door as his lips recapture mine, more demanding this time.

I don't know how long we've been making out when the door flies open. Ethan and I both snap up our heads, startled, staring at Jeff's angry scowl.

"What's wrong?" I ask.

"Sorry to intrude. Thought I'd save the two of you from embarrassment. Or, if you prefer to give the neighbors a side-show, I'll be happy to step back inside and let you two carry on as usual." On the surface, Jeff retains his usual amicable manner, but there's a distinct hardening in his blue eyes.

Ethan steps up, guiding me to the side. I see a twitch in his jaw. "Don't be ridiculous. I was kissing my date goodnight. Hope that's not a problem for you, brah?"

Jeff crosses his arm and heat spews from his glare. "Well, Dr. LeBlanc, it is a problem. My sister has a bad enough reputation as it is. Shall I add you to the growing list?"

"Jeff! That's enough." Tears well. I can't believe his visible disdain.

Holding his petulant gaze on Ethan, Jeff says crossly, "Anna, stay out of this." Then, he addresses Ethan. "I don't want my sister dating you."

"You think shaming your sister will run me off?" he laughs. "You don't give me much credit, do you?" Ethan stands his ground, crossing his arms like he did that night at the hospital. "Look! I realize you have done a lot for Annie. All the same, she is entitled to a life."

"Good idea. Maybe you should take your own advice. For hours, I've been on the phone with Kim. She's devastated. I don't want my sister in the middle of a love triangle," Jeff spews forth angrily.

"Whoa!" Ethan slams back. "I'm a free man and not tethered to Kim Rice. She and I were never a couple. If she gets upset, that's on her."

"Kim isn't fabricating untruths."

"Jeff," I intervene. "There is something wrong with Dr. Rice. She's ... weird."

"Oh, that's rich coming from you. You, my illeducated sister, should know better than anyone when someone is off."

Tears blur my vision, "I-I can't believe you said that to me!" I shriek. "Is that what you think I am ... a vacuous whore?"

Jeff clenches his mouth for several seconds. "Sorry, I don't care for the way you spoke of my friend. I strategically choose friends that are well adjusted, who are successful in business and life. Overachievers. Then, I have *you* for a sister. You embarrass me."

The insolence in his voice stabs like a sharp knife. "I embarrass you?"

Ethan steps up. "I think your sister should stay

with me tonight. I get that you foot the bill for her. Regardless, resorting to verbal abuse isn't the solution." Ethan pauses, his heated gaze on par with Jeff's enraged grimace. "If I ever hear you speak to your sister like that again, I'll coldcock you, brah."

"Oh, that's special!" Jeff sneers. "Throw your career away, why don't you? She's going to ruin your life. Get pregnant, cheat on you. Untrusting bitch!"

Ethan starts to throw his left fist at Jeff's face and I quickly jump in front of him as my eyes plead for him to simmer down.

I face Jeff. "Is that how you think of me? I thought you wanted me to find a nice guy?"

"I prefer you to leave Ethan alone, so he can go back to Kim. Despite his denial, they *were* a couple. He's better off with Kim."

Ethan speaks up. "Shouldn't that be my decision? Look! I have no intention of going back to Kim. Being with her felt like a cold bath. It baffles me why she's lying." Ethan takes my hand. "C'-mon, Annie, you can stay with me tonight."

He's speaking to me, but he's glaring at Jeff, daring him to protest. Jeff glowers at him but doesn't respond.

I nod, agreeing, unable to say anything for the aching knot in my throat. Not looking back, I hear Jeff slam the door. That's not a good sign. No doubt, when I return, Jeff will punish me.

GETTING ACQUAINTED

Standing in the middle of Ethan's apartment, I'm reeling over what has transpired. I make my way to the couch and flop down, bringing my knees under me. I place my face into my palms and sob.

I feel a tap on my shoulder, and I look up.

Ethan has a short, broad rim glass containing a deep gold liquid. "Drink this." He extends the glass to me. "It will ease your nerves."

"What is it?" I choke between tears.

"Bourbon," he answers tenderly.

I shake my head. "Thank you, but I shouldn't."

"Are you an alcoholic?"

"No. I abuse it, though." I wipe my tears with my fingers.

"One glass is not abusing alcohol. You need

something to take off the edge. I'll have a glass too," Ethan smiles, but it doesn't reach his eyes.

I exhale. "Alright."

I take the glass and sniff the drink. It reminds me of caramel. I take a sip, letting the liquid burn down my throat. It's not my first choice, but I could use the buzz. I take another sip.

Ethan sits down beside me. "Are you feeling better?"

"I am. Thank you," I look at the rim of the glass and circle my finger around the edge.

"I'm sorry about your brother's behavior."

"It's fine. Jeff's angry. Jeff is used to getting his way."

"His way or not, I have a huge problem with him talking to you like that."

"He was protecting his friend," I say, still playing with my glass.

"That's another issue I have. Jeff should've been on your side." Ethan shakes his head. "Something is not right with your brother and Kim."

"I don't want to harp on it all night. Can we change the subject, please?"

"Sure, I'm sorry. This was a good day, right?" He gently presses his shoulder to mine and flashes a lopsided grin.

"Yeah, I had a fantastic day. Thank you." I smile as he leans in and kisses me.

Ethan lifts his head from mine. "I don't want to

make this awkward, but I have a T-shirt for you to sleep in."

"Where will I sleep?" My face flushes.

"Hmm … I'd like to share my bed with you, but I'm not going to push. We can just sleep. I don't want to rush things with you."

I hesitate. It would be nice to cuddle. I really don't want to be alone, and the notion of Ethan's consoling arms around me would be paradise. I exhale. "Okay, why not, but first, may I use your shower?"

"Sure. Let me get you a towel and a shirt. You can use mine in my bedroom. Sorry for the Irish Spring. I don't have any girlie soap," he smiles shyly.

I giggle. "I'm sure the soap will do just fine."

"I'll be back." Ethan bounces off the couch and heads to his room.

I follow him. Why not? He's sharing his bed with me tonight. It's all entirely innocent.

When I enter his room, Ethan's going through his drawers. He looks up and appears embarrassed, and says, "I'm looking for a shirt without stains and holes." He smiles like a kid caught in the cookie jar.

I bite my bottom lip, hands clasped behind my back. "Holes are okay. Just something to sleep in is fine." He's so sweet. I totally get why Dr. Rice wants him back. I sigh. I like him too, and I think he likes me back.

"Ah! Found one!" He holds it up to the light and smiles.

"Yep, perfect!" I'm all giddy inside.

Ethan tosses me the shirt. "I placed a clean towel next to the soap. I'm playing my videos while you're showering." His eyes glisten with amusement as he begins to pass me in the doorframe but halts to give me a quick kiss before he heads off to his games.

"Thanks, I'll just be a minute." I smile, feeling a little awkward.

"No problem." He tosses a smile over his shoulder, sending chills to my core.

I can't think about sex. Pill or no pill, rushing sex is risky. I want to make sure whatever this is between Ethan and me is genuine.

I hit the shower. The warm blast of water pulsating my body lessens the earlier tension. The anger in Jeff's face tonight, his cruel words rack my brain. Does he think I'm trash? One thing I am certain about ... Jeff is becoming more agitated and controlling. And I blame myself for that too.

I step out of the shower and wrap the towel around me and head into the bedroom. I didn't have any clean panties, so I start snooping in his drawers. I find a whole drawer of boxers.

"Oh, yeah! I forgot. He's a boxer man," I mumble to myself as the memory of him answering his door in his boxers comes to mind. I snatch up a pair with red hearts. I giggle to myself. I recall the hearts that day. Such a cute thing to discover. A little boy inside the man. I laugh to myself.

After I dress, I head for the living room where Ethan sits on the couch, playing *Monster Hunter* on his Xbox. I know the game. I'd played it a couple of times over at Susan's house.

When I come into his visuals, he stops and looks up. "Wow, don't you look hot!" His gaze roams over me with approval.

My face heats like a furnace. "Thank you."

His gaze drops to my thighs. "What's this?" He fingers the shorts as his eyebrows pucker. "You dare to wear my lucky drawers." He plays like he's upset, but his eyes full of mischief.

"I hope you don't mind." I bite my bottom lip.

"Are you kidding? I like 'em better on you." His greens shine with pleasure. "Get over here!" he playfully demands.

I sit down beside him and he takes me into the circle of his arms and plants a playful kiss on my lips. "I'm glad you're here with me tonight. I hope we get to do a lot more of this."

He smiles and reaches over and kisses me on the forehead. "It's my turn. I'm showering next. C'mon, you can lie down. I'll dress in the bathroom."

"Are you sure? I can wait here."

"No way. I want you waiting for me in my bed."

"Ooo-kay." I'm a little nervous now. "Huh ... Ethan, we are taking it slow, right?"

"Of course, but I still want you in my arms. I promise I will be a perfect gentleman."

His green eyes cause my breath to stall. I'm not sure I can be as good as him. I want him, more than he'll ever know, but it terrifies me too.

"Alrighty, off to bed we go," I say, as Ethan takes my hand and we make our way to his bedroom. My heart is beating against my ribs and my hands are trembling. I feel like it's my first time. It's exciting. I feel alive, but at the same time, I'm terrified.

Although, tonight, I wish it'd been under better circumstances. Tomorrow, though, will bring its own set of problems. Jeff, for example. He'll either give me the silent treatment or yell at me and smash a few things.

I try to appease Jeff while living under his roof. Considering that he's paying my expenses. Nonetheless, I can't fathom why my brother is against Ethan. I shake my head, feeling the sting of his words.

Jeff needs to understand that, despite how crushed his friend, Dr. Rice is, he can't make Ethan take her back. I'm sorry, Ethan ended it. Either way, I'm not going to feel guilty for her feigned pain. That woman is as phony as a wooden nickel. I'm falling hard for Ethan, and unless he breaks up with me, I'm dating him.

I climb between the sheets, and a moan escapes my lips. The sheets are satin to the touch, and the bed is to die for. Not too hard or too soft, and very spacious.

Once settled in, with my left arm tucked under my head, I stare at the ceiling. My heart is attacking my ribcage; I'm so nervous and excited at the same time. I really hope he doesn't make a move on me. I'm not sure I want to go to that level. Sometimes sex ruins budding romances, but I can't help desiring him. Jesus! Stop thinking about sex! I shut my eyes tight, forcing my brain to drift elsewhere. But my body is tingling. I haven't had that feeling in a long time.

Suddenly, light flows through the room as the bathroom door creeps open and steam spills in. Ethan steps out and I bite my bottom lip. His locks fall over one side of his face, dripping water. I follow the beads of water rolling down, past the fine line of hair that dips below the band of his boxers. The thin cloth clings to his damp skin, leaving not much to the imagination.

Our eyes lock.

"Hey, you look mighty good in my bed." Ethan slips under the covers and slides over to me. He gets cozy, lying on his side and supporting his head on one palm.

"You ain't so bad yourself," I smile.

His arm lays relaxed on my hip.

"Thank you for defending me and … letting me stay with you," I say, feeling a rush of exciting sensations.

Ethan tucks a wet strand of hair behind my ear and says, "I like having you here. My bed gets lonely."

I laugh. "Oh, your bed, huh? What about its owner?"

Gathering me into the cradle of his arms, he holds me snugly. His closeness is so male, so bracing … my heart races.

His lips brush mine as he speaks. "He gets pretty lonely too!"

I quiver at the sweet tenderness of his kiss. It's too late for me to change my mind. I'm falling in love with him, and it terrifies me. Can I *dare* hope he might feel the same?

"Well, I can't have you getting lonely," I giggle as I slip my arms around Ethan's neck and bring his lips to mine.

He complies, crushing me to him. His mouth takes no mercy, capturing my lips. Before I know it, his body is halfway on top of mine, kissing me like the smoldering heat that joins metal. His breath smells like fresh mint, and the soap's manly scent makes me swoon.

I rake my fingers through his thick curls as I

find myself drowning in desire. I want to feel every inch of his hard body, skin touching skin. Eagerly, I arch my body, pressing hard against his. I ache for more. To feel him inside me, filling me completely.

As our kisses deepen, his smooth hands move under my shirt, and a groan flees my swollen lips. His skillful hands continue to take liberties.

Shivers dance across my body and a surge of yearning flutters through me. I want this man. More than I've ever wanted anyone. His skillful hands send shock waves through me. I arch my back, going mad. Our desire escalates as our bodies rock back and forth, and ends with an explosive ending.

He breathes against my earlobe. "You're so beautiful."

"I am?" I ask in short breaths. I suddenly want to know and ask, "Have you had many partners?"

Ethan rolls on his side, propped on his elbow, facing me. "No. I was married to Heather for ten years, never unfaithful. It was not until a year later after her death that I hooked up with a nurse in my second year of residency and then I met Kim." Ethan pauses. "What about you?"

I take a sharp breath. "Only Tad. He was my first."

"Tad is the *only* guy?" Complete surprise shadows his face. "You're kidding?" Ethan's sharp tone makes me blush a deep hue. "Why did you wait?"

"I was overweight and timid. Tad was the first to take a shine to me."

"So, you got with him because he paid attention to you?"

I roll my eyes, embarrassment hitting a cord. "I'm not used to being pretty or attractive. It wasn't like guys were beating down my door. In case you haven't noticed, I'm a little odd."

"No, baby, not odd. Cute, yes," he smiles and leans in, kissing me softly.

I lift my head from the kiss. "You think I'm cute?" I hold my breath.

Ethan's eyes glisten. "You're more than cute. You're sexy as hell. Besides, what's there not to like? You're breathtaking, tenderhearted and you make me laugh. You're one of a kind," he smiles. "You're my girl, and I'm here with you as long as you will have me."

"You want *me*, even after my messed-up life? I'm a train wreck."

He grins. "I like that train wreck. I like you too. Look, I'm a one-woman man. I'm only interested in you."

"You once told me you weren't up for any sorta relationship. What's changed?"

Ethan releases a long sigh. "There's something special about you. It's been a long time since this heart of mine has jump-started." Our eyes lock. "I'm mad about you, Annie."

"I feel the same about you too, but what about Jeff? He's not going to approve of us dating."

"Fuck Jeff! I'm sorry. I respect that he's your brother. Apart from that, he doesn't have the right to keep you from living your life. If he gives you too much crap, you can move in with me."

In one sweep, Ethan takes my lips. His kiss is urgent, demanding, and I surrender as a delicious shiver of yearning surges through me. He lifts his head from me and says, "You had me the first time I laid eyes on you." His green eyes ooze sexiness.

"Really? I liked you too but …" I smile, looking away. "I just thought you preferred more sophisticated girls. I'm nobody."

Ethan's eyebrows dip into a frown. "Don't say that about yourself. You're the most interesting person I know. You're real. You're not pretentious. And when I see your smile, my day is a much better place."

I smile into that handsome, chiseled face. I slip my hand through his thick black curls and bring his lips to mine once again.

Ethan complies as his tongue begins to explore the recesses of my mouth. Chills stream down my body, to all "those" spots. I yearn for him, to possess his mind and, yes, most of all, his heart. I want all of him. Every last piece.

Soon, our kisses plunge into a world that exists only with Ethan and me, leading us into a whirl of crazy passion. My body tingles, thirsting for his touch. I can hardly contain myself.

Ethan pauses for a minute as his eyes roam slowly over my body. I flinch inwardly, worrying he might not like what he sees. But then he smiles into my face with approving eyes that swim with desire. "You're amazing," he whispers, stroking the curves of my body, sending a rush of hunger through me. He quickly draws a breath. "Your skin is soft and tawny, as if you sunbathe daily at the beach." A faint growl escapes his lips, and I giggle.

I sigh as my eyes wash over him. He is stunning; his perfectly sculptured body and the thought of us making love makes me quiver with impatience.

Soon, our ecstasy soars beyond imagination as we explode, leaving us gasping for air.

That night, we fall asleep in each other's arms. For the first time in my life, I feel safe. I hope he's genuine and our feelings are real. That he's as wonderful as he seems. But, how could he not be?

His tenderness and caring bring tears to my eyes. Not tears of sadness but happiness. I'm where I should be … in the arms of the man I love. Gosh!

I exhale with ease. I'm happy for the first time in years.

BLACKOUT

The alarm goes off at six a.m. sharp. Both Ethan and I jolt awake to the blaring sound of Lady Gaga.

Ethan nearly smashes the snooze button as he drops back down onto his pillow and draws me into his consoling arms.

I smile against my pillow. "Good morning," I say drowsily, yawning.

"*Bonjour, mon amour!*" Ethan lifts up from his pillow and gives me a quick peck on the cheek.

I grin. "You're on dayshifts now?"

He yawns, throwing his long leg over my hip and I rest my head in the nook of his shoulder. "Yep, I gotta get dressed. You can stay sleep in, but duty calls me."

He offers a sleepy grin, kissing me softly on the lips, and a shiver of delight flutters through me.

"I wish you could stay." I stroke his day-old stubble, studying his chiseled chin, the strength it holds. Ogling Ethan is becoming a full-time hobby of mine.

"I'll be home around nine tonight. Why don't you bake a potpie for us?" Ethan's silent laughter jiggles the bed.

"You're teasing me," I smile.

"Only because you're adorable and you can't cook for nothing." He kisses the back of my head and jumps up, heading to the shower.

I get up and slip on my bra and his T-shirt and boxers. I grab my pile of clothes; I'll return his clothes tonight. He wants to see me again. I feel all giddy, like a kid on Christmas.

Ethan finishes dressing in his powder-blue scrubs and makes his way to me; I'm sitting on the edge of the bed with my phone in hand, looking through my missed calls. The mute button had gotten flipped, silencing my phone.

Ethan leans over and kisses me. "You look good enough to eat," he teases.

I roll my eyes, knowing dang well my hair is a disheveled mess. "I doubt that!" I laugh.

Then, he places a key in my palm. "Don't lose this. I'd like for you to be waiting for me when I get home.

I should be off by nine tonight, but it all depends if we get busy. I'll try to call if I'm gonna be late. And if your brother gives you any shit, you get your ass over here. I plan to have a heart-to-heart talk with him."

"Don't!" My gaze flies up. "It will only exacerbate the problem. I can handle Jeff. Really!"

All at once, his face appears grim. "If he gets anywhere close to last night, you march yourself back over here. I mean that!"

"Alright." I take the key.

"You, in the meantime, make yourself at home, and here is a little cash for dinner tonight." He slips several bills in my palm. "If I'm late, you're welcome to wait for me in my bed. I think you're growing on me, beautiful lady." He grins and, with a quick kiss, zips out the door, leaving me in an empty apartment.

Right now, I don't have it in me to think about last night, arguing with Jeff over Dr. Rice's whining. Nevertheless, I'm dreading Jeff this morning. I expect him to dish out some hardcore scolding. I know he's done a lot for me, but I have my limits. I sound ungrateful but I'm not. Regardless of my dating Ethan, I still plan to enroll in college and do something positive with my life. I have to make Jeff understand that.

What does concern me … is how many times Dr. Hunter has tried reaching me. I stare at my phone, gaping. I thought private doctors are off on weekends.

I let out a dreaded sigh as I listen to his messages. He sounds urgent. I guess now is as good a time as any to hear the bad news. It can't be good. Why else would he blow up my phone with more than twenty calls? It's bad. Really, bad. No point in wading through every message.

I hit his number and listen. I assume he's calling me from his private phone. His office number is different.

After the phone rings four times, a stranger picks up. "Hello," a woman's voice answers. She sounds stuffy, like she's sick with a cold.

"Hi, I'm a patient of Dr. Hunter's. Anna Baker. He's been trying to reach me over the weekend. Is he available?" I release a sigh.

The woman sniffles, choking on her words. "I'm sorry, there's been a tragedy. Dr. Hunter's house caught fire last night. I'm afraid he won't be able to come to the phone."

"Oh my God!" I gasp, as shivers skip along the back of my neck. "Is he okay?"

"No. I'm afraid he didn't make it." She sniffs. "The doctor and his family didn't survive."

Horror flows through me. The picture of Dr. Hunter's family sitting on his desk comes to mind. "I don't understand. The doctor's been trying to reach me all weekend long! I think it's important. Do you know what he wanted to discuss with me?"

"No. I wish I could help you. I'm afraid, I don't know anything about Dr. Hunter's patients." Her voice breaks.

"I apologize for disturbing you." I end the call, staring into the distance, submerged in unadulterated shock. Jesus! How unexpected!

Dr. Hunter and his whole family have been wiped from existence. Those words sound eerie. One minute, he's relentlessly calling me and, the next, he's gone.

I swiftly hit my phone for the doctor's messages and start playing each one back to back, and listen intently.

"Anna, this is Dr. Hunter. I have the results of your test. Please call me as soon as you get this message."

Each message becomes more intense, but the last one is the most frightening: "Anna, this is Dr. Hunter. Why are you not calling me back? You must return my call immediately. Your life is in danger. I have to warn you!"

Warn me? My eyebrows collide. About what? That I'm suffering from a personality disorder?

I tap my finger against my chin. Should I ask Jeff if he's heard anything from the doctor? I signed a permission form for him to receive my medical records. I assume Dr. Hunter sent my information to Jeff.

I bite the inside of my lip. My gut tells me to keep a tight lid on this. If Jeff brings it up, I'll play stupid. I'm good at stupid. I inhale a quivering breath.

Dreading the inevitable, I make my way out of Ethan's apartment and head to Jeff's. Every step feels like I'm walking to my death. I can feel Jeff's angry vibe seeping through the walls. He doesn't get angry often, but when he does, it can be frightening. I hope I can defuse his temper and, somehow, we can come to an agreement.

I unlock the door, and the smell of coffee hits my nostrils. For some reason, it unsettles me.

I spot Jeff in his chair, the one he never sits in. I spy a beer in his hand and several crushed cans sitting on the end table next to his chair. That's unlike him. He never drinks this early. Not a good sign.

I'm assuming he recently got off work; he's still dressed in his scrubs. I gather by the day-old stubble and his slumped shoulders that he's had a rough night. No doubt, I contributed to it.

I ease down on the couch. "How are you this morning?" I swallow hard.

"Why don't you get a cup of coffee and let's talk?"

"Huh … thanks, I'm fine. I have to get ready for work."

"Get a cup!" he grinds through his teeth.

I gape at him, blinking with shock. Why is he insisting? I roll my eyes. "Fine!"

I jump up and go to the kitchen. I see a white cup on the counter by the coffeepot. I fill the cup about halfway, not bothering with creamer or Splenda. What's a cup of coffee if it settles Jeff's ire? I see no point in exacerbating his foul mood.

I come back to the couch and sit. I hold the cup with both hands, waiting for Jeff to start his lecture. He takes a sip of his beer. The way he's slouching is a good give away that he's buzzed. Jeff is all about perfect posture.

"About last night." His words are slightly slurred. "I don't think it's a good idea for you to see Ethan. You just came off a bad relationship, and I don't want you hurt. It's too soon. You're not mentally stable enough to be in any sort of relationship."

I take a long, ragged breath. I knew this wasn't going to be easy. "Jeff, I respect your opinion, but last night, I felt you were more worried about your friend Kim than you were about me, your sister."

His blue eyes darken. "That's not true. You know I care! Have you forgotten that I support you?"

"How can I? You never let me forget." I swallow tears and the knots in my throat.

"Ann, you practically need a babysitter," he bellows.

"And you need tape across your mouth!" I shoot back. "You said some hurtful things to me last night!"

"Sorry, isn't the truth supposed to set you free?"

"The truth? You made it sound like I've slept with half of America!" I scream, coming half off the couch and slamming my coffee down on the coffee table.

"Why aren't you drinking your coffee?"

"I told you I don't want it."

"I do so much for you, and you can't even do something as simple as drink the coffee I made for you?" His words feel like sandpaper on my skin.

"Alright!" I swipe the cup up and take a huge gulp. The bitter liquid burning down my throat, "Happy?" I choke out.

"We're getting there. Drink more!" Jeff orders.

I narrow my eyes, confused. Maybe Jeff's trying to make a point here with the coffee. I polish it off and set the empty cup back down on the coffee table, still glowering at my brother. "I'll talk to you when you're sober."

I spring to my feet and storm to my bedroom. I'm dressing at Ethan's apartment. Jeff's acting too weird for my peace of mind. I gather my clothes for the day and all my supplies: soap, deodorant, shampoo, and blow dryer. I didn't spot one at Ethan's, so I'll take mine just in case.

I throw everything in a bag and head for the front door. I refuse to look Jeff's way until he's stopped addressing me with that icy voice.

"Wait!" he calls as he twists in his chair, half hanging over the arm. "You can't leave until we have resolved this problem."

I take a deep breath and reply, "Jeff, I appreciate everything you've done for me. You are always the first to step up to the plate. Yet this person I'm looking at now … *is not my brother*. When you're clearheaded, we'll talk again."

I open the door and leave without another word. For the first time, Jeff has frightened me.

I can't be happier, having Ethan's apartment as my sanctuary. My gut tells me to get away from Jeff. Apart from Dr. Rice's frame of mind and hurt feelings, I don't understand why he's upset at me.

SPECULATION

When my eyes flutter open, Ethan is checking my pulse. It takes a minute for me to become aware that I'm in his apartment on the floor. My eyes land on a bottle of bourbon. I feel my hair, and I realize it's damp with vomit. Suddenly, I panic. "What's happened to me?"

I hear Ethan's soothing voice. "It appears that you had gotten into the liquor and polished off the whole bottle of bourbon." His eyebrows are close together, revealing his concern. "Is there something you want to tell me?" His face takes on an agitated edge. He's upset.

I grab my head. My temples are throbbing. "I don't know," I cry, grossed out by how I must look.

"Let me get you in the shower."

Tears brush my cheeks. "Alright," I choke out.

He picks me up into his arms and I wince, knowing how gross I must smell with vomit in my hair and down my shirt. He sets me down in the bathroom, still holding me up with one strong arm as he flips on the water, waiting for it to warm.

In the meantime, he's checking my pupils and my pulse. A disturbing look crosses his face. "I'm removing your clothes, baby. Get you all nice and clean."

He kisses my forehead as he begins to strip me down to nothing. I am still wearing his clothes from last night. "Steady does it," Ethan says. "Take an easy step into the water. I won't let you go, I promise."

He grabs the soap and begins to lather my hair and my body. Under the haze of drunkenness, I am mortified. I don't understand any of this. Why would I polish off his bourbon? I don't like the taste. I don't remember getting it from his cabinet.

"Oh Jesus! My head is killing me," I say, hearing my voice echo as the steady stream of warm water flows over me.

"You're okay. We're almost done." Ethan's words fill my heart and feed my soul. There is hope in his voice.

He turns off the water and wraps a thick cotton robe around my shoulders and helps me to bed. Ethan starts looking through my bag and pulls out the clothes I'd planned to wear to work. With my clothes in hand, he makes his way over to me and begins dressing me. "I have to take you to the hospital. It looks like you have a good bump on your head."

He picks up a small flashlight and studies my eyes. A thin, worried line deepens between his eyebrows. "Your eyes are dilated."

Then he checks my pulse. His fingers press against my wrist. When his gaze catches mine, I see the concern. "Your pulse is a bit slow." He blows out a long breath. "Can you stay awake for me, doll?"

I nod, not completely understanding.

After Ethan rushes to dress me, he lifts my body into his strong arms and carries me to the lobby, past the glass doors. Drifting in and out of consciousness, I feel a raw chill freeze my damp hair. A shiver rips through me and I nuzzle my face against the his warm neck.

Ethan sets me down on the passenger's seat of my car and buckles me in. The next second, he slides in the driver's seat.

"Where are we going?" My words sound slurred to my ears.

"Don't worry, doll. I got you," he says, soothing me.

"Ethan, I didn't drink your liquor," I beg him to understand.

"I don't think you did either. That's why we're

going to the hospital. I need to run tests and get you set up with an IV. Don't go to sleep on me. Stay with me."

"I'll try," I mumble.

"Good girl," he says softly. "Almost there, just hang on. Sing to me. That'll keep you awake."

"Sing?" I faintly smile.

"Come on!" he insists. *"Yankee Doodle …"*

When I see past the blur, I find a clear cable traveling up an IV. My hand's heavily taped and stiff. I spot a needle inserted under the medical tape. The prick still lingers.

I notice the rails on the side of my bed and realize that I've been admitted into the hospital. Where's Ethan? I peer outside my door to the nurse's station.

Then, I spot a shadow in the corner of my eye, and a smile quickly plays across my face. Ethan is snoring, sound asleep, crunched in the chair next to me. A clump of soft curls swept over his face. Guilt hits me. He's been up since six this morning, and here he is back at the hospital tending to me.

I reach over and tap his knee. He stirs, dragging in a deep breath. He sits up quickly, his heavy eyes catch my gaze and he speaks, "Hey, sleeping beauty! You're awake." He smiles.

"Yep, I'm alive."

"The x-ray came back. No concussion."

"That's great." I stroke his cheek. "Come lie with me," I whisper. "You need to sleep too."

"That sounds like a good idea. I'm waiting on the results of the blood test, and later, you're getting an MRI. Doctor's orders." Ethan smiles at me as he slips under the covers. He draws me into his arms, and suddenly, I feel like the world is a much safer place.

"Ethan," I whisper.

"Huh, hmm?" He nuzzles the nook of my neck, half asleep.

"Ethan," I say again.

"Yep?" He gently yawns.

"I didn't steal your liquor. I-I don't even like the taste of bourbon," I stutter. "Coffee was the only thing I've had all day. Jeff insisted I drink it, The strangest thing. Jeff wasn't his usual, poised self. He was sorta drunk and very agitated."

Ethan lifts his head, catching my gaze as if an apparition has slinked past. "Are you sure you didn't have anything else?"

"Absolutely!" I say with conviction.

He jolts upright and drops his feet to the floor. "I'll be back."

He throws on his tennis shoes. "I'll tell the charge nurse, Joan, not to let anyone in your room. Hold that thought! I'll have the hospital's security come stand watch at your door. Don't speak to any-one." Alarm flickers in his eyes.

"I won't, but what's wrong?"

Ethan kisses me on the forehead and says, "I'll tell you when I get back." He smiles, but it doesn't travel to his eyes. "Don't worry." He holds my chin in his palm as our eyes latch. Worry is visible in his gaze.

"I'll be here waiting." I manage a faint smile.

I've drifted to sleep by the time Ethan returns. He gently shakes my foot. "Annie, wake up!" His voice is soft but amplified.

I pop open my eyes and spring up into a seated position. "What's wrong?" My eyes round with panic.

"I got your blood work back."

"You did?" My heartrate surges.

"I wasn't able to get a full report of your test. The lab report shows that you have no alcohol in your blood or urine. That tells me that someone staged this, but why? Can you remember what hap-pened after I left?"

"Hmm, I went to Jeff's apartment. As I men-tioned earlier, Jeff had been drinking. He was sit-ting in the living room, which is completely unlike him. He kept insisting I drink his coffee. To appease him, I had a cup. We got into an argument, and that's when I got my clothes and went back to your place. Everything else is a wipeout."

"Did you bolt the door?" Ethan asks.

"Uh, I don't think so. Just the door lock."

"Do you remember passing out?" His green eyes are dark with worry.

"That's sorta blurry. I remember heading to your bedroom, but then the room started spinning. After that, the room went black."

Ethan strokes my arms as I stare at him. "I think your brother gave you Rohypnol."

"What's that?" Panic rips through my chest.

"It's a tranquilizer about ten times more potent than Valium."

"A roofie?" I gasp.

"Yes. It's known as a date-rape drug."

"Oh my God!"

"Are you sure coffee is all you had to drink?"

I pause a minute, forcing my mind to push through the cobwebs. The morning was hazy but ... "I didn't even have a glass of water. Did you find ... what was the name of that drug?"

"Rohypnol," he repeats.

"Yeah, Rohypnol. Did it show up in my blood test?"

"No, it doesn't stay long in a person's system. That's why it's so handy for sex offenders. They can drug their victims and, by the time they awake, it's pretty much out of their bloodstream."

"Jesus! Why would Jeff do this to me?"

"I don't know. I did some snooping and found

that a bottle is missing from the hospital's pharmacy. No one signed it out."

"Do you think Jeff stole it?"

"At this point, I can only speculate. But I am certain you were victimized."

I gasp. "I … I gotta talk to Jeff!" I start scooting out of bed.

Ethan halts me, resting his hands on my waist and gently placing me back in bed. "You will do no such thing. If Jeff is a party to this, you're not safe around him."

"I can't believe my brother is capable of this sort of atrocity!" My eyes well with tears.

"Baby, I don't think he's trying to kill you. I think he wants you alive but contained."

"Contained? Like jail?" My eyebrows furrow.

"At this point, all we can do is speculate. We need to call the police."

"No! Please, not yet. Not until we know more," I plead.

"I get it! I agree, there are a lot of pieces to the puzzle here. For starters, how did someone get inside my apartment? No signs of forced entry."

I bite my bottom lip. "That's why I think we should wait to call the authorities. We have no evidence."

"Listen, I'll figure this out. In the meantime, I'm taking you to my cabin. It's down on the basin, and no one knows about it. You'll be safe there."

Everything seems so surreal. "I can't believe I'm hiding from my brother."

"I know, baby, but we can't take any chances."

"Do you think Dr. Rice could've drugged me? She has more motive than anyone."

Ethan draws in a fretful sigh. "At this point, *anyone* can be involved." He rakes his fingers through his thick sandy curls. "Get dressed. We need to get moving. I called Mom and told her what happened. She stacked the fridge with plenty of food."

Tears start to well. "You are a dream come true."

Our eyes lock.

"I take care of those I care about," he smiles and leans in and kisses me. "Now get dressed, hurry!" he urges as he clears my hand of the IV.

"Alright," I smile back, watching Ethan shut the door behind him. I grab the sack of clothes and hurry along.

CONFESSION

ast the city limits and deep into the basin, we arrive at Ethan's cabin. Talk about out in the middle of nowhere. This is a place to go when you need solace. It's very isolated. I don't recall seeing any neighboring homes. I suppose I can survive the wilderness for a few days.

We come to a stop, parking on a rocky dirt drive. Ethan unbuckles his seatbelt and leaps from the car. I hear the crunching of pebbles under his feet as he reaches my side. Like a chivalrous knight, he sweeps me up into his arms and carries me up the steep steps. I insist that I can walk, but he refuses to listen.

Once we reach the porch, Ethan sets me down and unlocks the door. He lifts me, and we enter the cabin. He doesn't put me down until we reach the back bedroom; then, he lies me down on a large bed with a headboard made of knotted wood.

The mattress feels soft and comfy, and is covered with a homemade quilt, patched with red and white squares. Country decor is the theme throughout the entire cabin. I notice deer heads on the wall. Not my taste, but it's part of the South. A lot of men hunt. When I was a teenager, my dad used to take me out deer hunting. Jeff was more the intellectual sort, nose in a book, all the time. Not the outdoorsy type.

There's a fireplace in the bedroom. Ethan gathers a pile of wood in his arms and dumps it into the fireplace and flicks a match under the kindling. In minutes, the fire is blazing. He places the screen back and climbs in bed with me. "What do you think of this place?"

"I like it, but I'm not sure how the deer feels," I giggle.

"The deer likes it just fine," he teases. "Hey, you got to be hungry. How do soup and a sandwich sound?"

Come to think about it, my stomach is gnawing at my ribs. "That does sound good." I smile. "Will you join me?"

"Absolutely!" He reaches over and kisses me. "I'll be back in a flash!"

"I can help! I'm not helpless. I feel much better."

"Stay put! We can have lunch in bed," he shouts from the kitchen.

I drop my head on my pillow, staring at the mounted deer on the wall. Sorta creepy, with its dead eyes fixed on me. My mind wanders through this web of deceit. I can't fathom Jeff's involvement. He's been there for me through thick and thin. I throw a hand over my forehead and sigh. Nothing adds up, and I'm not ready to point the finger at Jeff.

I do have my suspicions about Rice. I wouldn't put anything past her. I huff, filled with exasperation. I wish I could speak to Dr. Hunter but, sadly and horrifyingly, he's dead. Chills snake up my spine.

Too bad I can't just close my eyes and wake up to a world of happiness. And that this insidiousness is one big bad dream. Yet it's not a dream. It's the reality of my life.

Then, there's Ethan. God bless his soul. He's been with me throughout this whole debacle. There's no way he's involved. I can't deny my heart anymore. Whenever I look into his eyes, I'm as helpless as a kitten. Love is crazy like that.

Ethan comes into the bedroom with a tray and sets it down, across my lap. I slide up and realize he doesn't have a plate for himself. "I thought you're eating with me?" Disappointment veils my face.

He sits on the edge of the bed next to me and

takes my hand. "I need to go to the hospital, but I'll be back as quick as I can. I gotta find someone to cover my shif." Ethan pauses as guilt traverses his face. "I have to tell you something. Please hear me out, first." His sigh sounds full of regret, and I instantly get a sick feeling. "There's something that's been eating at me, and I want to come clean." His jaw twitches. "I haven't been exactly honest with you."

I sit up and set the tray to the side. "For heaven's sake, just tell me!" I stare back.

"I don't know how to tell you this other than just say it." He grabs my hand. "There was more to Kim and me than just hooking up. We were unofficially a couple. We'd been seen together at a few functions and around town."

My breath stops. "Come again?" Am I misunderstanding him, like I have Dr. Rice?

"Kim and I were more involved than I led you to believe. It was different. We had very little in common. My place was too meager for her expensive tastes, and she was funny about her place. That was the extent of our relationship. Nothing deep or meaningful. It was like being with Heather all over again. It wasn't healthy for either one of us."

"Oh, my God!" I glance away, unable to look him straight in the eyes. "So, she wasn't lying after all?"

"Not directly, but she made it sound like we were much more than what we were." He scoots closer to me. "Annie, you have to believe me. I don't have feelings for her." His eyes are filled with remorse.

"Is it true that you were planning to ask for her hand in marriage? That's what she told your mom."

"No, hell no!"

"The two of you never lived together?"

"That's a definite no!"

"So, it's true. That restaurant where Rice ran into us, she wasn't lying about the two of you. All this time, I thought Rice was crazy. But the real truth is ... that I'm the *other* woman!" I bellow, tears welling.

"No, Annie, you were never the other woman. Kim and I never had that connection like you and I have." He gently takes my chin into his palm, forcing me to look at him. "Look, you have to believe me! When we met, you jump-started my heart. Your long black hair, your hazel eyes, those soft curves of yours, but I saw past your beauty. You have a kindness one rarely sees. I started thinking about you more than I thought about myself." His voice breaks. "I hope you'll forgive me."

"You wait until *now* to tell me this?" Betrayal seeps deep within me and I struggle to find my voice. "Why didn't you just tell-"

"When I'd met you, Kim and I were on the brink of breaking up. I wasn't happy with her. Then, when I'd found out Kim was your psychiatrist, I didn't want to do anything unethical. I immediately ended my relationship with her. I was planning on ending it anyway, but you had given me a reason to end it sooner. I'd grown tired of Kim's aloofness."

"Jesus! All this time, I thought I had imagined things." Tears stream down my cheeks. "You knew Kim had been taunting me about you and her," I half shout.

Ethan reaches for me, and I slap his hand away. "No! You don't get to touch me after you've lied to me. I thought you were different. I believed you!" I choke through the tears.

"Baby, I wanted to be honest with you, but I was afraid if I told you the truth, I'd lose you."

"You should've told me anyway!" I shout.

"You're right! I was wrong," He scoots even closer to me. "I wasn't lying when I said I don't have feelings for Kim. I have feelings for *you*. Not Kim."

His voice is filled with pain and I instantly want to throw my arms around him, but I hold back. Confusion digs through my cloudy mind and squeezes my heart. There's so much doubt swimming around my brain.

Then, a light goes off in my head, and my eyes widen. "Oh my God! I'm right! Dr. Rice drugged me."

Ethan runs his tense fingers through his thick curls and gives way to a long sigh. "It's possible."

"If that were true, then Jeff is innocent!" Hope clutches my heart.

"Let's leave this to the police. We don't have any facts backing our story."

"It has to be Dr. Rice!" I insist with conviction. "You broke it off with her because of me. She knows, Ethan! She knows!" I shout. "She must have made a duplicate key to your apartment. Who else would have had the opportunity to duplicate your key?"

"I don't know. Kim gave her key back." Then, his face twists with regret. "I hope you will forgive me."

"Ethan, I wish you'd told me this in the beginning. This is your fault." I gaze away. I can't look at him.

"I know! I hate myself for it." Ethan reaches for me, but I pull away.

"I need to think about this, about us." Jesus! Maybe this was what Jeff was trying to warn me about. Perhaps I *am* losing my mind. Maybe I am insane, and maybe I was wrong falling for Ethan.

All at once, I feel stifled. I can't breathe, "I need to go," I cry. "Where are my clothes?" I ask angrily, sliding off the bed on the opposite side of Ethan.

He heads me off before I get very far and rushes

me into his arms, but I push away with all my might.

"Let go of me!" I insist. "All you've done is lie to me! I … I thought you cared about me, but that's all a lie too!"

"Listen to me!" His gaze captures mine. "I'm not perfect. I screwed up, but I do have feelings for you. That's real! But whether you forgive me or not, if you leave, it's only a matter of time before whoever is behind this finds you. You have to wait here and trust me."

Every fiber in my body tells me to run, but where? I'm pissed as hell at Ethan for ruining my perfect image of him. Now, it's fractured. Yet, he's right about this. If I leave, I may be jeopardizing my safety. If someone is willing to drug me, then what other lengths will they go to?

"Alright! I'll stay, but take your hands off me," I hiss. "When we find my attacker, you and I need to talk. I refuse to go through another bad round like I had with Tad. You claim you're coming clean, but I have to ask myself what the hell you were telling Dr. Rice. Were you making promises to her while wooing me?"

Ethan throws up his palms. "I have a lot to explain, and I will tell you anything you want to know. But right now, I need to get to the hospital and speak with the police."

"Why can't the police come here?"

"I just think it's best if I go to the police." He pauses. "I've been wondering about something, but I've never asked this. Do you think that your memory loss regarding your childhood could have anything to do with your brother?"

"Why would you say that? Jeff has been wonderful." My words sound weak, like I'm trying to convince myself.

"Sorry, I won't mention it again. But I can't help but question why Jeff became offended when you didn't want his coffee. It seems odd."

I hug my waist. I don't want to accept Jeff's part in any of this.

"Listen, we can talk about this when I get back."

"Okay." I shrugged limply.

Ethan places my cell in the palm of my hand. "You have my number. Keep this on you." He pauses, then nods. "I have someone for you to meet."

"Who?"

Ethan smiles and calls out, "Rerun! Come here, boy!"

I hear paws scampering across the wooden floor and, in a matter of seconds, a large Golden Retriever comes around the corner, entering the bedroom. I gasp with excitement.

"You have a Goldie?"

"Well, he's my mom's, but he's like family and a great guard dog. Nothing gets past him."

I squat down and call the dog. The large Goldie wags his tail and comes right to me. I have a feeling that Rerun and I are going to become great friends. Ethan? I'm still debating that one.

"Looks like Rerun is moving in on my girl," Ethan teases.

I look up, catching Ethan's gaze. "That wouldn't be hard, since he's never lied to me." Disappointment flavors my voice.

Ethan gathers me to my feet and pulls me gently into his arms. "I'm sorry. I plan to make this right. If you can find a way to forgive me, I promise, I will never lie to you again. I swear on my life."

I push from his embrace. "You have to give me a minute to process this." I feel Rerun's cold nose nudging my hand for another scratch.

Ethan gathers my chin in his palm, meeting my eyes. "May I kiss you? I don't want to leave with this between us."

A sudden bout of guilt washes over me. Ethan has been great. I smile faintly.

"I'll be back before you know it, lady." He kisses my nose.

"I'll be waiting," I say, unsure with so much encircling my life.

Ethan kisses me once more and leaves.

Quiet surrounds me except for Rerun's panting. I go back to bed and share my tray of food. Not long afterward, I discover he's a seventy-five-pound lapdog. He takes up my whole lap, but how can I deny those big brown eyes?

Listening to the sound of Rerun's breathing, I soon drift off to sleep.

UNEXPECTED GUEST

I awake to Rerun's growling. He's sitting at the edge of the bed, fur raised across his back.

I sit up with a jolt. "What is it, boy?"

I hold my breath, hoping Ethan's returned.

The sound of someone walking through the cabin with slow and steady steps doesn't register … until the person enters the bedroom.

The cabin's dark and I have to adjust my eyes. At first, I think the tall silhouette is Ethan, but then why would Rerun be growling?

I call to Rerun, and he returns to me, but his fur remains spiked and he is baring his huge canine teeth.

"Gosh almighty! Never thought I'd see you with a fancy doctor, sweetheart."

A familiar cold stone drawl pierces the dark.

Jesus! Tad! "H-h-how did you find me?"

Sheer darksome fright rips through me. "How did you find me?" My pulse is pounding erratically.

His sinister laugh wafts through the air. "You're such a stupid bitch!" he roars.

He takes a step closer, and Rerun starts to lunge, but I clench his collar as tight as I can, hardly able to contain him.

I suddenly hear a click and a glimmer of metal flashes, courtesy of the shaft of moonlight that is filtering through the curtain. I don't have to see to know Tad has a gun aimed at my head.

"Put the fuckin' dog up, or else I'll put a bullet in his head."

His words chill me. "Okay, okay!" I hold up my free palm while keeping a firm grip on Rerun's collar. "Don't shoot, please! I'll put him in the backyard."

I have no idea if there's a fenced yard. Either way, I'd rather have Rerun roaming the woods than getting shot. Tugging on his collar, I coax him softly with a pat to the head. "Come on, Rerun. Let's go outside."

I fumble in the dark, still clenching Rerun's collar, looking for the back door. I find a switch to the kitchen and flip on the light. Right away, I spot the door off to my left. Oh, good!

I open the door and quickly send Rerun outside.

He obeys and trots off, disappearing into a stand of trees. I glance around to see if Tad can see me.

I grab my phone and dial 911. I stick my cell in my back pocket with the speaker standing up. Hopefully, the call goes through, and it'll alert the police. The problem is … I'm not sure how great the service is out here in the sticks. With all the trees, I'm fretful there's no signal.

I leave the door unlocked. Just in case the police come. I step around the corner of the fridge and see Tad looming, with the gun pointed straight at me.

"Thanks, sweetheart! I like it when you're obedient." A forbidding grin materializes over his face.

"Was I ever not?" I hiss.

Tad snorts. "Hell, girl! I had to beat you into submission."

I stare Tad in the eyes as defiance saturates my voice. "What do you want? If you came here to kill me, then get it over with. Frankly, I'm tired of looking over my shoulder all the time."

He belts out hysterical laughter. "I tried to end your life, but you must be a cat with nine lives."

The hairs on my back bristle. "That night I went to the hospital, you were trying to kill me?"

In utter shock, I take a quick breath. How could I have been so blind? It's bad enough for Tad roughing me up, but the intention of taking my life is staggering.

"Choking the life out of you, I thought would be easy. No one figured you for a fighter."

"I don't understand!" I say. "What would you gain by killing me?"

"Someone near and dear hired me. I agreed, with the promise of a huge payment at the end of the job."

"Payment? Job?" I shake my head, unable to process his words.

"Damn, bitch! Don't you know nothin'?" His lips thin with impatience.

"Why don't you tell me!" I struggle to keep an even, placatory tone.

"Two years ago, before we met, a doctor treated me at a clinic. He saw my struggles. Knowing I was hard up for cash, he gave me a job. Hell, I'd done it for half of what he offered. I couldn't refuse. My momma taught me one thing … that you don't refuse a good offer no matter how dirty your hands get."

"What doctor? What freaking offer?" I shout.

"Shit, I guess I gotta spell it out for you. I was supposed to get rid of you. That night you were admitted in the hospital-"

"How can I forget?" My eyes narrow as I cross my arms, glaring.

"No one expected you to fight back. You damn near kicked my balls up my throat."

"Good! You deserved it," I snarl.

He chuckles. "The night of the hospital, remember when you thought your brother was defending you?"

"What about it?"

"He was furious, but not because I took my fist to you. Big brother was pissed at me for not completing the job he hired me to do."

"I don't believe you." I barely murmur the words.

"Your brother wants you dead, sweetheart."

"Why? Is he tired of carrying my weight?"

"I don't have all the answers," he snarls. "All I know is, if I kill you and take the hit when I get out of jail in a few years, your brother's gonna pay me one hefty fee."

"So, all this time, I've been sleeping with a monster and my brother is a part of my demise?"

"You're catching on," he snorts, wiping his nose.

"How do you plan to do it? Will you bury my body in the woods?" I lift my chin, daring him to meet my gaze.

A wide, menacing grin spreads across Tad's face. "Hell, I might burn you up in this cabin, just like that doctor you were seeing."

Terror slams into me with such rapid force that it steals my breath. "*You! You* started that fire at Dr. Hunter's house. He and his family ... *his children!*" I shriek, tears burning my eyes. "Why? What did he ever do to you?"

"That damn doctor was gonna ruin it for us. Jeff told him not to run that blood test that he'd covered all the bases. The doctor didn't listen. Stupid cocksucker."

"You killed an innocent man all because of a test?" I scream at Tad, wide-eyed, unable to believe my own ears. "Tell me *why*! What reason did Jeff have to hide the test results?"

"If I tell you," Tad punches his chest with his fist. "I'm gonna be dead, lying in a grave with you."

"I won't tell anyone. I'm as good as dead anyway. C'mon! Give a woman her last dying wish."

Tad spins in his shoes, banging his forehead with his palm. Then, he quiets and begins to reveal the truth. "Your brother's been feeding you Fluoxetine."

"Fluoxetine?"

"Yeah, if you give it in large doses, it can make you crazy."

"Oh my God! Seeing things that are not there, hearing things that no one has seen," I mumble to myself. "Of course, Jeff's been planning to declare me insane." It makes sense. But *why*? What does he have to gain, putting me in an insane asylum?

Without warning, flashes of my childhood charge through my mind. Jeff hurting my pet kitten, the beatings and hiding bruises under my shirt from Mom. Jeff was vicious as a boy. His behavior concerned Mom and Dad. To protect me, they sent him away to a boy's school, hoping his behavior would improve. Why didn't I remember any of this before now?

Then, a new thought surfaces. "Tad, listen to me. Jeff's going to frame you for all these crimes while he gets off scot-free." My words rush forth. "How else is he going to pull this off? Someone else has to take the blame. If you get charged with all these murders, you'll be in the confinement of prison for the rest of your life."

Tad's shoulders slump as he forces a weak smile. "Jeff won't betray me. I'm friends with him and that doctor woman. They're good people. They stick to their word."

"Woman? Dr. Rice?" Why am I not surprised? Of course, she's involved. What are they up to? Why would they scheme to have me committed?

"Yeah, a knockout too. I'd sure do her," Tad grins.

"Where are these good people now?" I ask. "Trusting folks, huh? Your fingerprints are all over this place, even the soil on the bottom of your feet will mark you as having been here.

"The police will know it's you. You have a record a mile long. Who do you think they'll believe? You, a known drug pusher? Or a doctor with a stellar reputation?"

"Shut up!" Blood rushes to his face as spit flies from his mouth.

"Hey, it's your funeral," I say tauntingly. I take him off guard by asking, "You hungry? This place is packed with food."

"Now, that sounds mighty nice. Why don't you fix me a sandwich, and coffee too? You know how I like it, sweetheart." He scratches his chin and smiles as he takes a seat in the recliner. He finds the remote and makes himself at home.

"Alrighty, one sandwich and coffee coming." I release a lengthy, silent breath.

I hurry, preparing his meal. He's quiet, watching some fishing show. I lay the butter knife down and place my palm over my heart. Jesus! It's racing.

The coffee pot finishes filling, and I look for a cup in the cabinet. I find one and pour a considerable amount in the powder-blue cup. Next, I lay a chicken-breast sandwich on a plate with potato chips.

I tiptoe to my purse and grab my gun, sticking it in the band of my jeans. I push my loose blouse over the gun. Before I gather his food, I steal a glance at my phone. Crap! No bars for service. No neighbors in these sticks either. The only chance I see is to shoot Tad and grab his keys off the table and run like hell.

Shooting him in the knee won't kill him. But it will render him helpless. The pain will be so intense, he won't be able to think. And he won't be in any condition to run after me.

I take a deep breath and grab the tray with his coffee and sandwich. I set the plate on the end table.

Tad is asleep; his eyes are closed, and his breathing is shallow. Swiftly, I pull my gun from the band of my jeans and aim straight for Tad's left knee and pull the trigger.

Fire flashes and Tad's screams resound throughout the cabin. Shock rolls through him as he leaps to his feet but is knocked back down by the shattered knee. Blood oozes as he screeches like a stuffed pig, palming his leg.

I don't waste a minute. I swipe Tad's keys and demand, "Give me your gun or I'll shoot you in the head." I hold the gun firmly against his head.

"You shot me, you fuckin' bitch!" His face is blistered with agony.

"Give me your gun!" I order as I cock my gun. Why not shoot the bastard? It'd be one less evil person.

Tad, with one hand raised, eases out the gun from his pocket.

"Thank you very much!" I take the gun and, without delay, I fire it again, missing his groin by an inch but striking his inner thigh. "That's for putting me in the hospital, you freaking loser!" My lips spread into a triumphant smile.

As I hear Tad's curses target my back, I dart out the door with his keys clenched in my hand, running for his truck. Holy crap! I pulled this off. Freedom never tasted so good! Excitement sweeps over me.

Then, out of darkness, I feel a blunt blow to the back of my head, and that's the last thing I remember.

FAMILY SECRETS

$\mathcal{M}$y eyes flutter open as reality sinks in. I'm tied to a kitchen chair. A thin nylon rope, bright yellow, is digging into my hands and feet. I no longer have either gun; both are gone, and only a throbbing ache remains.

There's moisture at the nape of my head. It feels plastered to my scalp, sticky. I struggle to touch it, but the rope restricts me.

I strain to get loose but to no avail.

When my eyes lift, I find Jeff sitting in a kitchen chair directly in front of me. Our gazes clash. He speaks first. "I gather you are probably wondering why I have you tied up."

"That did cross my mind." Sarcasm streams into my words.

My eyes comb the cabin. Dr. Rice is standing beside my brother, her manicured hand laid flat, resting on the edge of his shoulder. My eyes narrow at her.

I knew that bitch had a part in this scandal.

Tad is sitting on the couch, cursing under his breath. I notice white bandages laying around and half of Tad's pant-leg is missing. I hope the bastard never walks again.

"The police and Ethan are coming," I threaten.

The cabin fills with wicked laughter. I glare at my brother, as if he's a stranger. "I'm afraid your boyfriend won't be joining you. He's dead."

Shock sweeps over me and I gasp.

"Oh, don't worry! It'll be your fingerprints all over the gun." Jeff's face is a glowering mask of rage.

"Why would you hurt Ethan?" Tears stream down my cheeks. "No, not Ethan!" I vehemently fight against the cutting rope, but my efforts are futile. All I can do is break into sobs. I'm confused. Why is Jeff doing this to me?

I glare at Kim Rice. Could she have this much power over Jeff? Is she holding something over his head to convince him stoop to such sadistic behavior?

"You can blame yourself for this," Jeff snarls. "I tried warning you, but you wouldn't listen. You couldn't keep your hands off the son of a bitch."

"You're tying me up all because I went out with Ethan?"

"Sticking one's nose where it doesn't belong is very risky. Ethan visited my apartment. He wanted to know if I'd drugged you." Jeff belts out a sadistic laugh. "The thickheaded imbecile came to defend you. Left me no choice. I had to shoot him. Now he's dead, and you have yourself to blame. If you had just left well enough alone."

I shake my head, trying to gain an understanding. "You didn't have to kill him!" I screech through tears. "This never was about you defending your dear friend Rice and wanting Ethan to go back to her. It was about keeping me isolated so you could dispose of me without anyone being the wiser."

A wicked smile plays across Jeff's face. "You're quite perceptive, sis."

I'm stunned and fall silent as I become racked with tears.

Dr. Rice intervenes. "I'm afraid all the evidence points to you, Ann. With records of your psychotic outburst, the paranoia and illusions, on top of Ethan and your involvement of a love triangle, it will be effortless to prove."

"You bitch!" I lunge for her, yearning to wrap my fingers around her neck, but I'm quickly slammed back by the rope. My heated gaze shoots shards at Dr. Rice. "I always knew you were dirty."

She coos. "I'm afraid your suspicions will go

with you to the grave. This is the end for you, my darling."

"Jeff!" My gaze turns to his hardened face. "I'm your sister for Pete's sake. Are you taking orders from this sociopathic bitch?"

"Actually, she takes orders from me. And as far as blood, we are not blood-related."

"Come again?" My eyes widen.

"I'm your *adopted* brother. Our parents thought they couldn't have children until you came along. The Bakers were quite elated when they found out."

"Mom and Dad never told me. Not that that would have made any difference." I shake my head. "You're still my brother," I choke through the streaming tears. "I've always loved you!"

"Yes, tell that to your dead parents when you see them."

"They were your parents too!" I counter. "They loved you as much as they loved me!" I scream through tears.

"Are you quite sure, little sister?"

"As sure as I'm tied to this damn chair!" Anger bruises my entire being. I notice a plastic sheet under my chair, spread over a large portion of the plank floor. "Jeff, what are you doing?" My eyes grow apple-round with sheer fright.

"Our family had their share of dark secrets. Mother and Father tried to protect you from me."

I narrow my gaze. "What do our parents have to do with taking my life?"

Dr. Rice chimes in, "Jeff, honey, why bother telling her? After tonight, she'll hardly be a thought."

Jeff snaps, "I want her to know how much she's hurt me. How our parents loved her more than me. I want her to know the pain they inflicted on me. I want her going to her grave, knowing she's the reason our parents died."

"How am I responsible for their death?" I shout.

"I needed money to finish my education. I'd worked hard keeping my GPA a 4.0. My becoming a doctor meant everything to me. But Mother and Father disagreed. We got into an argument. I figured if they weren't going to support my medical school tuition, their death would. They had a will written. The inheritance was more than enough to live on for the rest of my life."

"An inheritance? What are you talking about?"

"I cracked the code to their safe and found their will."

I gape, stunned into total silence.

"I needed to end their lives to gain access to their money. Naturally, I had to cut the break-line to their Honda."

"*Naturally*?" I croak. "There's nothing natural about taking someone's life! You-you murdered our parents to get the will?"

"Correct. Our parents lost control of the car and crashed into ongoing traffic. However, I didn't plan for them to crash into a drunk driver. The drunk driver was a bonus. No one suspected a thing."

Appalled and mortified on so many levels, I need to single out Jeff. "Hey, let's make this a private discussion. Why do we need them here?" I nod to Tad, flinching in the corner and to Dr. Rice, smirking and standing over Jeff as if he's her puppet. "Just you and me?" I stare back at Jeff, challenging him.

Without taking his eyes off me, he speaks to Dr. Rice, "You and Tad take his truck. I'll catch up once I'm done here."

The look on Dr. Rice's face says it all. "I'm not leaving! We are in this together, remember?" Her ruby red lips pucker.

"Yes, darling, I am well aware of that. But things have happened that we did not anticipate, and we need to deal with the pending issues. Take Tad and try to mend him and I'll catch up with you as soon as I'm done here." Then Jeff catches her gaze, as if there is a hidden statement to what he's thinking.

"Fine! I'd rather not get blood in my Bentley." She snarls at Tad. "I can't carry him. Can you help me?"

I speak up. "I'll help. After all, I shot him." I glare at Jeff.

"I don't trust her," Dr. Rice exclaims, a mix of concern and anger in her expression.

"We have a gun pointing at her head. She won't get far," Jeff barks.

Dr. Rice throws her hands to her hips. "Fine! Untie her. She can carry him. Ruining my Gucci is not part of this agreement," she hisses, full of vinegar.

"Who cares about a little blood, when after tonight, you can buy the world, dear?" Jeff leaps to his feet and stomps to my side.

I flinch as he jerks free the rope. There's rage in his face. But why?

After my hands are free, I rub them from the rope burns. I wobble to my feet, feeling stiffness in my joints after being tied to the chair for hours.

Jeff nods for me to take Tad. He's the last person I want to touch me. Although, if I can get Tad alone, I might get him to rethink what he's doing. I gather my arm around his waist and have him throw his right arm over me. "Use my leg as your second leg and don't bear down on the injured knee.

Tad grimaces. "There you go, talkin' like you got a brain cell in your head. I know what the fuck to do!" he snaps.

"Oh, yeah! How stupid of me to forget," I mutter as Tad leans on me.

Jeff and Dr. Rice stay on my heels as I assist Tad

to the truck. The heat of the gun pointing at my back never lessens.

Carefully, I help lift Tad into the truck's passenger seat. With trembling hands, I buckle him in as I whisper in his ear, "They're planning to kill you. Please notify the police."

Our gazes collide and confirmation flitters in Tad's eyes.

I cling to hope.

Abruptly, I feel a firm hand gripping my upper arm; it jerks me backward, nearly knocking me off my feet. As Jeff drags me back to the cabin, I hear the truck door shut and the sputtering engine start. Lights cut on, and the truck rolls onto the dirt road and takes off.

I try to spot nearby houses, but the trees are too dense. It's a moonless night and pitch black.

Jeff shoves me through the door and pushes me roughly down on the couch. He doesn't bother tying me back up. A little ray of hope surges through me.

I stare at him as he takes a seat in the recliner. He doesn't lean back and drops his aim to the side, the gun tight in his grasp. Silence settles between us, but it speaks volumes. Unable to tolerate this madness, I state in the stale air, "Jeff, why don't you tell me what this is all about? Maybe we can talk this through."

He leers. "It's too late to go back. Remember,

I've murdered some people. First your boyfriend and thenTad."

Tears catch my breath, "I won't believe Ethan's dead until I see it!" I spit at him, enraged. "Why Ethan? You didn't have to hurt him."

"Ethan was getting in the way." Jeff's aloofness borders on self-importance.

"You could've convinced him it was my mental health. Anything but murder!"

"When Ethan came to my apartment and confronted me of his suspicions, I knew he was about to ruin everything. The insipid cad was coming to your defense."

"Oh my God! You killed Ethan for defending *me*?"

"Not exactly. He had to be removed from the equation. He was a whistleblower!" Jeff declares bitingly.

"Was Dr. Hunter a threat to your plan too? Is that why you took his whole family?" I shout through sobs, racking my mind with thoughts of escape.

"Yes, Dr. Hunter discovered the high levels of Prozac in your system. *Again* ... another person refusing to listen to reason. The doctor left me with no choice." The lack of empathy but overwhelming self-entitlement in Jeff's voice send an icy shiver down my spine.

"So, that's why you hired Tad to set fire to his

house, destroying his entire family." The doctor's family picture flashed through my mind. The children, the innocent children, a whole family wiped from existence. An urge to rake my fingernails across his angelic face courses through me, but I remain planted on the couch.

"Correct," Jeff answers, cold and flat, with no remorse.

"What do you have to gain by drugging me?"

Jeff laughs. "That takes me back to the death of our parents. After their burial, I met with the family attorney. I discovered that our parents were one step ahead of me. The will I'd found was no longer valid. The attorney had the official will kept in *his* safe.

"I was to receive only the money for my medical school tuition and nothing more. Everything else would go to you once you reach the age of twenty-five … unless you become mentally insane, or you die. Of course, I didn't want to kill you. You were my only sister. To spare your life, I decided to take another route.

"First, I needed you diagnosed with Schizophrenia. That's where Rice stepped in. If I proved your instability, the judge would deem you harmful to yourself. Therefore, the court would leave me, your only living relative, as your power of attorney. Giving me complete access to your inheritance. I'd also have the power to have you committed to a mental hospital. And you'd have no say."

"Wait! I have money?" A faint thread of hysteria drifts through my mind.

"Yes, for now. Since you have thrown up every roadblock there is in existence, preventing me from getting the inheritance, which is rightfully mine in the first place, you have forced me to resort to desperate measures: staging your death, a suicide." Jeff flashes a cold smile. "I regret that it has come down to this, *sis*."

"Tell me, Jeff, since I'm about to die ... what was in the coffee and who staged me, passed out on Ethan's floor, drowning in his liquor?"

Jeff holds a finger over his lips as if to stifle laughter. "I think you already know the drug I used. And Kim is the one who had access to Ethan's apartment. She made a duplicate key, just like she did with this place."

"How did you know about this cabin? Ethan said no one knows ..."

A menacing grin pulls at the corners of Jeff's lips. "Funny you should ask. When I saw that you and Ethan were getting too chummy, I had Tad do some snooping. He turned out to be quite a good little spy. He trailed Ethan's mother to the cabin. That's when Kim stole Ethan's keys from his hospital locker and made duplicates for his apartment and the cabin. Quite clever, I think."

"That inheritance must be out of this world for you to create such an elaborate plan. How much?" I laugh. "I hope it's worth all the blood on your dirty hands."

Pride casts a dark shadow on his face. "Three-hundred million, to be exact."

"It's a shame. All this for nothing. You're never going to enjoy it. The police will lock you up forever. And that semblance of a perfect image you have worked so hard to maintain will all be forgotten. Everyone will soon discover that you are a fraud," I hiss, anger surging through me. All this time, his preaching on how *I* should straighten my act was a ploy to break me—to shatter my confidence and it almost worked.

Almost.

"You're wrong. I have masterminded the perfect crime. The police will never suspect or prove my involvement. As for my stellar reputation, money can restore my image. The inheritance is more than a person can spend in a lifetime."

I look him straight in the eyes. "I'm disappointed in you, big brother. If the money is so astronomical, I would've shared it with you."

"It's more than the money. I win. I am a superior person. I deserve that money, not you! I was an exemplary student, top of the class. Never a mark of trouble throughout my entire school attendance. I got accepted to an Ivy League college, Yale. I passed with flying colors. Then there's you. The spoiled little brat that's Mommy and Daddy's favorite."

Jeff bolts to his feet and stomps over, his face ablaze as he leans in my face. "I earned that money." He pounds his chest. "It's mine! And I hate you for the loser you are."

I'm pushed to the corner of the couch, pressed against it, fear rushing to my face. "I get it. Fine, take the money. All of it! No one else has to die." My palms are now shielding my face from Jeff.

"You still don't understand. I don't want you to give it to me, sister! I want to pry it from your dead, cold body."

The fierceness of his hate singes my heart. Jeff is a psychopath. And all these years, he had me fooled. Despite my fear, I'm not going to make it easy for him. He has to pay for taking lives.

I speak up. "All your efforts are futile. In the end, you'll die just like everyone else, and most likely, it will be in prison, where you belong."

All at once, a car light appears in the window. Jeff takes his eyes off me for a second and I go into attack mode. I may die, but I won't die without a fight.

I lunge for Jeff, knocking him off his feet, and his gun goes sliding across the floor. We collide, struggling for the gun. It's do or die.

But Jeff is stronger and he gains the upper hand,

slamming his iron fist into my jaw, knocking me unconscious.

When I regain my senses, Jeff is looming over me, pointing the gun straight at me. Hope plummets as I stare into the barrel of a large pistol. I'm on my back, waiting. "How do you plan to explain my death?"

"Simple. You commit suicide. I found a letter you wrote back when you were a teenager. A suicide letter. I've saved it for a special occasion," he chuckles.

"It won't work. The forensic examiner will know that the paper is ten years old. Furthermore, how are you going to explain the lack of gunpowder residue on my hands? The police can tell, even by the angle of the gunshot, if I shoot the gun or someone else does. Didn't you do your homework?" I scoff.

"I don't plan to shoot you, sis." He grinds his teeth. "That's why you're going to ingest half a bottle of Valium. Overdosing is much cleaner than a bullet through your skull."

"You're kidding? You intend to force-feed me pills?" I laugh. "It will be a cold day in hell, big brother, when I make it easy for you."

"Take the damn pills!" He clenches his teeth as he throws the bottle at me.

"Is this another futile attempt, like you did with

the coffee? Giving me a roofie!" I shout. "What were you thinking?"

"Kim and I were hoping Ethan would think you're an alcoholic and he'd kick you to the curb. We didn't count on him falling for you. If he'd just left you alone, he'd be alive."

I choke on that last sentence. I can't believe he's gone. "You blame Ethan for his own death?"

"Of course. If you lie with dogs … I think you get my meaning."

"You make me sick," I spit angrily.

"Shut up!" He strikes me across my face with the butt of his gun.

Pain sears my whole being. I almost pass out.

Jeff doesn't' stop there. "I hated you from birth. I was supposed to be the only child. Father and Mother lied to me. When they died, I thought I could escape you, but no. The Bakers gave their money all to *you*!

"You have no idea how long I've been planning your demise. The joy it will give me to watch you die." Jeff's standing over me with the gun pointing at my face. "Start swallowing the pills or else I start smashing parts of your body."

I scoff, then flinch from pain. "Get me water!" I demand, glaring at him.

"Now you're talking." A wicked grin plays across his face.

I'd been eyeballing the deer over the fireplace.

Its horns would make a perfect weapon. Back in Dallas, I used to run the Katy Trail. I did it every day to clear my head. I'm pretty fast. I even outran a rapist once.

While Jeff has his back to me, looking through the cabinet for a glass, I leap to my feet and jump over the fireplace mantle, yanking the deer head from its frame. Before Jeff is aware, I charge, stabbing him in the back.

The sound of the horns piercing his skin and hitting bone makes my stomach roil. The horns slide between in his ribcage.

A terrifying scream escapes Jeff. And blood splatters my face. The deer horns still lodged in his back, Jeff turns to face me. That oh-so-familiar glower hits me like a bucket of icy water poured over my head—that same sadistic look he frequently used to give me.

Filled with rage, Jeff dives for his gun, which had slid under the table.

I leap to my feet and dash for the pistol, knowing if I don't get to it first, I'm dead. I collide into Jeff, knocking him back into the wall, shoving the deer's horns deeper. I hear crunching bone and see the shock on his face.

Jeff's blues grow cloudy as his breath expires. In seconds, his body slumps and hangs from the wall.

I drag in deep breath as I brace my hands on my knees. I look away. I can't bear to see him.

I drop to my knees, blinded by tears as memories flood into my mind. My childhood was nothing like what I thought. Jeff was a psycho. I now recall how he tried drowning me when I was eight. No wonder I fear water. He didn't have friends. The neighborhood kids feared him.

Sickness overcomes me, and I heave. All these terrifying memories. I lie on the floor, sobbing. I loved my brother—or the person I thought he was. I bury my face into the palms of my hands and wail.

Unaware to me, the door bursts open and police pour inside the cabin. Guns with lights are shoved in my face. They see blood throughout the cabin, and my hair and clothes are saturated in crimson.

One officer shouts at me, but I can't hear his words. He shoves me to the floor and handcuffs me. The cabin is swarming with deep voices. I assume they're securing the crime scene. I hear Rerun scratching and barking at the back door.

The policeman who cuffed me approaches again. "Miss Baker, we received a call reporting that you were being held as a hostage."

"How do you know me?" I try to peer from my side since I'm facing the floor.

The officer's voice appears from behind. "I have your photo ID. Are you hurt?" His voice expresses concern.

"No," I speak up, choking through tears. "The

man over there is Jeff Baker. He and his two ac-
complices, Kim Rice and Tad Taylor, were plotting
to kill me. I think they murdered my boyfriend,
Eth-"

"Yes, the suspects are in custody. But you will be
happy to hear that your boyfriend, Ethan, is alive.
He's injured, but he'll live. He's waiting outside. I
can't have anyone disturbing my crime scene.
You're welcome to join him. I'll be meeting you at
the hospital for further questions. Let me uncuff
you, ma'am." He releases me and helps me gather
to my feet.

"Thank you, officer!" I toss over my shoulder as
I rush outside.

A cool breeze hits my face as I see a familiar
head standing by an ambulance. I run towards the
dark silhouette.

Ethan meets me halfway and gathers me into
one arm. The other is in a sling, and I see past the
smile in his eyes that he's in a great deal of pain.
"Ethan, I thought you were dead! Jeff said-"

"-The *bastard* tried." He nods at his arm. "Lucky
for me, he's a lousy shot." His eyes glisten in the
moonlight and he still has his sense of humor. "I
was terrified for you. I wasn't sure if we'd make it
in time. Thanks to Frank … who found me knocked
out. He called the police, and that's when we realized Jeff and Kim's scheme."

"Frank?" My brow shoots up. "Who's Frank?"

I hear a familiar voice. "Gurl, you sure do look good, even if you are a little bloody and bruised."

Franny comes up to me and throws his arms around me and hugs me.

I gawk. "Wait, your real name is Frank, and ... and you're *real*?"

"Boo, I'm as real as they get. You don't get this good looking and are fake."

I turn to Ethan with wide eyes. "I thought you said you didn't know Franny?"

Ethan takes on that slow smile of his. "I don't. I know this fool, *Frank*."

"Fool! Who you callin' fool?" Franny purses his lips.

"We can argue later. We need to get this girl to the hospital and checked out. Fran, you drive. My girl and I want some time together. We're taking the back seat." Ethan smiles and, with his good arm, braces me up.

The two of us hobble to the car. Fran holds the door open for us as we slide into the backseat.

In minutes, Fran is driving and the distance from that horrible nightmare grows remote as the tires eat up the road. Joy swells inside me, knowing that it's just Ethan and me, with the whole backseat to ourselves.

Our eyes lock. "You scared the hell out of me," I smile. "Ethan, I'm not upset at you for holding back about Kim. All is forgiven. Life is too precious to waste on nonsense."

"I'm happy to hear that." His eyes well with tears. "I planned on making it up to you for the rest of my life, if that's what it takes to get you back." His voice breaks. "I thought I'd lost you forever."

Our gazes latch on to each other's, as if we were taking our last breaths.

"I'm sorry, too. I was wrong about Jeff. He fooled me and everyone." My voice trembles. "I took his life. I had to. It was him or me."

Tears begin to fall and Ethan takes his thumb and gently wipes them away.

"You did what you had to do."

"But I murdered my brother." Shivers rip through me.

Ethan draws me closer, stroking my hair. "Baby, I know you loved your brother, but he was a dangerous man. He can't hurt you ever again."

"I remember my childhood now. I had blocked out all the memories of Jeff hurting me."

Ethan kisses my forehead. "It's going to take some time, but the pain will ease. I promise you."

I push out a strained sigh. "I know I did the right thing, but it doesn't make me feel any better." I swallow the knot lodged in my throat.

"I know one thing. I'm never letting you out of my sight ever again. It's you and me forever, doll. I have a secret to tell you."

I bite my bottom lip, fearing what he may say. "You do?"

"From the first moment I laid eyes on you, I've loved you. I knew somehow, you were the one. I love you, Annie. I love all your flaws and every other quirk about you."

"I have a secret too."

"You do!" Ethan flashes a lopsided grin.

"I understand that I'm wealthy. My parents left me with a large inheritance." I release a faint smile. "I want one of those houses in the Garden District. And I want my man and my best friend to come live with me."

"That sounds tempting, but let's do this right. I want to marry you first." Ethan offers that lovable, lopsided grin.

Franny clears his throat. "Excuse me. That best friend better be me! But we gotta make sure the walls are soundproof. I ain't listenin' to y'all pantin' all night."

Ethan and I burst into laughter.

Dear reader,

We hope you enjoyed reading *Duplicity*. Please take a moment to leave a review, even if it's a short one. Your opinion is important to us.

Discover more books by Jo Wilde at
https://www.nextchapter.pub/authors/jo-wilde

Want to know when one of our books is free or discounted? Join the newsletter at
http://eepurl.com/bqqB3H

Best regards,
Jo Wilde and the Next Chapter Team

Duplicity
ISBN: 978-4-86747-473-0
Large Print

Published by
Next Chapter
1-60-20 Minami-Otsuka
170-0005 Toshima-Ku, Tokyo
+818035793528

19th May 2021